M000025420

Cheeky Swimsuits of 1957

July 1957

June 1957

Also by C.D. Payne

Youth in Revolt: The Journals of Nick Twisp

Revolting Youth: The Further Journals of Nick Twisp

Young and Revolting: The Continental Journals of Nick Twisp

Revoltingly Young: The Journals of Nick Twisp's Younger Brother

Son of Youth in Revolt: The Journals of Scott Twisp

Invisibly Yours

Brenda the Great

Helen of Pepper Pike

Cut to the Twisp

Civic Beauties

Frisco Pigeon Mambo

Queen of America

Cheeky Swimsuits of 1957

C.D. Payne

Aivia Press

Copyright © 2014 by C.D. Payne
All rights reserved

No part of this book shall be reproduced or transmitted in any form or by any means, electronic, mechanical, magnetic, photographic including photocopying, recording or by any information storage and retrieval system, without prior written permission of the publisher. This is a work of fiction. Names, characters, places, and incidents either are the product of the author's imagination or are used fictitiously. Any resemblance to actual events or locales or persons, living or dead, is entirely coincidental. For information or queries, address Aivia Press, 919 Midpine Way, Sebastopol, CA 95472.

ISBN-13: 978-1882647019

ISBN-10: 1882647017

To: L.A.A.F.A.D.L.B.

Special thanks to Till Hack for his editorial assistance.

"A man will go to war, fight and die for his country.
But he won't get a bikini wax." -- Rita Rudner

Chapter 1

I went in to see the old fellow as he was finishing his morning coffee.

"Good morning, Father. I'm back from Yale."

"Ah, sacked again were you, Colm?"

"Not this time, Pop. I graduated."

"Summa cum laude?"

"Hardly. But I understand there were several athletic chaps whose grades were lower than mine."

"Not at the bottom then. Well, that's something. I expect they'll be drafting you soon."

"I already had my physical, Father. I have a bum elbow from all that tennis and squash. The Army doesn't want me."

"So what's next for you, lad?"

"I was thinking of trying my luck in Hollywood."

"Acting is it then? The final disgrace for the family?"

"No, independent film production. This is 1957, Father. The studios are passe. There are splendid opportunities out there now for independent producers."

"I wish you the best of luck, son."

"Of course, I'll need a bit of capital to get started."

The old fellow smiled and sipped his coffee. He has only one sort of smile, always unnerving.

"You know your uncle Jonathan died."

"That was a while back as I recall."

"Your absence at his funeral was commented upon."

"It was the weekend of the Big Game with Harvard. I could hardly be expected to miss that."

"Jonathan left me his little company."

"That appalling firm that makes those hideous swimsuits?"

"I'm finding it a bit of a distraction. I'm thinking of putting you in charge of it."

I stood there stunned. Even for him it was a shockingly outlandish proposal.

"A generous gesture, Pop, but I have no interest in ladies' swim wear."

"I expect ladies' underwear is more to your liking."

"Even you were young once," I reminded him. "I think I could manage with $50,000."

The old fellow smiled again. Never a promising sign.

"Were you to prove successful in managing this business, I might consider investing in your film enterprises."

"Impossible, Dad. I've already promised Betty a big part in my first picture. She won't marry me otherwise."

"Then I'm saving that young woman from two ill-considered fates."

"Sorry, Pop. I must firmly decline your proposal."

"I understand, son. I suppose you could survive merely on your blue eyes and wavy brown hair."

"Aren't you forgetting my allowance?"

"A fellow offered a challenging position at a going concern is in no need of an allowance."

Blackmailed by my own father. What a foul day this was turning out to be. And me with a raging hangover. My head throbbed as I considered my options.

"How long would I be indentured to the dowdy swimmers?"

"Only for a year. That's half the time the Army would demand. I'll have my secretary arrange for your bus ticket."

"Bus ticket? Lots of my college friends are getting cars as graduation gifts."

(For example, one of those new Thunderbirds would suit me fine.)

"You've already crashed three cars, Colm. You're a menace on the highways."

But only when drinking, I considered retorting, then thought better of it. Sober I'm acknowledged to be a superb driver. And only two cars had been wrecked; the third was just moderately dented. Instead, I asked, "Bus ticket to where exactly?"

"Ukiah, California."

"Oh, is that a suburb of Los Angeles?"

"Possibly. Western geography is not really my forte. I'm sure you'll love it there."

That last part he added with his most ominous smile.

For the record I should note that my hair–inherited from my late mother–is a light sandy blond, not brown.

* * *

Three thousand miles on a Greyhound bus! Could purgatory be any worse of an ordeal? One realizes along the journey that large swaths of this country really should be ceded back to the Indians. Or broken off and redistributed to the hapless Canadians and Mexicans. Nebraska probably is the worst. Hot, dusty, and absolutely devoid of anything appealing to the eye. How people exist there is a complete mystery. Plus, it goes on forever. I'm told Nevada is dreadful too, but thankfully I slept through most of that desolate state. The bus pulled into San Francisco, which appeared intriguing, but then I had to board another bus heading north. We crossed the fog-shrouded Golden Gate Bridge, laden with tourists, then continued on for hours. Borrowing a map from my seat-mate, I was shocked to discover that we were headed in the *opposite* direction from Los Angeles. Fast-retreating Hollywood was hundreds of miles away!

Eventually, even interminable bus journeys have to end.

"Are you sure this is Ukiah?" I asked the portly bus driver.

"It sure is, pal. The one and only."

"Is this the distant outskirts of the city?" I asked, peering doubtfully out the window.

"Nope. You're right in the center of town. State Street is one block over."

"But we're in the middle of nowhere!"

"It's the seat of Mendocino County, kid. That's as exciting as it gets around here. They got their own courthouse and everything. Now move along, 'cause you're blocking the aisle."

Since no one showed up looking for me, I hoisted my grip and trudged over to what was making do as their "main" street. I checked into a Palace Hotel, which might more properly have been named the Sagebrush Hotel, as the grim lobby featured bas-relief cowboys molded into the plaster. Palatial it was not. I was assigned a room on the third floor, evidently the highest point in the entire town. I had a grisly dinner in the hotel's dining room, then fed coin after coin into the lobby payphone in a futile attempt to reach Betty. Her Provincetown roommate informed me gruffly that she was "out with a saxophonist."

My girl dating a horn player and me exiled to the frontier an entire continent away! Of course, I blamed my father. The old fellow seemed determined to sabotage my life. I decided I'll stick it out for a week, then chuck it all and head back to civilization. A week in Wilderness Hell should be enough to convince even my pater that I'd Made An Effort.

Impressions of Ukiah gleaned from a stroll in the fading light: Tall hills to the immediate west and distant hills visible in the east. Lots of rustic natives driving battered pre-war cars. Big trucks stacked with immense logs chugging noisily through town. Numerous bars and honky-tonks suggesting that beer guzzling was a prominent feature of daily life. Matrons window-shopping in hats at least a decade out of fashion. Swarthy loiterers in straw sombreros speaking a foreign tongue I gauged to be Spanish. Unbarbered louts roaring by on large, throbbing motorcycles. Stark marquee of the lone cinema advertising "Peyton Place" plus a newsreel and two cartoons. Not many patrons in line on this warm Wednesday night. Although this is alleged to be the West, no actual horses or cowboys were seen, but suspicious barnyard smells occasionally wafted by.

I bought an ice-cream cone for a dime, then returned to my hotel and its lonely (and lumpy) bed.

* * *

Unfortunately, the waitress at the diner where I ate breakfast had heard of Milady Modest Inc. and gave me directions to its location (five blocks south of my hotel).

"Yeah, we're sort of the bathing suit capital of the Redwood Empire," she commented, refilling my coffee cup. "My aunt's worked there in bra cups forever."

Not an appealing image; I put down my fork.

"Do you have one of their suits?" I asked to be polite.

"Not me, honey. I'm not quite old and decrepit enough for their styles, but I expect I'll get there eventually. What's your interest in them?"

"I think I'm supposed to work there."

That brought her up short. "Doing what, pray tell?"

"I'm not sure. Being the boss, I think."

"OK, honey, if you say so. You some kind of hotshot fashion wiz kid?"

"Hardly."

"I doubt even you could make their suits any uglier. So good luck."

"Thanks. I'll need it."

I was in no hurry to commence my day, but eventually I paid my bill ($.65 with $.15 tip) and wandered south on State Street. Milady Modest occupied a nondescript stucco building on a side street beside an alley. A sign on the battered metal door read: NOT HIRING TODAY. Nevertheless, I opened the door and entered.

A middle-aged secretary looked up with a start, then pushed a button on an intercom. "Mr. Slivmank!" she hissed, "I think he's here!"

A moment later a thin old guy, bald and stooped, bustled out from an office.

"Mr. Moran?" he inquired.

"That's me," I admitted.

He gave me a weak squeeze with a bony hand. His lint-covered suit hung on him like a costume prop in a low-budget play. "I'm Wendell Slivmank. We were expecting you yesterday. Was your bus delayed?"

"'Fraid not. Nobody met me, so I spent the night at the Palace Hotel."

"The Palace!" he exclaimed. "Goodness! That must have been expensive."

"It was $7.25 plus tax."

"That much! You must have got a deluxe suite with bath. That wasn't the plan. Since you'll be staying at your late uncle's house, the plan was for you to go there."

"Yeah, well, nobody told me that."

"How curious," he replied. "Well, you're here now, and welcome. Let me show you around and introduce you to everyone."

So I met the designer, the pattern-drafter, the cutter, and the bookkeeper–all elderly female occupants of the cramped and cluttered front offices. The stout secretary, Miss Page, doubled as the fitting model (whatever that is). She was the only one who could have been younger than 50. A swinging door led to the production room–smelling of steamy fabrics and mixed perfumes–where a dozen or so sewing machines whirled away, then abruptly halted.

"Ladies," said Mr. Slivmank," this is young Mr. Colm Moran–Mr. Jonathan's nephew from back east."

I heard someone whisper, "Well, at least he's not a beatnik."

"We'll see," someone else whispered back.

"'Morning, ladies," I stammered. "How, how's the sewing going?"

"Not bad," said a white-haired woman, holding up what appeared to be some sort of half-finished glove. "We're getting the hang of it."

Low tittering from the seamstresses.

"Mildred has been with us for 26 years," said Mr. Slivmank. "She's one of our veteran employees."

"Why is everyone sewing gloves?" I asked. "Are gals swimming in gloves these days?"

More tittering.

"We work far ahead of the season," the old guy explained. "The great majority of our orders for the 1957 lines have been shipped. In our slack months, we make a variety of utility gloves."

Mr. Slivmank and Joe in the warehouse appeared to be the only male employees. Joe's cluttered domain in the rear of the building was stacked high with dusty cardboard boxes and bolts of cloth. A long table held a variety of folded boxes and shipping supplies.

"'Lo," said Joe, shaking my hand. He was at least Mr. Slivmank's age and by far the shortest person on the staff. He must have bought his blue overalls in the boys' department.

"Any issues, Joe?" asked Mr. Slivmank.

Joe curled his lip into a sneer.

"Still waitin' on that Railway Express order."

"I'll give Sam at the depot a call." He turned to me. "We're always waiting on shipments of cloth from New England and mills in the South. Plus, they charge us extra for being west of the Rockies."

Personally, I'd charge them at least triple for being so far off the map.

* * *

The rest of the day crawled by. I wondered if work was always this depressing or just in the bathing-suit business. At one point Mr. Slivmank (who insisted I call him Wendell) asked if I'd care to examine the books.

"Oh, do you have a selection of popular titles?" I replied. "I've been meaning to read *On the Beach*. Say, if they make a movie out of it, perhaps we can get them to feature a few of our sexier designs."

"Ledger books," he replied. "Our business records. Would you care to look them over?"

"Oh, maybe some other time, Wendell. By the way, how are we doing?"

"Uh, well, sales were a bit disappointing this spring. It's possible people are staying away from the water because of the lingering polio scare."

Somebody in a nearby office harrumphed loudly.

"We have a very strong position in the marketplace," he went on. "If you're a woman who weighs 300 pounds, Milady Modest is really your only viable beachwear option."

"I don't know, Wendell, if any of the girls I know weighed 300 pounds, I don't think they'd be planning any outings to the beach. They'd be taking a cab to the nearest tall building for purposes of hurling themselves off the roof."

"Well, our styles do come in a variety of sizes, Mr. Moran."

"Call me Colm."

"We're very popular in your rural areas and smaller cities, although anyone with a problem figure is our target market. Our customers are rather conservative in their tastes."

Another loud harrumph. I was beginning to suspect there was some dissension in the ranks.

At last the clock rolled around to quitting time. Wendell locked up and gave me a lift in his aging Nash, Detroit's closest approximation to a bathtub on wheels. Uncle Jonathan's house was one of those shingled bungalows like your grandparents may have dropped dead in. Dark paneling, heavy furniture strewn with crocheted doilies, murky green roll-up blinds, and old-fashioned lamps giving off the feeblest glow. Good smells, though, emanated from the kitchen, where a girl about my age was stirring something in a pot.

"Who are you? I asked.

"I'm your housekeeper," she said, addressing the pot. "I'm reheating yesterday's stew because you never showed up."

"There was a mixup, sorry. You don't look like a housekeeper."

She wasn't beautiful like Betty, but she was the best-looking girl I'd seen since arriving in this town. Somewhere between slim and shapely, with a perky nose and bobbed brown hair.

"And what do housekeepers look like?" she asked, finally glancing my way. Her eyes were an arresting light hazel.

"Like Agnes Moorehead. That's usually who Hollywood picks. Or they get some fat Negro woman if they're going for laughs."

"Well, you'll have to make do with me. Name's Jean Valland. I make dinner, but not breakfast or lunch, so you're on your own for that. I also wash up, shop for groceries, do the laundry, and vacuum. If you're not disgusting in your personal habits, I might also clean the bathroom. Any questions?"

"What else don't you do?"

"I'll leave that to your imagination. Have a seat in the dining room, and I'll bring in your dinner."

Chapter 2

The stew was excellent, but the dining arrangements seemed awkward. So I picked up my plate and joined Jean at the yellow metal table in the kitchen.

"Dining with the help," she observed. "That's not generally done, you know."

"I hate eating by myself. You're a good cook."

"Thanks."

"Am I paying you? I found out today I'm only making $32 a week."

"No, the bookkeeper at your company is writing my checks and covering the grocery tab. Why such low pay? I thought you were the new big boss."

"That's a joke. I'm more like an apprentice. Mr. Slivmank says I'll be expected to learn all the jobs–including sewing."

"That could be a challenge."

"It's just my father's way of torturing me for being young and carefree."

"I always thought you had to be smart to go to Yale, but my dad says if your father is an alumnus and your family gives generously, they'll take any sort of nitwit."

"Very true. That's how I got in. Of course, they do hope you'll be borderline brainy enough to memorize the fight songs and not embarrass everyone with your table manners. So how did you make the leap from pretty civilian to my housekeeper?"

"I knew your aunt and uncle all my life. I grew up in the house next door. After your aunt Evelyn died your uncle knew I needed a summer job so he hired me to keep house for him."

"What were you during the rest of the year?"

"Going to art school in Oakland."

"So you're an artist!"

"Sort of. I'm your basic mediocre painter. After 50 years of struggle I'll die in obscurity."

"I'm sure you'll do better than that. Do you paint with oils?"

"Watercolors mostly. That's the hardest and most unforgiving medium. The frustration is nicely built in. So was it always your dream to make it big in the rag trade?"

"Not at all. I intend to go to Hollywood and produce independent films. This is just a detour to prove to my father I won't sink like a stone in the business world. I want to produce a movie so I can give my girlfriend a starring role. She's an actress."

"Ah. And where is she?"

"Doing summer stock on the Cape. I'm having trouble staying in touch. I can't call her in the daytime because she's sleeping. I can't call her at night until the show is over. That's usually after 11 their time. And when I do call her, she's always out."

"Doing what?"

"Raising hell with some horn player. Actors like to stay out late to work off all the adrenalin they pump out during the performance. I hope she's not allowing the guy to take any liberties. Those musicians are all wolves."

"Are you engaged?"

"That's a bit unclear at the moment. In the fall she'll be moving to New York to try out for parts, and God knows where I'll be."

"You could write her a letter."

"You haven't seen my spelling. And no one can read my handwriting, not even me."

Jean got up to clear off the table.

"I made a lemon pie for dessert–from the tree behind the garage."

"You're a wonder, Jean. You're the best housekeeper I ever had."

"And how many have you had?"

"A fair number. My mother died when I was eight."

"I'm sorry to hear that. My mother died when I was eleven."

"I'm sorry too. Did your father remarry?"

"Briefly. That was kind of a disaster. If he hadn't divorced her, I would have murdered her for sure. Were you blessed with any stepmoms?"

"No. Just housekeepers, cooks, and maids. I think my father's had some discreet ladies on the side over the years."

"What does he do?"

"I'm not sure exactly. He used to do something with stocks, but now he works mostly with bonds. Municipal bonds, I think. I know he rakes it in because he's always grousing about the income tax. How about your dad?"

"He's a doctor. He's right next door in case you show any symptoms of food poisoning."

"That's good to know. And are you right next door too?"

"I'm afraid so. Been in the same room since I was two."

* * *

I dried the dishes while Jean washed.

"I've got some bad news for you," she said.

"What?"

"There's no television in this house."

"That's OK. I don't watch it much. Never got in the habit. They had one in the junior common room in my dorm, but nobody watched it."

"Why not?"

"Because it shared the room with the dorm's only piano. And the musical guys were always sabotaging its vacuum tubes so they could practice undisturbed."

"So what do you do in the evenings?"

"Well at school I would go out and have a good time. Some weekends we'd take the train down to New York. Or visit Betty in Poughkeepsie. I'm not sure what I'll be doing in this town. Any suggestions?"

"The library's open until nine."

"Wow, I hope I can cope with the excitement."

I studied her lips. No lipstick, but they exuded a powerful attraction.

"So how many locals are lined up these days to take you out?" I asked.

"I get the occasional grudging volunteer."

"No steady?"

"Not really."

"Good. We should take in a movie sometime."

"I couldn't date my employer, Mr. Moran. What would people think? Besides, you're practically married."

"I never said that."

"At eight o'clock you're going to be on the phone with her."

"Maybe. Maybe not."

"Just remember: long distance is expensive. Especially for a fellow making only $32 a week."

"I should have kept that under my hat. No girl should ever know how much a fellow earns."

"You mean it should just come as a nasty shock on the honeymoon?"

"Yeah," I winked. "One of several."

* * *

I drove to work in Uncle Jonathan's 1938 Packard Super 8 touring sedan. Very stately automobile featuring a chrome cormorant hood ornament, twin side-mounted spare tires, bullet-shaped headlight enclosures mounted on the fenders, and green pinstripes highlighting the deep cream body paint. The classy interior was upholstered in tan wool. Started right up and drove pretty smoothly for a nearly 20-year-old car. When Jean showed me last night where the keys hung on a hook by the kitchen door, she cautioned that the car had been my uncle's pride and joy.

"Please don't wreck it," she said. "It's a sweet old car and deserves to be treated with care."

"Hey, I'm not 12 years old, Jean. I'm a responsible adult."

"Hmm, I hope so. I've heard some stories to the contrary."

"Don't believe everything you hear. Besides, people can change."

"It's a little balky going into second sometimes. Don't force it."

"I'll baby it like it was your own tender body."

She blushed. "That's enough of that, buster. Isn't it time for you to make your call?"

But Betty was out again when I phoned. I left my number with her roommate and told her to ask Betty to call me collect when she got in, "no matter how late." But no call came in. Should we start communicating via telegram?

I got assigned today to Madame Aranson, the designer. She's a petite old bird with silvery hair wound into a rock-hard bun, enough makeup for three normal women, an accent borrowed from Greta Garbo, and fairly tremendous breasts. A half-century ago she must have been pretty distracting to the gents. She was dressed today in a slinky crimson number that was not typical of the Ukiahan fashions I'd seen. She sat me down in a chair beside hers and grasped my hands.

"You are a most attractive boy, Colm. How tall are you?"

"Just a hair under six-two."

"Over 185 centimeters, that's good. You have intelligent eyes and your chin shows resoluteness. But you have the hairline of an Armenian peasant. I recommend selective electrolysis at the temples."

"Well, that's probably not going to happen."

"Please do consider it. Now let me see your teeth."

I flashed her my choppers.

"Good. You obviously possess a toothbrush. So many Americans don't, you know. Please be honest: do you like boys or girls?"

"Definitely girls."

"I sensed that from your dress. You have no fashion sense at all."

"Sorry."

I attempted to pry my hands loose, but she held on tight.

"Shall I tell you how I came to exist in this provincial place?"

"OK."

"I was young but very celebrated in Manhattan. Women of exquisite taste sought me out to dress them with my unique panache. You understand?"

"I get the picture. So what happened?"

"I became involved in a tragic love affair."

"He died?"

"No. He was married."

"Oh, right."

"He was torn, you see."

"How so?"

"He was torn between my precious love and his wife's fortune."

"Ah. Sounds like a bit of a cad."

"I understood, of course. It was during the Depression and so many souls were desperate for security. Have you ever known want?"

"Well, I wanted a car for graduation, but got a bus ticket to here instead."

"So, of course, I had to flee New York." She leaned closer and whispered, "For a time I was reduced to selling my body. Can you imagine? The louts I let paw me! To be rudely and uncouthly penetrated just to procure a crust of bread!"

I felt a change of subject was required. "So now you design swimsuits?"

"That is my fate and I accept it. In this small way I try to nurture my gift. Now, let us commence your studies."

* * *

I got my hands back when Madame Aranson went to retrieve some oversize sketch books. She flipped one open to the first page. On it was a stylized drawing of a hefty woman in a plaid swimsuit augmented with a kind of a flouncy skirt.

"Your impressions? she asked.

"Uh, well, it's, uh, very nice."

"No, Colm, it is utilitarian. It serves a function. How familiar are you with the female form?"

"Not as familiar as I'd like to be."

"Well, you are young. And the girls these days have been trained to tease, to withhold cruelly. Such inhibitions, of course, are not natural. When I was young we artists followed our passions. Now why do you suppose men's fashions change so slowly?"

"I have no idea."

"It is because the male body is innately easier to garb. Most men, even in Ukiah, look acceptable in their clothes. You young men can be devastating dressed simply in your dungarees and t-shirts. No?"

"If you say so."

"But the female form. Now that is the challenge. Shall I tell you a shocking fact?"

"OK."

"Ninety percent of women over the age of 30 despise their bodies."

"Really?"

"And their enmity is entirely justified. So now they must go to the beach. And reveal their loathsome body to the world. How do you think that makes them feel?"

"Uh, nervous?"

"Tormented! What do they see in their mirror? Bulges! Wrinkles! Sagging flesh! Grossly swelling bottoms! Puckered thighs like some hellish nightmare!"

"Wow. That bad, huh?"

"Worse than you with your flat stomach and broad shoulders and sweet tush can ever imagine. So now they must go and find a bathing suit. And what is the purpose of my designs?"

"Camouflage?"

"Exactly! Bold prints to distract the eye! A modest skirt to drape discretely and conceal the vast posterior. Perhaps a bit of lace along the neckline to suggest youth where time has writ age. And frequently a matching robe or skirt to hide the ghastly apparition as quickly as possible."

"Good job."

"But we are just starting to face the difficulties. Here's another challenging fact: every woman's body is different. Yet can we produce an infinity of sizes? No. A short woman with a large bust and no hips and a tall women with a flat chest and enormous hips must each find a suit off the same rack."

"How is that possible?"

"It is possible only if the designer possesses genius! Now do you appreciate my work?"

"I do, Madame Aranson. You are the key to this entire operation."

"Ah. You are a boy of intelligence. I thought so. Not like that dog Slivmank, who is determined to sabotage me at every turn. You know, of course, he was only the sales manager here before your uncle passed. He knows nothing of style and fashion. Better he should be running a pig farm in Fresno. Do I make myself clear?"

"Very clear."

"So, we must plan a coup d'etat as soon as possible. Loutish Slivmank must be deposed and returned to his adding machines!"

* * *

After lunch Madame Aranson set me to work looking through back issues of *Vogue* and *Harper's Bazaar* magazines. This was to help me absorb a "concept of fashion." Not my customary reading material. The models in the ads and photos were quite beautiful, but hardly the type of girl you'd feel comfortable inviting out to the movies. Many of them were skimpily dressed in improbable-looking undergarments. You wonder if they ever felt self-conscious about that, like maybe guys they went to high school with might see them and have a good laugh at their expense.

Of course, I paid special attention to the swimsuits, none of which looked much like what Milady Modest produced. Some of the poses, frankly, were more than a little titillating, making me lament my separation from Betty even more. Not that Betty let me take many liberties. She wasn't that type of girl. Still, we'd graduated beyond first base.

Some of the bathing suits in the magazines were those trendy two-piece designs that put non-controversial sections of the torso on public view. This is a positive development that might reach Milady Modest in about 2003, assuming any of us here live that long.

It was sort of educational and kept me away from those dreaded sewing machines, but all in all I think I prefer *Sports Illustrated* or *Road & Track*.

I stopped on the drive home and gassed up the Packard. It took nearly $3 of high-test. Driving this swanky car could get expensive. The grease jockey who washed my windshield and checked the oil knew the car well.

"You must be old man Moran's nephew."

"That's right."

"I guess you're in the ladies' bathing suit business now." This he said with an undisguised smirk.

"Hey, it beats pumping gas for a living," I said with a wave as I floored it.

Jean, my cute housekeeper, had chicken baking in the oven when I got back. The kitchen table, I was pleased to see, was set for two. And lipstick had been applied and possibly a daub or two of perfume.

"You're like a vision out of *Vogue* magazine," I said, resisting the urge to make a grab for her.

"What would you know about *Vogue*?"

"Oh, I'm all up to date. I've been reading them all afternoon."

"Oh? Were you getting your hair done at the beauty parlor?"

"Purely research and fact-finding for work. You wouldn't believe what I know now about foundation garments."

"You can keep that knowledge to yourself. How do you feel about gravy?"

"Chicken is naked without it."

"OK. Dinner will be delayed five minutes while I thicken the drippings."

I found a church key in a drawer and punched open a can of beer. It was a west coast brand I'd never heard of. I offered one to the lady of the house, but she declined.

"It's the weekend, girl. Time to relax!"

"And you had such an arduous week in the salt mines, Colm. Two entire days."

"It felt like an eternity at times. I missed you."

"More talk like that and you can eat in the dining room."

The chicken dinner was delicious as I knew it would be. Some girls just have the knack.

Dessert was cherry cobbler. As I was digging in I asked Jean a question.

"Do you think my hairline is too low?"

"Too low for what?"

"I don't know, Madame Aranson thinks I should get it altered by electrolysis."

"Madame Aranson is several bonbons short of a box. I think you can safely ignore her beauty tips."

"I was planning on it. Speaking of plans, I see they've held over 'Peyton Place' another week. I'm thinking of seeing it tomorrow night. Perhaps you'd care to walk to the theater with me and possibly sit in my general vicinity."

"And who would be buying my ticket?"

"I'm open to negotiation on that point. Afterwards we could possibly grab a bite to eat. That way you wouldn't have to make me dinner."

"I don't make you dinner on Saturday anyway. It's my day off."

"Oh, OK. That's fine with me."

"I guess it would be OK if we went dutch, and it wasn't an actual date. No groping in the theater or elsewhere."

"Right. It would be like two nuns on an outing."

"I doubt two nuns would be seeing 'Peyton Place.' I hear it's quite racy for Ukiah."

"Well, we can storm out of the theater if it gets too offensive."

Chapter 3

The telephone by my bed rang very early Saturday morning. I groped for the receiver.

"I have a person-to-person call for Mr. Colm Moran," said the operator.

"I'm Colm," I said. "Betty, is that you? Why haven't you been returning my calls?"

"I cannot elucidate such mysteries," said the old fellow.

"Hello, Father," I yawned. "You know it's the middle of the night here."

"It is, I believe, 8:12 a.m. your time. How are you getting on there?"

"OK. Old man Slivmank is threatening to stick me behind a sewing machine."

"It is the wise captain who can perform every duty on the ship."

"I'll keep that in mind if I ever join the Navy. The pay is really rotten, I suppose you know that."

"But your room and board are provided for. Thirty-two dollars cash money in your hand every Friday is a magnificent sum just for frivolities."

"Yeah, in 1912. Any more on your mind, Pop? I know you like to keep your long-distance calls as brief as possible."

"Just ascertaining the tenor of your mind, son. You appear to be adjusting well. Keep up the good work. Good-bye."

The old fellow hung up. I wish it had been Betty disturbing my sleep.

I did some scouting around the house and found a portable typewriter in the closet of the guest bedroom. So I sat down and typed a letter to Betty. I said I missed her a lot and was concerned that I hadn't heard from her. I asked her to call me collect as soon as possible. I gave her my number here and also the number at my job. I found a three-cent stamp in a drawer, stuck in on the envelope, and slipped it in the mailbox on the corner. I'm beginning to suspect she's punishing me for putting an entire continent between us–not that I had much choice.

Ukiah may be a million miles from nowhere, but at least the

weather's pleasant. Nothing but sunny, warm days since I got here. I'm told it almost never rains here in the summertime. I dragged out the garden hose and washed the big Packard. I'm glad it's painted a light color. Otherwise, I'd feel like I was heading up a funeral procession every time I drive it. The Packard's not really appropriate for guys my age, being your classic old man's car.

It's a shame that the huge Packard factory in Detroit shut down recently. Packard merged with Studebaker, and now the company is making a "Packardized" version of the Stude in South Bend. From the sales figures I've seen it's not going over so hot with your diehard Packard drivers. When I start producing hit movies, I'm only going to buy cars from the smaller companies–just to help keep General Motors from taking over the world. They own more than half the market, and everybody and his grandma drives a Chevy. I suppose, though, I would have accepted one of GM's sporty Corvettes had the old fellow laid the keys on me. Now that's a young person's car.

* * *

While we were waiting in the ticket line at the theater, three different guys passing by said hi to my date.

"Does every fellow in town know you?" I asked Jean.

"Hey, it's a small town. I grew up with those boys. And don't stand so close. People will think we're together."

"You're smelling terrific. Like a whole patch of roses."

"I happen to love roses. I splashed on a little rose water, but not for your benefit."

"I'll try not to breathe in your vicinity."

The movie was not as racy as the publicity promised. I doubt many nuns would have been offended. There was a skinny-dipping scene, but they didn't show anything–the Hollywood Production Code saw to that. In New Haven a few months back I saw an Italian movie that showed a girl with her top off. Bare nipples and everything. Hollywood, of course, will never dare be so bold. The Catholic Church and other morality watchdogs would scream for the head of any producer responsible for such an outrage. So "Peyton Place" was kind of a dud, but I did like Hope Lange, who reminded me a lot of Betty. They are both stunning blondes. And the film's doing fantastically well at the box office. I should have such a hit.

Not much is open late in downtown Ukiah, so we headed over to a burger joint on the Redwood Highway. We sat at the counter because sharing a booth could be interpreted as being out on a date.

After we ordered Jean asked what I had for lunch.

"The rest of your tasty chicken and the leftover mashed potatoes."

"Did you reheat anything?"

"No, I didn't mind them cold. The gravy was a bit gelatinous."

Jean sighed. "If it were up to you men we'd still be living in caves."

"I wouldn't mind sharing a cave with you."

"And where would you put Betty? In the next cave over?"

"Let's not bring her up. So when can I see some of your paintings?"

"Probably never."

"That's not fair. I'm planning to show you the first bathing suit I design."

"You could model it for me. I'd like that."

"I want to see your art."

"Why?"

"Because I'm sure your stuff is great."

"Your optimism is misplaced. I assure you I'm not that talented."

"Damn, Jean, I think you have one of those inferiority complexes."

"No, Colm, I just know good work when I see it. And so far I haven't seen any from me. But I'm getting a little better. Mostly though my colors just lie there on the paper gasping for air. What are you looking at?"

"You. You're much prettier up close."

"Back off, buster. This is not a date, remember?"

"Why couldn't it be a date?"

"Because you're not free. And you're probably not sticking around very long."

"Madame Aranson says artists should follow their passions."

"Then I suggest you invite her out on a date. She's probably waiting for your call right now."

* * *

The evening was still warm when we walked up the hill toward our street. I wanted to touch her, at least to hold her hand, but I knew better than to try. We chatted about this and that as we sauntered along. Too soon we came to her house. It was a bungalow too, but done in stucco instead of wood shingles.

"I'm glad our paths happened to cross, Mr. Moran."

"Yes, Jean, it was pleasant seeing you at the theater. And what a coincidence that we ran into each other at that restaurant."

"Good night, Mr. Moran."

"Good night, Miss Valland. See you soon."

How cruel that fate denied me the pleasure of a parting kiss.

Later my girl phoned as I was getting ready for bed.

"Hi, Colmy! How come I haven't heard from you? Have you forgotten me already?"

"Betty, I've been phoning you non-stop. Haven't you been getting my messages?"

"Oh, it's a madhouse here. Just crazy! I did mail you a surprise gift though. Guess what, honey?"

"What?"

"We're doing 'The Skin of Our Teeth' next and I got the part of Sabina. That's the starring role! Guess who played her on Broadway?"

"Who?"

"Only Tallulah Bankhead and then Miriam Hopkins! Jimmy says there could be some scouts coming up from New York."

"Who's Jimmy?"

"This amazingly talented director. He really likes my work."

"That's great. Well, I've been missing you terribly and–"

"Got to go, Colmy. The gang's leaving now. Try not to be such a stranger! 'Bye, darling!"

Either we got disconnected or she hung up. Kind of a short conversation, but it was great hearing from her at last. Sounds like she's having a much more stimulating summer than I am. Her manner was decidedly friendly, so she must be missing me at least a little.

* * *

When I emerged from my bedroom this morning, Jean was vacuuming the living room rug. I bent down and pulled out the plug.

"Damn, that thing is loud enough to wake the dead. What's it powered by–the engine off a DC-7?"

"It roars away, but the suction is lousy. You haven't shaved."

"At Yale one often didn't shave on Sunday."

"You have left your college days behind, Mr. Moran."

"Don't remind me. They were four splendid years. Except for all that studying. What a nuisance."

"I hear you didn't do much of that."

"God, you're lovely in the morning."

"I thought we were discussing vacuuming."

"No, the topic was my grooming habits and your loveliness. What are we doing today?"

"After I finish slaving for you, *I'm* going sketching by the river."

"Good. I'll tag along."

"You weren't invited."

"Fortunately, I'm not one to stand on ceremony."

We drove to the river in Jean's VW beetle. This is a curious little car they've started importing from West Germany. It looks a bit like the stunted bastard offspring of a '37 Plymouth. Tiny engine and very stark interior, but then Germany did lose the war. Jean said she bought the car because it was "cute and cheap."

"You know your engine is so loud because it lacks coolant cavities to dampen the noise of the timing chain," I pointed out, trying to be heard above the din.

"How do you know that?" she asked.

"Because when I'm not absorbed in *Vogue* I like to read car magazines. For what you paid for this foreign job you could have bought a decent used American car."

"But I didn't want a *used* car. Who needs somebody else's problem car?"

"No, it's fine," I lied. "I'm sure this car will serve your needs."

"I love my car," she insisted. "It has character."

"Yes, that it does."

"You men are so condescending when it comes to cars. I find it rather infuriating. I'm sure this car will be *very* popular."

"You could be right," I lied again.

The river, named the Russian, wasn't much: just a sluggish stream flowing over a gravelly bed. Its banks were heavily wooded, with here and there patches of sun breaking through in clearings. Jean said the river was more impressive in the winter and prone to flooding in rainy years.

"It's pretty here," I said. "You live in a very scenic place."

"You should see it in the spring when the prune and pear orchards are in bloom. This valley is like heaven on earth. But I expect you'll be gone by then."

"Why rush me out of here before I've even settled in? How about you strip, and I'll do a nude study of you?"

"In your dreams, buddy. I'm going to sketch the river. Want to join me?"

"Sure. I'll give it a try."

Jean lent me a drawing pad and some of her colored pencils. We sat down on the river bank and went to work. Some time later she glanced over at my pad.

"You faker!" she exclaimed. "Why didn't you tell me you were an artist?"

"OK, I took a few art classes in high school. Big deal. I'm no Rembrandt."

"You're very good! Look at how you've captured the light."

"Well, my mother was an artist. She definitely had the knack."

"How did your mother die, if you don't mind my asking?"

"It was a freak accident. In New York. During a freezing cold winter. Ice broke part of a stone parapet off a building. She never knew what hit her."

"That's terrible. How did you ever cope?"

"How does any kid cope? I just went to school and tried to get on with things. We Morans are fairly stoic by nature."

"No eight-year-old is stoic."

"I was. How did your mother die?"

"She got sick. Cancer. A long slow decline. So I had a chance to get used to the idea that she would be leaving us. Still, her absence was a terrible void for so long."

"I'm sorry. It must have been hell watching her suffer. OK, now it's your turn to show me your sketch."

She held out her pad. It was a lovely drawing that left my crude work in the dust.

"That's wonderful," I said. "Remind me never to pick up a pencil again."

"Let's not be competitive, Colm. There's plenty of room in the world for two more struggling artists. Except you could be first-rate if you applied yourself. You have a gift."

"I'm a mere art peon and you know it. What's in your basket?"

"I brought some sandwiches and some fruit. And a few slices of that lemon pie. But we're not having a picnic."

"Oh, what are we having?"

"Just a bite to eat to assuage our hunger."

"And what if I have a hunger for you?"

"Then you'll be missing out on lunch. And facing a very long walk back home."

Despite the example of skinny dipping in last night's movie, we kept our clothes on and only dipped our bare feet in the cool water.

After our non-picnic we lay back in the shade and both fell asleep. I was awakened by some bug crawling down my shirt collar. I found her leaning against a tree and looking at me.

"What are you thinking?" I asked, scratching my neck.

"Nothing I'd care to divulge to you, Mr. Moran."

"You know now I can say that I've slept with you."

"Only in the narrowest sense of the term. And I wouldn't go blabbing that to the world. My reputation is imperilled enough just being seen in your company."

"I'm fairly respectable."

"We're supposed to be having a business relationship. Remember: I spend a lot of time *inside your house.*"

"Not enough if you ask me–especially at night."

"It's time to go. You'll be expecting your dinner."

"Any chance I could kiss you first?"

"Absolutely none."

Chapter 4

Madame Aranson had a surprise for me Monday morning. "How would you like a sneak peek at our 1958 line?" she asked.

"That would make my day," I lied.

Madame Aranson swung open a door and there stood our chunky secretary Miss Page in a purplish swimsuit. Rather shocking to see so much bare flesh in an office environment. She was hardly nude, but still her beefy contours were on display. Her legs were entirely bare and the neckline of her suit was plunging precipitously. She stood there calmly as our designer tugged here and there on the stretchy fabric.

"What do you think, Colm?" she asked.

"Very, uhm, striking."

Madame Aranson pushed up on Miss Page's breasts. "Do you think the bodice needs more support?"

"I couldn't really say," I gasped.

"Well, don't be shy. Feel for yourself," she said, grabbing my hand and placing it on our model's ample left breast."

"Forgive me, Miss Page," I said, blushing.

"I don't mind, Mr. Moran. Being the fit model is part of my job. You can touch me anywhere."

If only I heard those magic words from Betty. (Or Jean.)

Madame Aranson wasn't satisfied until I got a real feel for the fit of the suit, touching Miss Page on many of her intimate areas. Had our secretary been 20 years younger, I might have embarrassed myself with an inadvertent physiological response.

"Now let's see this one," said Madame Aranson, handing our model a pale yellow suit.

With no hesitation, Miss Page wiggled out of the first suit and calmly struggled into the second, flashing a brief interregnum of total nudity.

Suddenly the bathing suit business was not as dull as I had assumed.

After enhancing my familiarity with the female form, Madame Aranson passed me on to Vera Schall, the pattern drafter. Lined up in her cramped office were a half-dozen headless mannequins on metal stands. Vera's a petite older gal with severely plucked eyebrows and masculine-looking horn-rimmed spectacles that seemed too large for her face. Strapped to her left wrist was a velvet cushion bristling with pins.

"What do you think of the Czarina?" she asked.

"Madame Aranson? Uh, she seems very competent."

"Oh, you think so, huh?"

"I gather it's tricky designing suits to fit all those different shapes and sizes."

"It is indeed, Mr. Moran. Which is why our design queen leaves that task to me."

"Really?"

"What does she do? She scrawls some vague picture, attaches a fabric swatch, and dumps the mess on my desk. Then she saunters off and flirts with Slivmank."

"No, I think she hates him."

"Shows what you know, kiddo. When his wife died, she made a major play to be the next Mrs. Slivmank. He wasn't biting though. I hear you were fondling Miss Page."

"Only in a professional capacity."

"OK, what's the difference between Miss Page and this fabric?" Vera held up an eye-fatiguing floral pattern.

"Miss Page is warm and breathing?"

"Well, you should know. No, this fabric is flat and Miss Page is anything but. See the problem?"

"I think so. One has to contour the fabric to fit the compound curves of the three-dimensional body."

"Exactly so. You're fairly astute for a male. That is what I do. I drape and cut the fabric to fit the body. Then I have to create patterns for all the different sizes we make. Does that sound like a challenge?"

"It certainly does."

"Well, it gets worse. Most of our competition makes suits in at most a half-dozen sizes. We customarily make 10 and sometimes a dozen sizes."

"Why so many?"

"Because we endeavor to fit those jumbo ladies and those super-jumbo broads. Most makers don't even try. Now at least we're getting some decent synthetics that stretch. When I was your age we hit the beach in wool knits. Scratchy when dry, and clammy and scratchy when wet. Plus, they took about a week to dry. You know what you can get lounging around in a wet bathing suit?"

"Wrinkled and puckered?"

"That and a nice painful bladder infection. Be thankful you're a man."

"I am. Daily."

* * *

The kitchen smelled like Italian food when I got home.

"Hello, darling. I'm home!" I called.

No answer. I walked into the living room and there stood Jean with a distinguished-looking older man. Jean was blushing and he was peering at me with eyebrows raised.

"Father, this is Mr. Moran," she said.

"How do you do, Dr. Valland?" I said, extending my hand. He shook it reluctantly. "I should explain my greeting was in jest. Jean cooks my dinner, which is rather in the manner of a wife. I was being facetious."

"And what else does she do for you in the manner of a wife?" he asked.

"Absolutely nothing, I assure you. You have a remarkable daughter."

"I am aware of that," he replied. "I met your father at the funeral. He did not speak highly of you. Nor was your uncle very complimentary while alive."

"Well, I'm older now. I've graduated from college."

"So I understand. I lived next door to your uncle for nearly 20 years. Jonathan was a most respectable and decent fellow. He took his business seriously and was concerned for his employees because he knew they depended on him for their livelihoods."

"Yes, I've heard nothing but admirable things about my uncle. I hope to emulate him if I can."

"I'm glad to hear that. OK, I'll leave you to your dinner. Just remember, Jean is my darling, not yours."

"Yes, sir. I fully understand. I apologize again."

Jean gave him a kiss as he departed, then turned and faced me.

"Well, you certainly stepped in it that time."

"I don't see why I shouldn't call you darling. Darling implies dearness, and you're certainly dear to me."

She sighed a big sigh.

"What's for dinner, sweetheart? It smells delicious."

"Lasagna. And one more endearment out of you, buddy, and you'll be scraping it off the walls."

In the spirit of repentance I confessed to Jean during dinner that I had spent the morning ogling and fondling Miss Page, our secretary.

"How bare was she?" she asked, appalled.

"At times just as nature made her. The word Rubenesque came to mind. But really it's no different than those life-drawing classes you took at art school."

"Not quite. We drew the models; we didn't go up and grope them."

"I imagine the blind students did."

"We didn't get that many blind artists at our school. Perhaps this new job perk will make you less inclined to leave."

"Mostly it makes me want to hire a younger and prettier secretary/ model. Want to switch jobs?"

"I can't type."

"I'm willing to overlook that."

"You need to develop new interests, Mr. Moran. You need a hobby besides trying to seduce your housekeeper."

* * *

Another session this morning with Vera, our pattern drafter. I watched as she cut out sections of tissue paper and pinned them to a mannequin. Remarkably exacting and tedious work. Fortunately, she didn't expect me to try my hand at it. She said pattern drafting is a skill that takes years to acquire, and very few master it as she has.

"It's not like designing," she said. "To do that all you need to know is which end of the pencil to hold."

"I can see, Vera, you are the key to our entire organization."

"It's nice to be appreciated, Colm. But don't expect to see any fashion magazines fawning over the geniuses in my profession."

I sensed a certain bitterness over the general neglect of pattern drafters. It's true that until a few days ago I was not even aware that her craft existed.

After lunch I was passed on to Mrs. Mona Bramley, our cutter. She's a brawny gal whose vivid red hair seemed somewhat incongruous with her otherwise grandmotherly appearance. Her job consists of laying out each set of patterns on multiple layers of cloth and cutting them out with a vibrating vertical knife.

"Looks easy don't it, Mr. Moran?"

"Not really. And please call me Colm."

"But right here in the cutting room is where you determine whether or not the company makes a profit."

"Really?"

"A good cutter will lay out the patterns to minimize waste. You're looking at as much as 50 percent more product out of the same yardage. That's pure profit in the bank."

"That's impressive."

"You also have to watch the direction of your cloth. And with many fabrics you want the patterns in the cloth to line up on the garment. Kinda tricky, you see."

"It looks endlessly difficult."

"Sometimes I have to alter a design slightly to squeeze everything together. Or I make a change or two so that the panels are easier to sew together or truer to size. But I only do that if I think it will improve the appearance of the suit. In some respects I'm the designer of last resort."

"I can see you are the key to our entire organization."

"Tell that to Slivmank. Ol' Aranson's got him so entranced he thinks it's only the unwashed peasantry past her door."

"I'm sure he values your contribution–as do I."

Today Mona was cutting regular 9-inch squares out of a greenish brown cloth woven in a sort of waffle pattern. I couldn't quite see how those squares could be sewn into gloves or bathing suits.

"Slivmank scored a real deal on this fabric," she commented. "He bought a carload of it cheap. Only it has kind of a strange sheen when wet. Gals were emerging from lakes and pools looking like large lizards. It was a real bomb."

"So what are we making with it?"

"I'm not supposed to tell you. It's kind of a surprise. OK, Colm, now you take over."

The knife buzzed through the thick stack of fabric almost effortlessly. But it constantly wanted to wander off the line. Plus if you weren't careful, you could run the blade across the cord–severing it and possibly electrocuting yourself.

"You're getting the hang of it," said Mona. "I think you've got the knack."

"I was always sort of a cut-up. What happens if you run the blade into your hand?"

"You better hope you can grow some new fingers."

* * *

Busy at the stove, Jean informed me that tonight's dinner was a ham and potato casserole.

"Sounds excellent," I said, hanging the Packard keys up on their hook.

"You got a package in the mail."

"Oh? Where is it?"

"On the dining room table."

The package was from Betty. Something told me I should wait and open it later, but my impatience got the better of me. Inside was an 8 x 10 head shot of you know who mounted in an expensive-looking silver frame. She had signed it "To Colmy, Love ya! Betty." Under her signature was a bright-red lipstick imprint of her lips.

"Very nice," commented Jean, looking over my shoulder. "Your fiancee is quite pretty."

"We're not engaged."

"So you say."

Jean pulled out one of the dining room chairs.

"Have a seat, Mr. Moran, and I'll serve you your dinner."

"Come on, Jean. Don't be that way."

"You may address me as Miss Valland. This is where the previous residents of this house always dined. Get used to it!"

"But I don't like to eat alone!"

"You're not alone. You've got her picture for company."

"Jean!"

"Sit down!"

I sat. She returned to the kitchen. Cupboard doors slammed, dishes clattered, and pans were heaved about. I sighed and lit a cigarette. She returned with my napkin, silverware, and a bowl of soup.

"Since when do you smoke?!"

"I smoke when I'm stressed."

Jean flung the items down on the table, spilling the soup. She glared at me, then returned to the kitchen. She was back a few seconds later with an ashtray that she plopped down in front of me."

"My father is a doctor!"

"I know. I've met him."

"He reads the medical journals. He's aware of the latest research findings. He says that smoking is very bad for your health."

I flicked off the accumulated ash and took another puff.

"It's only bad for people with weak lungs."

"You're an idiot!"

She returned a moment later with a glass of water. I half expected her to heave it in my face, dousing my cigarette, but she slammed it down on the table."

"I don't smoke that much," I coughed. "A friend of mine gave me a gold cigarette case and a nice Dunhill lighter for Christmas. So I started smoking. I don't mind it that much."

"You mean a *girl*friend, don't you?"

"Uh, possibly."

"Some gift! She gives you something that is harmful to your health. What is she giving you for next Christmas? A gunshot wound to the head?!!"

"Jean, please calm down."

"The name's Miss Valland, Mr. Moran!"

Someone knocked on the front door. I got up to answer it.

"I heard yelling," said Jean's father, entering without being asked.

"It's OK, Dad," said Jean. "We were having a bit of a disagreement over the health hazards of cigarettes."

"They don't call them coffin nails for nothing," he pointed out to me. "You know that big-time smoker Humphrey Bogart just died from esophageal cancer."

I snuffed out my Chesterfield.

"OK," I announced. "That was my last cigarette. I'm giving them up!"

Dr. Valland seemed impressed. "I like a fellow who can heed sound medical advice. I hope you're serious."

"I pledge to you on my sacred honor: That was my last and final and ultimate cigarette."

"No cigars either?" he asked.

"No cigars!" I affirmed.

"Good. There may be hope for you yet, young man. But a fellow should not be yelling at his housekeeper."

Mostly she was yelling at me, but I apologized anyway.

Dr. Valland spotted the new addition to my decor.

"Who's the beauty in the fancy frame?" he asked.

"His fiancee," said Jean icily.

"Congratulations!" exclaimed her dad. "You've made my day."

"Er, why's that?" I asked.

"Because some other lucky man gets the honor of having you as a son-in-law."

I didn't eat much of my dinner that night. Too upset. Jean continued as frosty as January in Moscow. She only deigned to speak to me once.

"You realize when your girlfriend planted that kiss she was kissing herself, don't you?"

"Girls often leave an impression of their lips on a photo as a gesture of affection. It doesn't mean that she's some big-time narcissist."

"Ha!" she scoffed, returning to the kitchen. It was a hard night for the crockery, but I don't think anything got broken.

Later in bed when I was not falling asleep I decided the fault had been mine. You can't romance one girl while you're semi-engaged to another one. It's too stressful on all concerned.

* * *

The next morning I typed out an apology to Jean that I left on the kitchen table. I said I was sorry for coming on so strong and hoped we could still be friends. The photo I put in an inside pocket of my grip that I stashed away in the back of my closet. I know what Betty looks like; I don't need her smiling image causing discord with Jean.

On my way to work I stopped at a pawnshop downtown. I told the gent behind the counter that I wanted to sell the cigarette lighter and case outright instead of hocking them. He gave me $26 for the pair–probably a lot less than Betty had paid. He said he'd have given me $5 more if the case wasn't inscribed. Under the lid Betty had had this message engraved: "To Colmy. Think of me when you light up! Love ya, Betty."

I wonder if guys think of their girls when they light up. I never did. And why did Betty choose to write "love ya" instead of the usual three words? Did "love ya" carry as much import? I suspect not.

Today at work I was assigned to Mrs. Ethel Yeater, the production supervisor. She's a serious gal not given to gratuitous smiling. Her office is four steps up from the production floor in one corner of the room. Two large interior windows give her a sweeping view of the sewing stations.

"What would you like to know, Mr. Moran?" she asked.

I hadn't realized I was going to be quizzed. I tried to think of a suitably sober question.

"How much do the sewing ladies make per hour? I asked.

"They're paid by the piece, not by the hour. For the gloves we're producing today they receive 12 cents per pair."

"Really? That little?"

"If a girl sticks to the job and doesn't dawdle or indulge in idle chatter she can sew ten pairs in an hour. That's $1.20 an hour, which is quite an acceptable wage."

More than I was making per hour.

She went on: "Our gloves wholesale for 52 cents and retail for 99, so we could hardly pay them more."

"How do you keep track of their output?"

"Each girl has a box by her machine where they put their finished gloves. Every hour I do a count and inspection, noting the total for each worker in my register. Gloves with flaws I put aside separately. These are sold as seconds to jobbers at a discount."

"How much do the girls earn for gloves with flaws?"

"Nothing. We don't pay for sloppy work."

"How much do they make for bathing suits?"

"The piece rate varies with the complexity of the design and size. The larger sizes take longer, so they pay a higher rate. Some of our best sewers routinely earn over $2 per hour."

"And the flawed suits, do we sell them as seconds?"

"Never. The garment is returned to the girl to correct. Milady Modest is known for its high quality and fine tailoring. It's my job to ensure that our reputation is upheld."

"That's good to know."

"A firm hand is required over production, Mr. Moran. Without it, we would soon descend into chaos. Orders would be delayed, product could be rejected, and profits imperiled. All of our girls are on call. I summon only as many as are needed for that day's production. Naturally, I choose the most skilled and the fastest. This keeps the girls on their toes. Slackers soon realize that they are at the bottom of my call list."

I for one would not want to be at the bottom of any of her lists.

"I can see, Mrs. Yeater, that you are the key to our entire operation."

"I do my best, Mr. Moran," she replied, unsmiling.

I thought of another question. "I notice, Mrs. Yeater, that all of our sewing ladies appear to be Caucasian. Do we ever employ Negroes or Mexicans?"

"We do not, Mr. Moran. I would not wish racial disharmony to interfere with production."

"I see. Well, you know best."

I left her office with the impression that the bathing suit business was far more Dickensian than I had imagined. Mrs. Yeater turned me over to one of their veteran seamstresses, Mrs. Justeen Snyder. She was a pleasant older lady who cracked an actual smile.

"Nice to meet you, Mr. Moran."

"Please call me Colm."

"Oh, I couldn't do that. Mr. Slivmank would have a fit."

"Sorry. How do you like Mrs. Yeater?"

"Oh, she's OK. She's firm but fair. She's much better than our previous supervisor who risked scissors in her back every time she stepped out on the floor. And there wouldn't have been any witnesses either, if you catch my drift."

"That bad, huh?"

"It was nice to see Myrtle go. There were no tears shed at *her* farewell party. Now, what do you know about sewing machines, Mr. Moran?"

I gulped. "Pretty close to zero. I believe some sort of thread is involved."

"Don't worry. We'll get you up to speed in no time."

Chapter 5

Everything about Mrs. Snyder's machine was bigger and more intimidating than the few home sewing machines I had seen. The industrial motor, for example, was the size of the motor on a table saw. It should have no trouble plunging a needle through my finger. Very likely it wouldn't stall even when it hit the gristle and bone.

Mrs. Snyder showed me the numerous small orifices where you applied a drop or two of oil at the beginning of your shift.

"If you take care of your machine, Mr. Moran, your machine will take care of you."

That's what I was afraid of.

Next she showed me how to wind thread on a small device called a bobbin and insert it in a compartment below the needle. Then she demonstrated how to guide the thread on the intricate path it took from its big wooden spool to the small hole through the needle.

"What happens if you don't get the thread over all the places?" I asked.

"Then you will not have a happy time at your machine."

She showed me how to adjust the thread tension and stitch length, and how to operate the presser foot.

"OK, now it's time to sew," she announced, grabbing a box and removing some of the fabric squares I cut out yesterday.

"What are we making?" I asked weakly.

"Potholders! Won't that be fun? It's ol' Slivmank's bright idea to use up some of the excess acreage of lizard cloth. He thinks they'll make great gift items, like for Christmas I guess. Should be a real wife-pleaser, don't you think?"

"I couldn't say."

She leaned over and whispered, "Well, just between you and me, I wouldn't suggest givin' 'em to your best girl. Not if you wish to make an impression."

"Thanks for the tip."

In about 30 seconds Mrs. Snyder had sewn two potholders, complete with fabric loop on one corner for hanging and a tiny Milady Modest label. Each consisted of two squares sewn together around the perimeter, with something called seam-binding tape neatly concealing the raw edges.

"OK, now it's your turn, Mr. Moran. Don't worry, it's kind of like driving a car. This lever extending down from the machine is your accelerator. Just press it sideways with your leg to control your speed. Some girls like a pedal on the floor, but I prefer the lever-operated style. Any questions?"

"Is it time for lunch?"

"Sorry, it's time to sew. Let's do it!"

So I gave it a shot. The first problem was that the machine appeared to have only two speeds: zero and 90 miles an hour. Even the slightest pressure from my leg sent the fabric rocketing under the needle.

"Why can't it go slower?" I demanded.

"Don't forget, Mr. Moran, you're getting paid by the piece. Very soon 'slow' will not be a option you'd want on your machine. Besides, just remember: the faster you go the straighter you sew. But I suppose I could slow it down a bit while you're learning."

She adjusted a dial. Now the machine's one speed was a mere 60 miles per hour. After a half-hour of struggle, I produced my first finished potholder. A thing of beauty it was not.

"It's, uh, not bad for a first effort," said Mrs. Snyder.

She held it up, and all the other ladies applauded politely.

"I doubt if it will pass Mrs. Yeater's inspection," I said.

"Don't worry about that. All the potholders you sew today are being donated to the thrift store up at the hospital."

"You think someone would pay actual cash money for that?" I asked doubtfully.

"Sure," she replied. "Probably at least five cents. Maybe even ten."

"Mrs. Snyder, you are the supreme optimist."

"Thanks. Now let's cut the chatter and sew."

* * *

Eventually, I got a little better. The straight sides started to be easier, although turning corners was still a challenge. I got a little less fearful of the needle. I sewed one especially neat seam, only to discover that my bobbin had run out of thread. By then I'd entirely forgotten how to load more onto it, and had to have Mrs. Snyder demonstrate it again for me.

"You're doing great," she said.

"Is it time for lunch yet?"

"No, but we're due for a coffee break."

I sipped my coffee outside in the parking lot with my fellow workers. Many of them were smoking cigarettes.

"How come you don't smoke?" asked a gaunt-looking woman named Ida Stipe.

"Had to give it up. Doctor's orders, you know."

"My doctor smokes like a chimney," said a Mrs. Cikowich, whose first name I hadn't caught.

"Mine too," said Mrs. Snyder. "My gynecologist always has a stinky cigar on the go while he's poking around up there."

Everyone snickered at my blush.

By the end of the day I was turning out potholders at the rate of one every six or seven minutes. Many of them looked virtually semi-professional. The best example I tucked into my pocket to take home.

"So, Mr. Moran, how do like sewing?" asked my instructor as we were getting ready to leave.

"It's a hard job, Mrs. Snyder. My back hurts, my butt aches, and I'm kind of seeing double. A week of this and I'll be ready for the Mayo Clinic."

"So you see who has the tough job around here?"

"I do indeed. You gals are the key to this entire organization."

* * *

I was relieved to see when I got home that Jean was no longer on the active warpath. I was disappointed to see that the kitchen table was set only for one.

"Good evening, Mr. Moran," she said.

"Hello, Miss Valland," I replied, handing her a surprise gift.

"What's this?"

"A potholder. I sewed it myself."

"Really? It looks quite professional."

"Thanks. I'm sorry about last night."

"Yeah, well I was going to hand in my notice, but I guess I can't if you're bribing me now with potholders. I'm sorry I got upset. It's none of my business if you want to smoke yourself into an early grave. I wish, though, you had taken your pledge to my father more seriously."

"What do you mean?"

"It's none of my business, but you reek of tobacco smoke."

"I haven't been smoking! Not a one! I'm taking my coffee breaks now with a bevy of heavy smokers. We can call Mrs. Snyder right now if you don't believe me."

"Relax. I believe you. Dinner is chow mein. I went light on the strychnine."

"Glad to hear it. I hope we can still be friends."

"We'll see."

So we ate our dinners separately again in adjoining rooms. Very dumb if you ask me, but she didn't. I insisted, though, on my right to dry the dishes while she washed.

"The theater's getting a new movie on Friday," I pointed out.

"It's about time. What is it?"

"'I Was a Teenage Werewolf.' I'm willing to give it a try if you are."

"Sorry. I'm going to a barbecue at the Sons of the Forest that night."

Not good news.

"Oh. You don't look much like a son of the forest."

"That is not a requirement."

"Are you going with someone?"

"Yes, Elwyn Saunders. Do you know him?"

"How could I know him? I just got here. What does he do?"

"He's working in his uncle's law office this summer. He's starting law school at Berkeley in the fall."

"Do you like him?"

"I don't know. I suppose. I've known him since I was five."

"If you've known him that long, you should be tired of him by now."

"No, it's only those recent acquaintances who wear out their welcome."

"How about Saturday night then?"

"Sorry. I'm washing my hair."

"You have short hair. Washing it could not take longer than five minutes. I'm willing to wait."

"I'm washing my hair and then I'm performing other assorted tasks. You should ask out another girl."

"All the other females I know are over 50 and mostly married."

"There are ways to meet girls in this town besides hiring them to cook your dinner."

"Where's the nearest women's college?"

"That would be Mills in Oakland."

"Too far. I think I'll stick with you, but only as a friend."

"My friends quota may be full up."

"Then I'll just have to be even more ingratiating."

* * *

The first thing I did at work today was have Mrs. Snyder call Jean and assure her that I've been boycotting cigarettes. They spoke for several minutes.

"How did it go?" I asked when she returned to her machine.

"Miss Valland seemed surprised to hear from me. I told her you were a very nice young man with no bad habits."

"What did she say?"

"She expressed a certain skepticism on that point. She also wanted to know if you had in fact sewn the potholder that you gave her yesterday."

"Wow. I didn't realize my credibility was so low."

"I assured her that you were making wonderful progress and were demonstrating a natural aptitude for sewing."

"Thank you, Mrs. Snyder. You're a great teacher."

"We make a nice team. OK, let's cut the chatter and go to work."

Our machines whirled away as we assaulted the mountain of lizard cloth squares. No longer terrifying, sewing soon became tedious and boring. I was turning out a presentable potholder every couple of minutes. My seams were straight, my loop was affixed firmly, and my label was tucked neatly into the binding. My output now was going into a box for critical inspection by the exacting Mrs. Yeater.

"Mrs. Snyder, doesn't all this non-stop sewing get a little tiresome after a while?" I asked while reloading my bobbin.

"You get used to it, Mr. Moran. Bathing suits are better 'cause the work is more varied. Gloves are the worst. Very repetitious. I've come home from a day of that and spent the whole night sewing gloves in my sleep."

"And after all the work of making a pair you only earn 12 cents. Isn't that discouraging?"

"Well, Mr. Moran, your father owns the company now. Couldn't he raise the rate?"

Very true. I hadn't thought of that.

"Good point, Mrs. Snyder. I'll discuss it with Mr. Slivmank."

I waylaid the linty old guy during my coffee break.

"Out of the question, Colm," he replied. "Our profit margin on gloves is razor thin as it is. In fact, we really should reduce the rate to nine cents."

"I hardly think so, Wendell. The sewers are working for peanuts as it is. Why don't we raise our wholesale price?"

"We can't. We're getting lots of competition now from gloves from Japan and Hong Kong. Our quality is better, but their gloves are retailing for 69 cents."

"Damn, that's 30 cents cheaper than our price."

"I know, Colm. It's very discouraging."

I returned and reported the bad news to Mrs. Snyder. She sighed and said she didn't think that any of the sewers would mind if we gave up on gloves and switched to something else.

"Perhaps these potholders will work out," I suggested.

She looked doubtful. "Mr. Moran, I'd be very surprised if anyone ever got rich in the potholder biz."

"Why not?"

"Because most people have a grandma or aunt who crochets and knits. They churn them out by the dozen for Christmas gifts. It's hard to compete with free."

During our lunch break I asked Mrs. Snyder if she knew anything about the upcoming Sons of the Forest barbecue.

"Oh, yes. It's one of their big fund-raising events of the year."

"Do you have to be a member to go?"

"No, you just need $4 for a ticket. It's pretty expensive, but the men do a nice job barbecuing the salmon. I should warn you they charge extra for beer. Are you thinking of going?"

"I'm considering it."

"You know my granddaughter wants to go, but she doesn't have a date."

"Oh, really?"

"It's not that she's unattractive. She's a very lovely girl. Senior year she was both homecoming queen and queen of the annual Prune Festival."

"Doesn't she have a boyfriend?"

"Kind of. But he got drafted and is now all the way over in West Germany. He drives a tank. Are you facing the draft?"

"No, I'm 4F."

"Flat feet?"

"No, bum elbow. Do you think your granddaughter might be willing to go with me?"

"She'd be thrilled. I've told her all about you."

"Then tell her I'll pick her up at seven. What's her name?"

"Juanita Howe."

"Howl as in howling at the moon?"

"No, Howe as in how now brown cow."

Wow, I've got a date with Juanita Howe. My first blind date arranged by a grandmother.

* * *

I had a letter waiting for me on the dining room table from Betty. Too bad one's housekeeper always gets first peek at one's mail. I slipped the envelope unopened into my shirt pocket and waited for my dinner to be served. The main course was liver and onions–not on my list of top ten favorite foods. I gagged it down anyway.

"Anything interesting in the mail?" inquired Jean, bringing out my dessert: some sort of gruesome rice pudding.

"Not really, Miss Valland. How was your day?"

"Not bad. I waxed your kitchen floor."

"I thought the linoleum exhibited a new and attractive sheen. Thank you."

"Don't mention it."

She returned to the kitchen.

I removed the envelope and tried to open it as stealthily as possible. Jean returned with a surprise cup of coffee; I quickly tucked the envelope away.

"Are you still working on your pudding?"

"I guess so. What are those slimy bits?"

"Chopped prunes. Ukiah is a major producer of prunes."

"I know. I have a date tomorrow with one of your former prune queens."

"Oh, who's that?"

"Juanita Howe. Know her?"

"Of course. I hope you have a lovely time."

She returned to the kitchen. I removed the envelope. She promptly returned with an ashtray. I tucked the envelope away.

"I'm continuing not to smoke," I informed her. "As I intend to do for the rest of my life."

"I thought Juanita was engaged to Reggie Dowling."

"He's manning a tank in Germany as we speak. He's our first line of defense against the thousands of Russian tanks deployed by the Warsaw Pact nations."

"In which case we're all in big trouble. Reggie Dowling is a major flake."

"I wouldn't know about that, of course."

Jean returned to the kitchen. I removed the envelope. She came back with a small bowl of mixed nuts. I slipped the envelope back in my pocket.

"How do you know Juanita?"

"I don't. It's a blind date. Should I be worried?"

"Her reputation is not the best."

"Good. I'm a lusty young fellow–as I expect is your Mr. Saunders."

"Elwyn happens to be a respectable gentleman."

She returned to the kitchen. I gave up trying to read my letter and waited for her to return.

She came back with a tray.

"Shall I remove your pudding, sir?"

"OK. Prunes aren't really a favorite of mine. You can go easy on the liver in the future also."

"Your uncle loved liver."

"Well, that was him and I'm me."

"If you say so. I'm merely your housekeeper."

"And my friend too, don't forget."

No reply. She returned to you know where. A cupboard door slammed. I sipped my coffee and munched some nuts. She returned and took back the ashtray.

"So where are you going on this date of yours?"

"To the barbecue, of course. I love grilled salmon. So you don't need to make dinner for me tomorrow."

She contemplated that news.

"I hope you're not going there to spy on me."

"It's the farthest thing from my mind. Grilled Pacific salmon is just not something you can get back east. Nor are blond prune queens easy to come by either."

"Juanita happens to be a redhead."

"So much the better."

"At least she had red hair the last time I saw her. It tends to vary."

"Good. I like a girl who gets creative with her appearance."

Jean turned and exited, then poked her head out the door.

"You can read your letter now, Mr. Moran. I don't need any help with the dishes."

"OK, if you say so."

Here's what Betty wrote:

> Hi Colmy,
>
> Thanks for the letter. "The Skin of Our Teeth" has got to be the CRAZIEST play ever to escape from some nut's typewriter. I keep asking what does it all mean? We open in 3 days!!! Assuming I don't go mad first!! Wish you could come to see my debut. Write me again soon!
>
> Love ya,
>
> Betty

Not very informative, so later I tried phoning her. Her roommate said she was at the director's hotel "going over scenes."

That was a scene I kept going over. And I didn't much care for what I was imagining.

* * *

I got yanked out of the sewing pool today. I think Slivmank feared I was beginning to identify too closely with the proletariat. I got assigned to Joe, our diminutive warehouse czar. The little fellow seemed rather hostile. The first thing he did was ask if I'd come to spy on him for "old man Slavemonk."

"No, I'm just making the rounds to get a feel for the various operations of the company," I replied.

"I seen you sewin' all them potholders. Seems like a queer job for a fella to be doin'."

"It's good to try all the jobs, Joe. Those ladies have it really tough. From now on when I buy clothes I'll appreciate all the work that goes into making them. So you keep track of our inventory?"

"Yeah, and ship orders and take in supplies and all the other jobs they dump on me. Been doin' it for 19 years, so I guess I know what I'm doin'."

"I'm sure you do. The shelves, though, look a bit, uh, chaotic."

In truth our warehouse looked like San Francisco after the 1906 quake.

"I know where everything is."

"And what if you call in sick? Can other people find things?"

"I don't miss work. And I don't get drunk and wreck cars neither."

Apparently news of my youthful follies had reached even this remote outpost.

"Well, carry on, Joe. I'll just sit here and observe."

Joe muttered something unintelligible and handed me a ratty broom. "Floor needs sweepin', kid."

So I swept the dusty floor. Then he had me take inventory of the bolts of fabric on the uppermost shelves. These, of course, were out of sight to him. He did not seem pleased when I found seven more rolls of lizard cloth.

"We could corner the market in potholders," I joked.

Joe took my list and crossed out that line. "Just forget you ever saw 'em."

"Can I ask why?"

"No, you can't."

"I'm the owner's son, you know," I reminded him.

"I'm not stealin' nothin'. Them lizards have caused enough trouble already. We'll stash 'em up there and then I'll find 'em in a year or two."

"OK, Joe, whatever you say."

Of course, in a year or two he could be pensioned off or deceased. Just then, Mrs. Hazel Simmerman, the aged bookkeeper, entered with our paychecks. Mine was for $11.32. Two day's pay (for last week) minus assorted deductions. Shockingly meager, but it was the first money I had ever earned. My income can only go up from here (I hope).

A long-distance call gave me a welcome break from warehouse tedium. It was Tom Brannan, a college buddy.

"Damn, Colm, nobody's heard a peep from you. We're beginning to think you defected to the Commies."

"It's great to hear from you, Tom. Thanks for tracking me down. Who's paying for this call?"

"My employer, naturally."

"I figured as much. How's the wholesale liquor business?"

"You know all those gangsters who got into booze during Prohibition?"

"Yeah."

"Well, they never got out of it. You should see the characters I have to call on. Like their photos should be up on the Post Office wall. But now I know who to call if I ever need anyone rubbed out. How's things in bathing suits?"

"More interesting than I expected. It's not too bad."

"Where are you exactly?"

"About three hours north of San Francisco. It's where the known map ends and unexplored territory begins."

"Sounds rustic as hell."

"There are more sawmills here than people. How's New York?"

"Great as usual. Katie and I caught Coltrane at Birdland last weekend."

"So you two are still together?"

"Yep, got my foot snared in the trap. I've been gnawing at my leg, but she may have hooked me."

"Good. I always liked Katie."

"Please don't remind me that you dated her first. How are the locals out there? Accommodating?"

"I'm working at it. Tonight I'm going to a Sons of the Forest barbecue with a former Prune Festival queen."

"Damn, Colm! You've gone native!"

"Yeah, Tommy. You may be right."

Chapter 6

I found Juanita's house without much trouble. It was south of downtown on a street of modest homes. She bounded off the front porch when she saw the Packard pull up. Vivid yellow blouse and matching shorts. Nice legs. Medium height. Hair now blond, not red. Not quite as pretty as Betty, but much more buxom. Scorching red lipstick. Friendly blue eyes and creamy complexion. Close to any fellow's dream blind date.

I got out to open the door for her, but she beat me to it.

"Right on time, Colm," said said, hopping in. "What's with the jacket and tie?"

"My housekeeper said it was a dressy event."

"Well, she lied. Heck, it's just a barbecue in the park. We'll strip you down when we get there. This car is a gas!"

I pulled away from the curb at the Packard's usual stately pace.

"You look very nice," I said.

"You're not so bad yourself," she winked. "I hear if we hit it off, I could in be for a free potholder or two."

"Damn, I should have brought you one. I make them you know."

"Better that than one of your bathing suits. So how do you like Ukiah?"

"It's quite a change from the east."

"I hear you went to Yale. Is that in Boston?"

"No, New Haven."

"What's that college in Boston?"

"There's an obscure one near there called Harvard."

"Oh, right. You're the first Yale guy I ever met. I suppose the girls back east are really fast. You know, being so sophisticated and all."

"They tend to vary. Not so fast in many cases. How are the girls here?"

"Wouldn't you like to know. God, this car is so-o-o old. Are you going to sell it and get something new and modern?"

"I wasn't planning on it."

"Kinda twitchy going into second, isn't it? You know they got cars now that shift automatically."

"I'm aware of that. I don't mind shifting myself."

"Well, the thing is that big ol' knobby gear-shifter shaft kind of separates a fellow from his date. If we ever reached the state where some closeness was desired, I could get a nasty bruise from you shifting into third."

"I hadn't thought of that. You're right. This car is completely unacceptable."

"I thought you'd see the light," she smiled.

We parked on a street near the city park. I removed my jacket and Juanita swiftly denuded me of my tie.

"There, you look better," she said. "Not so stuffy. Who's your housekeeper?"

"Jean Valland. Know her?"

"Sure do. She was in my high school class. Very artistic. We always got her to paint the signs for our pep rallies. She's keeping house for you, huh? Well, that's a shocking scandal."

"Our relationship is extremely close, I mean chaste. We dine in separate rooms."

"I should hope so. Is she live in?"

"No, she sleeps 50 feet away in the house next door."

"I bet she's itching to cross that divide."

"You are so wrong, Juanita. She wants nothing to do with me."

"A cute Yalie like you? I don't believe that for a second."

* * *

We entered the park under a giant banner that read, "Your Generosity Can Put Someone in an Iron Lung."

"Is that to be desired?" I asked my date.

"Sure. They're raising money to buy iron lungs for polio victims. That's why they're clipping you so much for the eats."

Throngs of festive barbecue-lovers were dining at long tables and enjoying toe-tapping tunes provided by a band playing hillbilly music. We joined the long line snaking toward the ticket booth. Many passers by of both sexes nodded greetings to Juanita. Two sets of remarkably alluring girls stopped to chat and be introduced. Both groups also inquired about the health and well-being of Reggie.

"He's fine," Juanita replied both times. "I got a letter from him today."

"Reggie's a guy I used to go out with who's in the service," she explained to me.

"I know. Your grandmother mentioned him."

"I'm not formally engaged to him or anything like that."

"I understand."

"People were just used to seeing us together. You know, it being a small town and all."

"I know how people can be."

Eventually we bought our tickets (I paid), got our hands stamped for the privilege of buying beer, were served our food on paper plates, and found places to sit at a table in the shade. A man carrying a tray filled with paper cups of foamy beer came by as we were sitting down. Our two beers cost a buck each.

"You know that's more than you pay for drinks at the Essex Hotel bar in Manhattan," I pointed out.

"Don't worry, Colm. I'm your basic cheap date. One beer does me fine."

"I don't mind," I lied. "It's for a good cause. This salmon is great."

"They get it fresh too. It was swimming in the ocean this morning."

I looked around. No sign yet of Jean and her date.

"So, what do you do, Juanita?"

"I manage the photo department at Flamperts. That's a variety store downtown."

"I've seen it. So you sell film?"

"Yeah, and cameras and flashbulbs and filters and such. I can even sell you a tripod if you've got the shakes."

"Do you develop film too?"

"No, we send it to Kodak in Frisco. We offer pretty fast turnaround. If you get it in by 2:00 p.m., we'll have it back in two days."

"Do you ever look at the photos?"

"Sure, sometimes."

"Ever see anything naughty?"

"Once in a while."

"Do you call the cops?"

"I haven't. So what if a guy snaps a photo of the missus with her girdle off. Big deal. Now say you're going out with a girlfriend of mine, and I spot a photo of you hanging out with some other dame. I'd probably make sure she finds out about that."

"You chicks stick together."

"We have to," she laughed. "You guys are *not* to be trusted."

* * *

I spotted Jean and her escort as we were finishing our meal. She was making a big point of not looking in our direction. She was dressed as casually as Juanita, confirming her blatant misdirection of me. Her fella was this beetle-browed oaf in a seersucker jacket and baggy linen trousers.

"Elwyn's a fine looking specimen," I observed.

"He looks like an overgrown boy, if you ask me," commented Juanita. "He'll look like that until he turns 35. Then he'll switch overnight to looking like a prematurely old man."

"What can you tell me about him?"

"Elwyn? He was a big brain in high school. Kind of obnoxious in your know-it-all department. Always sweet on Jeanie, but she didn't have much to do with him. I'm surprised to see her with him tonight. Not so good in sports, but I think he made the wrestling team."

That sweaty oaf grappling with my pretty housekeeper: not a scene I'd care to imagine.

"Oh, and he was big in the Bible Club. His family goes to one of those churches where everyone stands up and hollers for Jesus.

Jean and Elwyn got their food and headed for a table on the opposite side of the park. The sight of that unnatural pairing was so annoying, I resolved to ignore them.

A woman strolled by displaying desserts on a tray. Juanita selected the German chocolate cake; I got a piece of apple pie. Another $2 subtracted from my beleaguered wallet. That was it: my paycheck was spent.

"You have good table manners," said Juanita, savoring her cake. "Your nails are not chewed to the quick, and your cuticles are neatly groomed. You smell faintly of some nice soap. You have the longest eyelashes I've ever seen on a guy. Also cute dimples in your ruddy cheeks when you smile. You went to a fancy college. Your family is big in bathing suits and you drive a block-long car. You know what that tells me?"

"I have no idea."

"Somewhere there's some smart east coast gal who's got her claws into you. Or had them."

"I suppose next you're going to tell me her name."

"It won't be anything ordinary like Annie or Ruthie."

"Would you believe Betty?"

"Betty I could see. That's pretty classy. Bet she went to a fancy college too."

"Very perceptive. She just graduated from Vassar."

"But she's not here hanging around your neck, so what is she, a career girl?"

"Actress. She's playing in summer stock on the Cape."

"Actress, huh? So she's pretty too."

"Very."

"And you phone her a lot, but she hasn't got much time for you."

"Have you been talking to my housekeeper?"

"Didn't have to. But she's doing just enough to keep you interested."

"You're in the wrong job, Juanita. You should hire yourself out as a psychic."

"You're not so hard to figure, Mr. Colm Moran. Hey, it's too hot to dance. I know a place up in the hills with a nice view across the valley. Might be a breeze up there too."

"Let's go before they come around to collect rent on these chairs."

* * *

I was thankful I'd downed only one overpriced beer as I was navigating the treacherous road up the hill to Juanita's parking spot. The last segment was a steep quarter-mile climb up a rutted dirt road. We pulled into a turnout that offered a sweeping view of the valley. Far below the lights of Ukiah twinkled in the fading light.

"Nice spot," I said, shutting off the motor and yanking up the parking brake. "Where's this road go?"

"Back into the woods. It's an old logging road."

"Do you come up here with old loggers?"

"Sure do. As often as I can."

She slid over in the seat toward me.

"You smell great," I pointed out.

"Thanks. Got this perfume with my employee discount."

"Very sensible."

Tiring of the view, I kissed her. Eventually I liberated several of her buttons and slipped my hand into her bra.

"You have magnificent breasts, Juanita."

"Thanks. It's generally acknowledged I have the nicest pair in town. How do they compare with Betty's?"

"She's not even in the running."

We kissed again, then she pulled away.

"There's something we need to discuss."

"OK," I said, reluctantly withdrawing my hand.

"I have two older sisters: Ramona and Margarita. They both gave birth nine months after their weddings. You see nature designed us Howe girls to attract men and have babies."

"Well, you're certainly doing the former."

"For example, you could go to the back seat and jerk off . . ."

"Not a very gentlemanly thing to do."

"And I'd still get pregnant."

"Really? Across that distance?"

"No doubt about it. It's guaranteed."

Alarming news, but at least she wasn't squeamish about discussing sex–which is more than I can say for Betty.

"There is such a thing as birth control," I pointed out.

"Doesn't work with us. My sisters have tried everything. They still get knocked up like clockwork."

"So you and Reggie have never, uh . . ."

"No, never. Not once. And it's been a real strain on him. He's about the horniest guy I've ever met. He was talking dirty to me way back in the seventh grade. That's why I suspect he's over in Germany wallowing in fräuleins. Those continental girls are known to put out."

"They do have that reputation. So you can't have sex until you're married?"

"I don't dare and it's a real drag. Plus, I'll have to find some guy who wants a big family. I may have to move to Utah and marry a Mormon."

"Why's that?"

"Mormons go for big families. How many kids do you want, Colm?"

"I never gave it much thought."

"Would nine or ten be too many?"

"Probably."

"Aren't you Catholic? Your name sounds Irish."

"We're from the Protestant section. We wear orange on St. Patrick's Day and get punched in the nose by drunken papists."

"How about seven or eight kids?"

"That's still quite a crowd. I was an only child, so big families are a mystery to me. Aren't there times of the month when you can't get pregnant?"

"Maybe. But only for a second or two. Well, that's my situation, Colm, as far as sex goes. You can take me home now if you're disappointed."

"Not at all, Juanita. Let's stay a while. I was just limbering up my lips."

Chapter 7

The roaring vacuum cleaner got me up early Saturday morning. I shuffled into the living room and pulled the plug.

"I thought Saturday was your day off," I said.

Jean inspected my flannel bathrobe with distaste. "I switched it to tomorrow this week. I'm sorry if I disturbed you and any guests you may have."

"I have no guests. Are you taking tomorrow off so you can spend the day in church with your beau Elwyn?"

"He's not my beau. Anyway, he asked me, but I declined. How was your date?"

"It was very likely the most spectacular blind date a fellow could hope for."

"That figures. She *would* appeal to you."

"Your escort looked like quite a splendid example of manhood. How come you didn't come by and introduce me?"

"I might have if you'd stayed longer. Dare I inquire where you went?"

"Just off for a spot of platonic necking."

"I see. Are you going to plug my machine back in?"

"Not until I find out what's wrong with it."

"It's not the bag; I just changed it."

Under the bag was a filter screen clogged with years of crud. I cleaned it off and tested the machine. It now ran quieter and sucked as designed.

"Thanks," said Jean. "You've made my day."

I switched off the motor again.

"So what are you doing tomorrow, Jean?"

"Driving over to the coast to do some sketching."

"Good. I'll go with you. But let's take my car."

"Why?"

"Because I prefer to travel in style and luxury."

"OK, buddy, but you're buying the gas."

Frankly, I expected her to put up more of a fuss about my tagging along. Was it possible she was just the slightest bit jealous?

* * *

After lunch I did something unusual for me. I went to the library. Like most small-town libraries, Ukiah's occupies an imposing neoclassical building donated by the ever-generous (except to his employees) Andrew Carnegie. As I recall Mr. Carnegie made his millions in steel, not bathing suits. I found a heavy tome titled *Introduction to Business Accounting.* But to issue me a borrower's card the librarian required a form of local identification. I explained my situation re: Milady Modest Inc. and showed her the keys to my uncle's Packard, a well-known local automobile. She decided that would have to do.

To have any sort of career in business, one ought to have at least a vague idea of what those lines of figures in a ledger book mean. This book, however, proved virtually unreadable. I slog through a couple of paragraphs and my eyes glaze over. The type starts to shimmy and all the concepts explicated by the author quietly exit my brain as I nod off. Jean says this is because I lack a facility with numbers. She claims that math-inclined people find business accounts exciting. I suspect the only way I could get through this book is if I tear out the pages one by one and read them between Juanita's extravagant breasts. Now there's a figure my brain can get excited about.

My housekeeper produced a more palatable dinner tonight. Even though we dined separately we managed to find topics to fight about. We were discussing current popular music, when she expressed an enthusiasm for that unwashed hillbilly crooner Elvis Presley. I pointed out that Mr. Presley, although inexplicably popular now, would surely prove a flash in the pan. Clearly, the best new singer of our times had just scored with his popular hit "Love Letters in the Sand."

"Pat Boone is the Bing Crosby of our generation," I called through the closed door.

"You're an idiot!" Jean replied from the kitchen. "All he does is remake songs by Negro singers."

"Pat's at least as good an actor as Bing in his movies," I called.

"Hah! That's not saying much."

"He was excellent in 'April Love.' Elvis in his movies is as wooden as a cigar store Indian."

"At least he has sex appeal. Pat Boone looks like someone your parents would want you to marry."

"What's wrong with that? Someday I hope to produce a movie starring Mr. Boone."

"That will be the end of your career, buster. And his!"

After Jean did the dishes and left I called Juanita to reserve next Friday for another date. She was happy to hear from me.

"I half expected you not to call, Colm. Some guys disappear for good after I give them the speech."

"Well, that's shallow."

"Are you watching Perry Mason?"

"No, I don't have a TV."

"What do you do in the evenings then?"

"I'm reading a book on business accounting," I lied.

"That's impressive, Colm. A handsome business success with a sparkling personality. What girl wouldn't go for a guy like you?"

Unlike Jean, Juanita always makes me feel good when I talk to her.

Later I got a collect call from Betty, sounding distinctly cool.

"I don't know if you're interested, Colm, but the play opened this weekend."

"Of course I am, darling. How did it go?"

"Very well. I got a nice notice in the *Cape Cod Times*. The review said, "Fetching newcomer Betty Platt was sparkling in the demanding role of Sabina."

"That's great. I'm sure you stole the show."

"I thought you might at least have sent some flowers. It being my big opening night and all."

Damn, the thought never occurred to me.

"I wanted to wire you a lavish bouquet, Betty, but I only make $32 a week."

"So now you're pinching pennies? You never cared about money before."

"That's when I was going to college and spending my father's generous allowance. When I'm doing better, I'll smother you in roses."

"I hope so. I'm thinking of changing my name."

"Why?"

"Jimmy says catty reviewers will always be tempted to write "Betty Platt fell flat" or "Betty Platt went splat."

"You could change it to Moran."

"Moran? Wouldn't that be confusing? People might think we're married."

"I meant you change it via marriage to me."

"How could I marry you, Colm? You live on the other side of the world!"

"It's not quite that far."

"I could never leave New York, you know that. Unless I got an attractive offer from Hollywood."

"Marriage might improve your love life," I pointed out.

"You mean *your* sex life–until the novelty wears off."

For being a lovely young woman in the prime of life, Betty's not exactly steeped in romance. I'd wire her some repentance flowers, but I have to make $6.12 last until Friday.

* * *

To get to the coast we drove north to a small town called Willits, then took an absurdly winding road west to Fort Bragg. At every turn the Packard swayed queasily on its aging suspension. It's a good thing I'd eaten a light breakfast. The joke about Fort Bragg is there's no fort there, nor is there much to brag about. You can't see much of the ocean either because a giant sawmill sprawls along its waterfront. Jean said the other major industry in town is fishing. We also passed a few modest motels for intrepid travelers determined to escape civilization.

Our destination was an even more forlorn town ten miles south called Mendocino. Its sawmill closed years ago and the place has been moldering ever since. Just a bunch of weathered Victorians amid overgrown vacant lots. Reminded me of the seedier sections of the Maine coast. Jean says a few artists have moved there because the rents are so cheap. God knows what they do in that isolated, fog-bound place. The town occupies a rocky bluff overlooking the Pacific. Scenic yes, but how long can you sit in the chilly dampness staring at the ocean before you get an urge to off yourself?

Thankfully, the fog lifted as we were setting up our easels. Our task was to paint some windswept pines above a road meandering down to the turbulent sea. Probably a scene that would have inspired Winslow Homer, but it made me anxious.

"I've never been any good at watercolors," I complained to Jean. "I muddy my colors and produce ugly blotches."

"Welcome to the club. Well, try your best. And remember, Colm, we're not competing here."

Laughably untrue, of course. The clash of our personalities rendered us incessantly competitive. If I ever got a chance to kiss her, we'd probably compete to see who was best at that.

"I bet you don't have anything back east as wild and beautiful as this coast," she remarked, sorting through her brushes. (See note above re: competitiveness.)

"I don't know, our millions of tourists seem to find plenty to gawk at. The Palisades across from New York are fairly spectacular, and the Hudson River Valley offers the visitor many scenic delights."

"You sound like a Chamber of Commerce brochure."

I tentatively applied a daub of watery blue to my paper.

"Have you noticed, Jean, that nature's spectrum is infinite, while I'm stuck here with a tin of ten colors?"

"Turner did OK with his. You can feel the sun radiating out of his paintings."

"Yes, but he wasn't spending five days a week flogging bathing suits."

"Or keeping house for some messy bachelor."

"My Yale roommates regarded me as excessively neat."

"Then I can only imagine what a slum your dorm room must have been."

Jean worked with her usual intensity, while I casually dipped and daubed. Paint dripped onto her pants, but she didn't seem to notice. She was wearing clamdiggers the color of tomato soup, although no clam-digging was planned.

Not to be competitive, but I preferred my primitive effort to Jean's more polished painting. I think my grayed-down colors limned the scene somewhat better. She may have felt that way too because she sulked a bit through our non-picnic down on the damp sand.

"It's nice that you get sunsets over the Pacific," I said by way of appeasement. "We have to make do with sunrises over the Atlantic."

"But you can go in the water there. Ours is always freezing. Plus the undertow wants to drag you to your doom."

"That's fine. It helps keep the crowds away. We have this entire beach to ourselves. Back home I usually had to battle for a few square inches of sand."

"More apple pie?"

"Sure. You know I paid a dollar for a slice at that barbecue. And it wasn't nearly as good as yours."

"But I'm sure Juanita was impressed by your largesse."

"I expect so. I blew my entire paycheck on her. She thinks I'm pretty terrific."

"Keep in mind she's comparing you to Reggie Dowling, a fellow who learned to tie his shoes in the 11th grade."

"She's afraid Reggie's going to come home with a German war bride."

"It would serve them right for starting that war."

* * *

I didn't blab to Jean about Juanita being incapable of having sex without a ring on her finger. She confided that to me in private, and it wouldn't be right to gossip about her fertility problems.

On the drive home we talked about our war years. Pearl Harbor happened around when we were starting school. Even for six-year-olds it had a momentous impact. After years of war we almost couldn't remember when it wasn't a central occupation of everyone. Jean said she remembered the day when her Japanese classmates disappeared from school. Their families were rounded up and hauled away to guarded camps; many lost their farms and orchards for good. The few Chinese-run businesses in town displayed signs in their windows proclaiming their nationality.

Jean said the war brought prosperity to Ukiah after the grim years of the 1930s. People could afford to pay their doctor bills again, and Jean's dad bought one of the last cars produced by Detroit before the car factories switched to war production. The town's sawmills put on extra shifts to meet the demand caused by all the military installations going up in the Bay Area. Stacks of Mendocino lumber also filled supply ships bound for Hawaii and points west.

"Did you know anyone who got killed?" I asked.

"Mr. McKenzie, my second-grade teacher. His ship was torpedoed off Okinawa. We planted a tree in his memory on the school grounds. A boy named Ray on our block died in the invasion of Sicily. How about you?"

"Nobody really close to me. Some of my schoolmates lost brothers and uncles. A former beau of my mother had his optic nerve cut by shell fragments and was blinded. She visited him a few weeks before she died."

"Was your father in the military?"

"No. Too old. He worked in a war production office coordinating the allocation of boxcars to keep freight trains running efficiently. I hardly ever saw him. Do you know if Milady Modest kept on making bathing suits?"

"I remember hearing they got a contract to make duffle bags and rucksacks. It helped your uncle upgrade his sewing machines. Did you do the scrap drives?"

"Yeah, we collected paper and metal. Also kitchen fat. Why do you suppose they wanted that?"

"For making munitions I think. The rationing probably helped our teeth. Not so many sweets. Were you ever scared the war would come to you?"

"Sometimes. We thought we might get bombed. Rumors would go through school that the Nazis were deploying big aircraft-carrying submarines. Everyone seemed to have a lot of respect for German engineering, so we did too. Naturally, they'd have bombed New York first. We did have enemy subs patrolling off our coast. Quite a few ships went down out there. We were lucky the war happened before they had missiles and long-range jet bombers."

"The Japanese launched thousands of fire balloons toward the west coast, but they didn't do much damage. I think they killed one unlucky person. It was all hushed up at the time. We didn't hear about it until the war was over."

"Yeah, I read about that. Hitler was our big demon. I spent a lot of my youth hating that guy. We used to fantasize about what we'd do if we ever got hold of him. Really gruesome stuff."

"Our target was General Tojo and his gang. I think all those years immersed in the hyper-patriotism of the war effort affected us much more than the kids growing up today."

"Except now they're watching all those old flag-waving movies on TV: John Wayne marching through Bataan and single-handedly winning the war. And now they have to worry about getting nuked by the Russians."

"God, Colm, the world is a mess."

"It usually is–one way or the other."

Chapter 8

Very hot day. Even with all the windows open the sewing room was stifling. I sat in front of a whirling fan in Mrs. Simmerman's office while she went over the ABCs of bookkeeping. It all made more sense from her than trying to learn it out of a book. She showed me how she recorded each item under income or expense. Everything got noted in two places so you could check for errors by balancing the figures.

It seems the big problem in business is getting paid. Our terms are full payment within 30 days, but stores often stretch that out for months.

"So what do we do about that?" I asked.

"I send out statements every month. Our sales reps don't get paid their commissions until the stores pay us, so they try to collect as well."

"Do they threaten to sue?"

"No. Mostly they beg and plead."

"Can't we sue them?"

"Not really. Everyone tries to be polite. We want to keep them as customers. They usually pay eventually. Sometimes stores are slow to pay because our goods aren't selling."

"Do they send stuff back?"

"No. Our policy is no returns except for defects. And Mrs. Yeater makes sure there aren't many of those."

"Do we ever run out of money?"

"Frequently. Fortunately, we have a revolving credit line with the bank. You always have to make the payroll. That's a given. And you have to pay the government: workmen's comp, unemployment insurance, and withholding. If you don't do that, they come in and shut you down. Then we pay our other expenses as we can–for supplies, for example."

"So we're late paying too?"

"Oh, yes. Frequently. I'm always getting calls from irate creditors. Of course, you have to keep up or you risk getting a bad Dun & Bradstreet rating. Then your suppliers want cash up front."

"It's quite a balancing act. I can see now, Hazel, that you are the key to this entire organization."

"I do my best. Some garment-makers use factors to improve their cash flow."

"What's that?"

"Companies who pay you up front for your accounts receivables and then collect on them."

"Why don't we do that?"

"Your uncle considered them leaches. You don't get the full amount. They only pay you a percentage."

"This is all so depressing," I sighed.

"Business is competitive, Mr. Moran. If you have a lucrative business, people always will notice and try to enter your field. And it's very easy to get in the bathing suit business. There are always new companies starting up. All you need are a couple of sewing machines and a few employees. The barriers to entry are low–unlike, for example, the gasoline business."

"How so?"

"Well, to go into that field you have to drill oil wells, build a refinery and a pipeline network, buy a fleet of tanker delivery trucks, and start a chain of gas stations. The barriers to entry are very high."

All in all, I wish my uncle had gone into that business. I could fill up my Packard for free. And nobody refuses to buy gas because the neckline is too low. Or it makes their butt look big.

Hazel showed me how she prepares a P&L (profit and loss) statement every Friday. This provides a quick snapshot of how Milady Modest Inc is doing. She gives a copy to Mr. Slivmank and mails one to my father. The most important figure on this page is the final entry: the proverbial bottom line. Last week's P&L showed a figure of $38,624.

"So we're earning a profit of over 38 thousand?" I asked, impressed.

"No, you'll notice there are parentheses around the number."

"We're losing that much!"

"Well, we have over 63 thousand in accounts receivables. Things will balance better when those funds come in. Of course, our accounts payable are rather high. And every week our ongoing expenses add to that."

"Does my father ever call up to complain?"

"Not usually. It could be that your father is willing to accept losses from this business to offset other income. I imagine he is in a very high tax bracket."

"Probably the highest."

"That's helpful then. Mr. Slivmank tries to bother him as little as possible. We suspect he is not entirely pleased to be in the bathing suit business."

Right, and that makes two of us.

She went on, "That's why we were so happy to have you join us. It demonstrates a commitment by your father to our company."

She would not be so happy if she knew my father's opinion of me.

On Tuesday Mrs. Yeater did not call in any sewers. She said it was too hot and there was no pressing need for more inventory. The ladies got the day off to stay cool at home, but they earned no income. I got the job of phoning delinquent accounts, introducing myself (as if they cared), and asking for payment. No one seemed overjoyed to hear from me. Naturally, I stressed I was phoning long distance at my own expense to bring this matter to their attention. I heard a variety of excuses and promises, none particularly credible. The stores clearly did not want to part with their cash. I can't blame them. I was down to my last two bucks and was in no mood to spend even a nickel.

Hazel said times seemed particularly tough this summer. Shopping centers were popping up in all the suburbs and putting the squeeze on the big downtown department stores. Several long-established stores had gone bankrupt recently.

"Aren't we selling to the shopping center stores?" I asked.

"We're trying to, Colm, but it's tough. Most of them cater to young families. And those gals don't wear our suits unless they have a weight problem."

"Why aren't those gals eating more and getting fat like they're supposed to? Surely some of them are bored with marriage."

"I think it's TV. Too many of the girls they see on TV are slim and beautiful."

Calorie-counting! Another unforeseen threat to my business success.

* * *

That night as I was drying the dishes I shared these business concerns with Jean.

"Well, the solution is perfectly obvious," she said.

"Close down and try something else? Gasoline retailing?"

"No. You need to fire Aranson."

I nearly dropped a plate from shock. "How could I do that, Jean? She's my friend. She's taught me everything I know about fashion."

"Which is precious little. Face it, Colm, your designer is way over the hill. It's time for some new blood."

"But she'd have to go back to prostitution! I doubt she could drum up much business at her age."

"So you give her a pension. Plus, she's got Social Security. She'll be fine."

"I could never fire her, Jean. She's been too nice to me."

"You don't have to. You phone your father and say you've discovered why the company is losing money: your designer is 400 years old. So your dad will call Slivmank and tell him to fire Aranson."

"I'm not sure Wendell would have the guts. I heard she was after his body."

"He'll fire her if he knows his job is on the line."

"But what will we do for a designer? I doubt we could find anyone better in this town."

"You put an ad in the San Francisco papers. That city is full of talented people. I'm sure you could find somebody good. Designing bathing suits is not rocket science."

"How would we know whom to pick?"

"You have them submit six sketches with their application. Then interview the candidates with the best designs."

"But would somebody talented want to move here?"

"Well, we live here don't we?"

"I live here because I have to. I'm not sure why you do. To be close to Elwyn?"

She socked me in the face with a wet dishrag.

* * *

The next morning I called the old fellow from my home phone. I didn't want to risk having Madame Aranson overhear my treasonous treachery. I didn't call collect because too many such calls in the past involved pleas by me to be extricated from some unpleasantness. No point starting off with him expecting the worst. His secretary tried to put me off, but I insisted on being connected.

"Couldn't this wait until the market closed?" he snapped.

"It's about the business, Father. I know our P&Ls have been disappointing lately."

Coming from me, I think that statement may have astounded him.

I went on, "But I'm working diligently to reduce the arrears in our accounts receivable."

Silence on the other end. Clearly, the old fellow was flabbergasted.

"That's very encouraging, Colm," he gasped at last.

So I launched into my analysis of the problem at Milady Modest Inc.

"Is Aranson the old bag with the affected accent and enormous bosom?" he asked.

"That's the one."

"Then by all means fire her. She was making eyes at me all through my brother's funeral."

"OK, Pop, but I'll need you to call Slivmank and give him the order. You see I have no authority here."

"Right, son. I'll do as you say."

Now it was my turn to be astounded. The old fellow was taking my advice.

By Friday the deed was done. When the hysterics abated, I assured Madame Aranson that I had fought for her tooth and nail. I'm not sure she believed me. Jean says I am not mentally equipped for deviousness.

At my insistence she was awarded severance ($300), a monthly stipend ($100), and a one-way bus ticket to New York.

"What's this for?" she demanded, referring to the last item.

"It's so you can return to Manhattan," I explained. "You can visit old friends and resume your career."

"Fat chance of that," she said. "If you're handing out bus tickets, I'd rather have one to Florida."

"Oh. In that case I'm sure you can exchange it at the Greyhound depot. Their cross-country fares are all about the same."

"Tell me the truth, Colm. Was it Slivmank who stabbed me in the back?"

I looked around and lowered my voice. "Confidentially, he's always been tremendously envious of your talent."

"The man is a peasant. They all are. While I was reaching for the stars, they were in the muck hoeing their cabbage patch."

Our want ads are set to appear in this Sunday's *Examiner* and *Chronicle*. The ad specifies that the applicant must be willing to relocate to "a cosmopolitan city in a scenic area." How shocked they will be when they find out it's Ukiah. We're having them send their replies to the newspapers, who will forward them to us. This is generally how it's done. When hiring someone one must tiptoe about and be sneaky. Don't ask me why.

During my lunch break I cashed my meager paycheck at the bank, then dropped into Flamperts to see Juanita, who tried to sell me a

Kodak Brownie camera outfit for $12.95.

"See, Colm, it's complete with camera, strap, film, flash attachment, and four flashbulbs–all in an attractive gift box."

"Very nice, Juanita, but if I bought it, I'd have to radically economize on our date tonight. How does panhandling in front of Safeway sound?"

"I've had worse dates."

I wanted to kiss her, but Flamperts frowns on that sort of activity.

* * *

Somehow we had missed the teen werewolf movie. Just as well, they can be fairly predictable. The make-up artist shows off his craft while the audience sits there wishing they'd seen the western instead. If I ever produce a horror movie, I'm going to make sure it's truly terrifying. I want popcorn scattering in all directions from shock and dread. I want involuntary screams from skeptical men. I want children traumatized for life. I want incoherent victims being carried out on stretchers. That's what sells tickets.

Tonight's movie was more to Juanita's liking anyway. Titled "The Wayward Bus," it starred Jayne Mansfield and Joan Collins as busty travelers looking for love on a bus ride through rugged mountains. The novel was by John Steinbeck, but I suspect Hollywood took some liberties with his story. It held my interest, but I don't think the rowdy teenagers up in the balcony were entranced. If I had produced it, I'd have gone for a stronger male lead. Dan Dailey is OK if the script calls for tap-dancing, but he's no Cary Grant. Me, I'd have cast Dana Andrews or Tony Curtis.

We watched it on the opposite side of the theater from Jean and Elwyn. The guy draped his gorilla-like arm over her shoulder, which I can only hope seriously impaired his blood flow. I don't think any necking took place, because I checked often. No introductions again, which is fine with me.

On the drive to the theater I told Juanita I had budgeted $1.50 for the movie, 35 cents for popcorn, and $3 for eats afterward. She suggested a Chinese restaurant she likes called the Golden Carp. I had my doubts, but it was surprisingly decent. With tip, the tab came in only a dime over budget.

As we were finishing a little Chinese boy came by to refill our water glasses.

"What's your name?" asked Juanita.

"Steve."

"Is this your father's restaurant?"

"Yeah. And my uncle's."

"What do you want to be when you grow up?"

"A race car driver. Or a elephant trainer."

"Not a waiter?" I asked.

"Too boring!"

Afterwards, we went back to my place. Juanita commented that my house was even more out-of-date and obsolete than my car. Being a modern girl she likes everything clean, spare, and streamlined. Nevertheless, she was willing to sit amid the doilies on my mission oak settee and neck. Kind of garlicky, but both of us persevered. I got rather overstimulated, but I knew relief was unlikely. Fellows my age aren't really inclined by nature to stop at second base, spectacular though it may be.

We'd reached the point where both of us were semi-nude from the waist up when the phone rang. I reached a free arm over and picked up the receiver. Kind of an awkward moment, but I told the operator I'd accept the collect call.

"Hi, Colmy!" said Betty. "Guess what?"

"Er, what?"

"I've decided on my new name!"

I gave a start as Juanita began softly stroking the bulge in my trousers.

"What's it going to be?"

"I'm changing my name to Betty Hilton."

"Oh, really. Hilton like the hotel?"

"Exactly. I think it'll be easy to remember. Even if they forget my name, producers can say get me that girl with the name like the hotel."

"Good plan. Let's hope there are no actresses named Betty Ritz or Betty Sheraton."

"Oh, right. I should check into that."

"And it's a little close to Betty Hutton. She's a blonde too."

"Except she's more of a singer and dancer."

The stroking continued. Rather reckless of my date considering her fertility issues. An involuntary moan escaped into my phone.

"Is something wrong, Colmy? You sound distressed."

I put a firm hand over Juanita's, but she persisted.

"I'm uh, I'm uh . . . Oh, God!"

"Colmy! What's the matter?"

My speech function returned a moment later. "Oh, nothing. I just had to sneeze."

"Is somebody there with you, Colm? I hear what sounds like giggling. Female giggling."

"Must be the radio you hear. Well, thanks for calling, dear. Good luck with your new name. Talk to you soon."

I hung up.

"Who was that?" inquired Juanita, taking the precaution of escaping to the opposite end of the settee from my now dangerous state.

"The east coast girl with her claws into me."

"Oh, Betty. I thought so. Next time you should let me talk to her too."

"And what would you say?"

"I'd tell her that her boyfriend's an extremely sexy guy. And a great kisser too."

* * *

I passed the night alone as usual. Spending even a platonic night with Juanita was out of the question. She said if we tried it, her father would be over with his shotgun. Then either I'd be deceased or commencing that journey toward extreme fatherhood. Her dad is inclined to be overprotective because growing up she was always his "little baby." In fact I can't have a third date with her without being introduced to her parents–that's a standing rule for all new guys on the scene. Fortunately, her grandmother (Mrs. Snyder, my sewing mentor) has been putting in a good word for me.

No sign of Jean all day Saturday. I hoped she wasn't out with that creep. I washed the Packard, then drove to a tennis court I'd spotted previously. I played a few sets with some locals, who didn't provide much competition. I stopped when my elbow began to complain. Then I drove down the road to a crossroads town called Hopland and had a burger in a diner. I had two beers in a bar there, conversing with a thin, chain-smoking girl who looked like trouble, then drove back home alone. In the mail was a phone bill for $11.86. On that depressing note, I went to bed.

Sunday morning I phoned my housekeeper.

"Hi, Jean. What are we doing today?"

"I was planning to come over and do your laundry. You're almost out of clean underwear."

"That's a detail I wish you didn't know. Want to go swimming instead?"

"Where?"

"I don't know. You're the local. Is there a swimming hole in your river?"

"Yeah, but they tend to come with pestering boys. There's the hot springs, but it's kind of a dump. I usually go to a pond up in the hills. The water's clean and pretty warm."

"Sounds fine. Should we take a non-picnic lunch?"

"I could pack one," she sighed. "Give me 45 minutes."

There were three other cars parked in the turnout by the pond. One big family group and a couple with two golden retrievers. We walked up toward the stream that fed the pond and found a shady spot for our blanket, towels, and basket. Jean took off her top and shorts. I studied her trim one-piece bathing suit and the nice figure it showed off.

"Who makes that? I asked.

"Jantzen. I bought it at Capwells in Oakland."

"You don't buy local, huh?"

"I should say not. You could give your eyes a rest, mister."

"I wasn't staring at you, just your suit."

"Oh, I see."

"If girls didn't want guys to look, they could wear something less revealing."

"Generally, we wear what's the fashion. Why did you pick your bathing suit?"

"I didn't. It's what they require at the Yale pool."

"Well, you're not there any more. You could buy something that reflects your tastes."

"I don't think much about it. Swim trunks are just something you grab on the way out the door when you're going swimming."

"You guys have it so easy."

"That's what Madame Aranson says too."

We paddled about in the pleasantly cool water, then toweled off and tackled Jean's sandwiches.

"How come you didn't invite Juanita?" she asked. "If you wish to study bathing suits, I imagine she has much to offer. More than me that's for sure."

"You were the one who said I should go out with other girls," I reminded her.

"So why aren't you today?"

"If you see a girl more than once a week, you're, uh, turning a corner."

"Is that a guy rule?"

"It's generally accepted to be true among males, yes."

"Turning a corner to what?"

"You know, Jean. That you're getting serious. For example, if you saw your fellow yesterday, that means you were with him two days in a row."

"Oh, I see."

"So, were you?"

"I don't see how that's any of your business."

"I'm sorry I asked. But you asked me why I wasn't with Juanita."

"That's true. I did. Do you want chocolate cake or raspberry pie?"

"Both, of course. You kind of spoil me, you know."

"I'm merely trying my best to be a conscientious employee, Mr. Moran."

Chapter 9

The mail on Monday at work brought in over $4,000 in checks. Mr. Slivmank thinks those pleading phone calls I made to deadbeat stores may have done some good. He had me take the checks to the bank and introduce myself to our banker, Mr. Morgan (not the famous one). He was a sober older gent who reminded me of those unsmiling college deans I used to face for various infractions. Milady Modest Inc. banks with a branch of a big San Francisco bank that also finances some of the Hollywood studios, so you know they're willing to take risks. Local banks here want nothing to do with a firm that makes bathing suits for fat women. They prefer to deal with real companies that do substantial, paying work like cutting down forests and sawing them into lumber.

Leaving the bank, I dropped in at Flamperts; Juanita did not appear overjoyed to see me. Since it was close to her break time, she let me buy her a cup of coffee at their lunch counter.

"What's the matter, honey?" I asked.

"I heard you were up at Johnson's pond yesterday with your housekeeper. What was *that* about?"

"It was about cooling off on a hot day. We never got heat this torrid back east."

"It wasn't so bad. This is normal for Ukiah."

"Yes, and I believe for the Sahara desert as well. And did your spy also report there was no physical contact between us?"

"She said you looked like you were having a good time."

"Well, that's a right guaranteed by the U.S. Constitution. Besides, you know Jean has a boyfriend."

"Elwyn? That's a joke."

"Then why is she going out with him?"

"To make you jealous, of course."

"That's merely your supposition with no basis in fact."

"No girl as attractive and smart as Jean wouldn't be caught dead with Elwyn Saunders unless she had some ulterior motive."

"Really? You think so?"

"Absolutely. So, do you like Jean?"

"Of course not," I lied. "She's pleasant company and she packs a great picnic lunch. That's all there is to it. Are we having a date on Friday?"

"You're having dinner at my house with my parents. If you want to."

"I'd be delighted."

Another falsehood from my lips. My second of the morning, or third if you count telling the banker I was pleased to meet him.

I thought about all this on my walk back to work. Was it possible that Jean was seeing that creep just to make me jealous? If it were true, then it could only mean one thing. And how did I feel about that? But if she cared for me, why would she encourage me to go out with Juanita?

That evening I watched Jean as she was making dinner. Her demeanor toward me seemed at best pleasant. No sly loving glances. Not much lipstick either. Girls usually glamorize to the max if they're stuck on you. Could it be Jean's dating Elwyn to make some *other* guy jealous? She's not at all forthcoming about her love life, whereas I'm pretty much an open book. I'd ask her if she's in love with me, but I doubt I'd get a straight answer. And I don't need another wet dishrag in the kisser.

I tried calling Betty later, but got nowhere as usual. Just as well, since I haven't figured out yet how to explain the mystery giggling.

* * *

Friday's mail brought two big packets of responses to our want ads. Over 50 in all. Who would have guessed that so many people wish to devote their work lives to squeezing oddly shaped gals into swim attire? About three-quarters were clearly unqualified to design anything more complicated than a handkerchief. Their material went into the wastebasket. But we had nine promising prospects: seven women and two fellows. Could we hire a man for this job? They do have male designers (*Vogue* dotes on them), but I assumed they were all over there in France.

Mr. Slivmank has a plan. A party consisting of himself, Vera Schall (our pattern drafter), and me are to drive to San Francisco in his Nash sedan next Monday. We are to interview selected applicants in a hotel room, spend the night, then drive back on Tuesday. Well, it could be tolerable, and I might get to see something of that famous city. It does concern me that thrifty Wendell is reserving only two hotel rooms. I'm hoping that he and Vera are planning a discreet fling.

Some of our sales reps have checked in. The lizard potholders are proving a tough sell. One store in Omaha ordered a dozen as a trial. Meanwhile, we have 14 gross in the warehouse. According to my math, that works out to 2,016 potholders (67 of them sewn by me). Nor have our donated rejects proved popular in the hospital thrift store. They've sold two so far at seven cents each.

* * *

Even though Juanita holds a managerial position, her salary is modest. She resides with her parents in their compact three-bedroom home. I showed up as specified at 6 p.m. (they are early diners). I brought a pound of assorted chocolates known to be popular with her mother. These Juanita had purchased with her employee discount and dropped off at my workplace on her way home. She's not the type of girl to leave these small gestures to chance.

Mr. and Mrs. Howe greeted me with the wary pleasantness one expects from parents of attractive single girls being preyed upon by men. They are handsome people whose best features have been combined and improved upon in their daughter. Their comfortable living room, done in Early American maple, was dominated by dozens of framed photos of smiling grandchildren.

"It's so nice to meet you, Colm," said Mrs. Howe, accepting my gift. "You're even handsomer than my mother said."

"Your mother is a very patient teacher. I never expected to be able to sew a stitch."

"You like that sort of work, eh?" asked a dubious Mr. Howe.

"Well, it's just part of learning the business."

"Bathing suits," he replied. "Is there any money in that?"

"Oh, yes, sir. Just this week we received nearly $5,000 in revenue."

That at least impressed the old buzzard.

Dinner was a ground beef and potato casserole with a mystery ingredient Mrs. Howe later identified as sliced radishes. After four years of eating dorm food, I downed it without a struggle. The only cocktail offered was iced tea. I expect it's best to face these ordeals sober.

"Do you like large families?" Mrs. Howe inquired, serving me another dollop of creamed peas.

"They could be rewarding," I hedged.

"We have nine grandchildren and two more on the way," she said proudly. "We love them all to bits, don't we, Bert?"

Bert grunted a grudging assent. "Seems like they could give it a rest once in a while," he growled. "I hope my Juanita steers clear of men."

I felt that comment was directed at me.

"What do you do, Mr. Howe?" I asked to be polite.

"Daddy drives a logging truck, Colm," said Juanita. "I told you that."

Must have been some other guy.

"Why is it?" I inquired, "when you're rounding a hairpin curve up in the hills there's always a logging truck speeding toward you at 60 miles an hour? And usually in your lane?"

"They don't pay us to poke along," he replied. "Time is money. We're the safest drivers on the road. You timid drivers should get the hell out of our way. We're longer and wider than you are."

We had our dessert (Jello with fruit bits and mini marshmallows) in the living room. Mrs. Howe introduced me to all the grandkids via their photos. A blizzard of names and faces–all fair-skinned and blond. No one in the family appeared to have any Mexican ancestry. So I asked why her three daughters received such Hispanic-sounding names.

"Guess you never read *Ramona* by Helen Hunt Jackson," she replied.

"What's that?" I asked.

"It's my mom's favorite book," said Juanita. "She's read it 58 times."

"Fifty-nine times, dear. I got a little restless last night."

"It's a romantic novel set on the ranchos of old California before all us Anglos showed up," explained Juanita.

"You really should read it, Colm," said Mrs. Howe. "It's a wonderful story. And so appropriate for a newcomer to our state."

"I'll look for it at the library," I replied.

"You would," grunted Bert from his rocking chair in front of his gun rack.

I don't think that fellow likes me.

* * *

We got out of there in time to catch the later show at the theater. As we were waiting in the line to go in I spotted my housekeeper exiting with a different guy.

"Who's that fellow with Jean?" I asked.

"Never seen him before," replied Juanita. "He's kind of a hunk too."

"There goes your theory about Jean and me."

"Not necessarily. She may have decided she needs to date *two* guys to make you jealous."

One had been doing the job quite well–a fact I kept to myself..

Tonight's movie was "Godzilla, King of the Monsters!" (Their exclamation point not mine.) It featured an oversized reptile laying waste to large sections of Tokyo. Raymond Burr showed up to save the day. Kind of a Japanese version of "King Kong." More amusing than scary. The special effects were strictly bargain basement, and the actor's voices were crudely dubbed into English. The kids in the balcony seemed to enjoy it though, and I hear it's doing well at the box office. I bet there are smart producers down in Hollywood scouting now for other Asian films they could adapt.

"That rampaging lizard reminds me of your father," I said to Juanita as the credits rolled.

"My father's a sweetie. He just wants you guys to keep your hands off me."

"My hands are the least of his worries."

"Oh. Are we shopping for rings tomorrow?"

"I wasn't planning on it."

"Then my father has nothing to worry about."

Nevertheless, we went back to my place and engaged in intimacies that likely would have earned his severest censure. I fear I may spend my bachelor years exploring the erotic limits of second base.

* * *

Saturday morning I noticed a dusty war-surplus Jeep parked in front of the Vallands' house. I went out to reconnoiter and spotted four legs extending out from underneath Jean's VW.

"Engine problems?" I inquired.

Jean slid over and peered up at me. "Hi, Colm. Peter here is showing me how to adjust my valves."

Peter, the hunk from last night, looked up and said hi.

"Hi," I replied in my most neutral voice. "You know, Jean, many modern engines have self-adjusting valves."

Not intended as a joke, but she found it funny.

"Colm is the fellow I keep house for. He's an artist too, although he doesn't admit it. Colm, Peter is a friend from school. We're going camping in his Jeep, but I left you two days of lasagna in your frig. Promise me you'll heat it before consumption. There are salad makings too if you get ambitious."

"Where are you going camping?" I asked, not at all pleased with this development.

"Not far. Up in the national forest past Potter Valley."

"You're going to some sort of resort?"

"Hardly. We'll be roughing it on our own."

"Aren't there bears and snakes out there?"

"Possibly. And perhaps a hostile Indian or two."

I felt the need to drop a competitor's name. "Is Elwyn accompanying you?"

"Elwyn is staying home. He's not the outdoors type. If you like, I could call him up and you two could plan an activity together."

Sarcasm from my housekeeper. More salt in my wounds.

"Well, have a good time," I said, sauntering away.

Despite the inappropriateness of the hour, I went back to my house and called Betty. Her sleepy roommate answered on the 12th ring.

"Betty's not here. She's in New York."

"What's she doing there?"

"Making a TV commercial."

"Really? For what?"

"For the exposure and the money, I guess. They're paying her $500."

"No, I mean for what product?"

"Rheingold beer."

My girl's doing a commercial for Rheingold beer and she didn't even tell me. That's hard to figure since I've probably drunk my weight in Rheingold beer many times over. I'd imbibe a case of it right now if they sold it out here. I can just imagine the TV commercial. It will be making the not-so-subtle point that if you drink their beer you can date a beautiful girl like Betty. That, of course, is the *reality that I used to enjoy*. In fact, I met her at a Yale mixer where it was more than likely I was holding a lukewarm can of Rheingold at the time.

That's a nice financial windfall and possible career break for Betty. She could use part of her $500 to come visit me. Fat chance of that.

What a wretched morning. I felt like strangling someone. Instead I went in the kitchen and dumped Jean's lasagna in the garbage. I could hardly be expected to choke that down while imagining her activities out in the woods.

* * *

I decided it was time to get very seriously impaired. Drunkenness was a mental state I'd been avoiding for too long. It was Saturday night, and I was single, over 21, and had just got paid. I left the Packard in the garage and walked into town. Not a hardship since this burg is so small. I had my choice of bars. Most of them I knew were the haunts of rowdy tree-fellers and log-sawers. Guys who made Juanita's dad look like a model of refined elegance. Not really my type of crowd. So I strolled into a place called the Peacock Grill, which had a Cadillac or two parked among the Fords and Plymouths in its lot. The upscale interior featured a dimly lit bar with adjoining dining room. About half the tables were occupied.

"One for dinner?" asked a pretty waitress.

"Can I eat in the bar?"

"Sure thing, honey."

"Do you have steaks?"

"Best in town."

I had the porterhouse. Grilled as requested, but sized for Godzilla. I made a sizeable dent in it as I downed a local cocktail called a margarita. Heavy on the lime juice and a Mexican booze called tequila. A surprise coating of rock salt ornaments the rim of the glass. Easy to drink and packing a kick that sneaks up on you. I was working on my fourth when Juanita walked in with two of her cute pals I'd met at the barbecue.

"Well look who's here," she said, sliding into the booth beside me. Her companions sat down opposite us. "What are you drinking, honey?"

"A margarita like your sister. Want one?"

"Sure. You buying for everyone?"

"Of course."

I gave her a sloppy kiss.

"Bet you a dollar, Colm, you don't remember our names," said the stunning brunette in the low-cut top.

My brain felt profoundly numb, but I tried twirling some gears. "You're Alice and your friend . . . let me see. . . She has a trickier name . . . something like, uh, Ora?"

"That's impressive," said Ora, dressed in shimmering blue to match her eyes.

"I never forget a breast," I slurred. "I mean a face."

The girls found that amusing. I'd stolen that line from a classmate who'd bedded at least one girl from all Seven Sister colleges. Unbidden, their names swam into my mind: Mount Holyoke, Vassar, Wellesley, Smith, Radcliffe, Bryn Mawr, and Barnard. So many distinguished girls and all pointedly avoiding Ukiah.

"You lost your bet, Alice," said Ora. "Pay up."

"How about we go out to your car, Colm, and I'll pay you in kind?" she said with a wink.

"Damn! I didn't drive!"

"Just as well, honey," said Juanita. "Hey, I wondered what you did on your Saturday nights. How come you didn't call me, baby?"

Caught in the net. I didn't dare tell her that seeing her twice in one week meant commitment and marriage and children (by the dozen) and life insurance and dental bills and grandchildren and annuities and old age. Then a somber funeral with the widow (grieving? relieved?) wondering why it all went by so fast.

"I figured you'd be busy with your other fellas," I replied.

"This girl does nothing but talk about you, Colm," said Ora. "You've made a BIG impression on her."

"Yeah, Colm," said Alice. "And when you get tired of Juanita, you can give me a call anytime."

"Sorry, Alice," said Ora. "I already called second dibs on him."

We had more margaritas and then switched to daiquiris. Very fruity beverages. I'm sure I was getting lots of vitamins along with the alcohol. Definitely warding off scurvy. In time my brain shut down completely, but apparently the rest of me kept on going. That's as much as I remember.

I woke up–alone—around 11:30 Sunday morning. Wildly hung over, but that was to be expected. I was nude in my bed. My clothes were neatly folded on the chair beside it. There was one dollar in my wallet.

My phone rang as I was getting out of the shower.

"Hi, Colm, said Juanita. "How you feelin'?"

"Like I died a while ago and the funeral's been delayed. Who put me to bed?"

"We did. You were a bit inebriated."

"Whose idea was it to strip me naked?"

"Alice suggested that. She was afraid you might strangle yourself on your t-shirt."

"And my undershorts?"

"We didn't want anything to get twisted."

"That's not usually a hazard. Did I behave myself?"

"Mostly. And don't worry, we all liked what we saw."

Chapter 10

Monday morning I packed my grip and stopped at the pawn shop on the way to work. My gold cigarette case and lighter were displayed in the window and priced at $89.95. The gent behind the counter remembered me.

"Selling or buying today, young man?"

"Pawning: This nice watch. It's a Waltham. Twenty-four jewels, keeps perfect time, nice gold case."

"It's gold-filled. I'm familiar with this model. Gold-filled case and matching expansion band. Your crystal's pretty beat up. I can lend you $20 on it."

"Could you make it $25?"

"Sorry, that's the best I can do."

We did the paperwork and he gave me the cash. I now had $21 to fund my trip to San Francisco. I was hoping Wendell wouldn't ask me to chip in for gas.

To conserve cash, the day before I'd eaten salvaged lasagna for lunch and dinner. It tasted only slightly off, and I tried not to think about its maker as I gagged it down.

I looked at the date on my pawn ticket. "Is it really July 1?" I asked.

"Yeah, we'll be closed for the holiday on Thursday."

I was starting my second month in Ukiah–something I'd have bet would never happen.

Slivmank and Vera Schall were waiting impatiently when I arrived.

"Good morning, Colm," he said. "You're here at last. We have a long journey ahead of us, so let's get started."

According to my map, our trip to S.F. was about 115 miles. Not exactly a trek by mule across Siberia. In east coast terms it's about the distance from New York to Hartford. Even drunk or hung over I could do that in a couple of hours.

I stashed my grip beside the others in the trunk of Wendell's Nash and grabbed the back seat. I'll say one thing for Nash: their upside-down bathtub styling was unique. No other car on the road looked like it. Nash offered a sprightly V-8, but Slivmank had opted for the economical six. Not a lot of go, but it was motoring heaven compared to Jean's VW.

Slivmank drove like the old man he is. His passengers had lots of time to study the scenery along Highway 101 and check out the small towns along the way.

By Santa Rosa Wendell and Vera had run out of idle chatter, so I decided to lay out this brainstorm that had come to me during yesterday's hangover funk.

"Hey, Wendell, that movie 'Godzilla' is really popular with kids. How about we take some of our surplus lizard cloth and do a line of bathing suits for boys? We could sell it under the name Beachzilla. Unlike gals, boys might dig looking like a big reptile."

"That's a thought, Colm, but we've turned all that stock into potholders."

"No, I think you'll find Joe has seven more bolts stashed in the warehouse."

"Well, that's depressing news," he sighed.

"The patterns would be simple to do," commented Vera. "The fabric's stretchy so we'd only need three sizes to start. And they'd be quick and easy to sew."

"We'd have to research the name for trademark registration and get labels made," said Wendell. "It's awfully late in the season."

"We could market to Florida, southern California, and Hawaii to start," I pointed out. "They sell bathing suits year round."

"OK, Colm," said Wendell. "But I'm leaving all the details to you. You can be in charge of that project."

Wow, just like that I was a bathing suit designer and marketing executive. All for $32 a week.

* * *

San Francisco is no Manhattan, but it's a big city with a busy waterfront and imposing downtown. Lots of fancy hotels catering to well-heeled tourists and international businessmen. Not where we were headed. Wendell's choice was a semi-seedy flophouse at 6th and Mission. Centrally located and just a block off Market Street, which may be why all the derelicts and winos chose to hang out there. We did have sort of a view of the Bay from our adjoining fifth floor rooms. Be better if they washed the grime off the windows. Even though television had only been around a decade or so the battered set in our room looked to be about 20 years old. At least Wendell had splurged on rooms with private baths. Only one double bed though, featuring a prominent cigarette burn in the bedspread.

"Uh, where am I sleeping? I inquired anxiously.

"The bellhop will bring up a cot later for you, Colm," he replied. "I hope you don't mind roughing it."

"That's OK. But why such a budget hotel, Wendell? It's not going to make a very good impression with our applicants."

"Exactly, Colm. We don't want them to think just because we're in the fashion business we're paying exorbitant salaries. I like to make that plain right from the beginning. Besides, hotel prices in this city are outrageous. We're not some out-of-state tourists to be exploited."

No, we're more in the "rubes from the sticks" category.

The fog had lifted, but the temperature was like New Haven in March. A big change from the non-stop heat of Ukiah. After a quick lunch at a nearby hotdog stand (Wendell paid), we returned to our room just in time for our first interview.

I let Wendell and Vera do most of the talking. It must be tough looking for a job. (I got mine the old-fashioned way: via nepotism.) All the applicants were so hopeful and polite and eager to please. They brought their big portfolios and spread them open on our sagging bed. We inspected page after page of stylish women's suits, elegant evening gowns, casual wear for those smart occasions, flamboyant hats, shoes to warm a starlet's heart, and beach outfits of every imaginable sort.

Only one applicant, a refined gal about 35, said she couldn't possibly move to Ukiah. She had grown up in Cloverdale and was done with Rural Life.

"I thought your ad referred to someplace like Monterey or Santa Cruz," she said, gathering up her materials.

"You could try New York," I suggested. "I think you'd do well there."

"I'd love to," she said wistfully. "But my lover's a native Californian too, and she hates the cold."

Not a statement you hear every day in Ukiah.

At the end of a long afternoon, two applicants stood out: a man named Gene from the city and a girl named Norma from Berkeley. He'd been designing men's ties on a freelance basis (could there be any money in that?), and she was a recent fashion grad from Boston's upscale Emerson College. Interestingly, they were also the best-looking candidates. Do talent and good looks go together? They didn't particularly at Yale.

Gene was your tanned Tab Hunter type with a thin build and blond mustache. Nice suit and tie, but the yellow socks were a shock. Norma reminded me of that young actress Audrey Hepburn. Petite, with great cheekbones and luminous dark eyes. No shape to speak of, but stylishly dressed in an outfit of her own design.

We hashed out our decision over at dinner in a cafeteria on Market Street. Wendell chose it because it's one of the few places in San Francisco where you can get a three-course meal with dessert and coffee for 85 cents. Strictly separate checks for this extravagance. The good news is the company was picking up the tab for my cot.

In the end I voted for Norma, but my companions went for the guy. They said he had more work experience and his designs seemed more practical. Vera said it was obvious he had an innate grasp of the female body. Could be, but I'm willing to bet I've grasped a few more than he has. So Wendell called him from the restaurant's phone booth and told him he had the job. Gene wasn't thrilled with the proposed salary (much higher than mine), but he accepted our offer.

We went back to the hotel to phone my father with the news (I wasn't sure he cared), when a call came in. It was Gene saying he'd thought it over and changed his mind. He said his roommate advised him that if he went to work for Milady Modest Inc. he'd never get another job in the fashion world. A harsh assessment that could be true for all I know. Good thing I don't aspire to move up to a high-profile designer job in New York.

So Wendell called Norma and made the same offer to her. She seemed genuinely pleased and accepted our financial terms without complaint. I hope she works out because we're all in the soup if she doesn't. Vera for one is skeptical. She thinks a petite girl with no bust may have trouble "conceptualizing designs" for big gals with problem figures. I pointed out that at least she's a female, which gives her one leg up on snobby Gene.

* * *

Wendell and Vera, being elderly, were ready to turn in, but I felt like exploring.

"I'm not sure this neighborhood is safe after dark," Wendell warned.

"I'll be fine," I assured him. "I'll be as quiet as possible when I come back."

"Try not to be too late. The criminals here are known to prey on unwary tourists."

"Thanks, Wendell. I'll keep that in mind."

I walked over to Market and took a streetcar down to the Ferry Building. I hiked up from there to the Italian district called North Beach, famous for its coffee shops, beatniks, and unwashed poets.

Not many of them about on a foggy Monday night. I had a beer at an Irish bar, then walked a few blocks over to Chinatown. I spent 50 cents to sit through part of a Hong Kong action movie. The film had subtitles, but only in Chinese. Not helpful for the lone Anglo in the audience. I figured out that some bad dudes were menacing a pretty girl and her dad. Every so often guys would duke it out kung fu style. Nobody had any guns which might have settled matters faster. Interesting as a novelty, but I think that genre is too foreign ever to appeal to Western audiences. I expect any American producer who got involved in that would lose his shirt.

I had a bowl of noodles in a blue-collar joint, where I wrote a note to Betty on a postcard I bought at a Grant Street gift shop. I dropped it in a mailbox and headed back to the hotel. I slept like a log on my creaky cot–missing out on the fleas that visited Wendell. He was anxious to leave first thing in the morning, but I said I wanted to stay another day.

"Why on earth would you want to do that?" he demanded, scratching his neck.

"I thought I'd check out the bathing suit displays at the local stores. I should know what the competition is doing. I can return tomorrow by bus."

"Well, all right, if you must."

"How about giving me $20 for expenses?"

A shocking request, but I managed to get him to pry open his wallet. Of course, he made me promise to save all my receipts.

I had a leisurely breakfast, then packed my grip and checked into a better-class budget hotel on Geary. The room was clean and the windows had been washed in my lifetime. I phoned around to trademark lawyers and found one who would research Beachzilla and file the paperwork for a flat $100. Even better he said he would bill us for the work. I used my new authority to tell him to go ahead.

I walked over to Union Square, a block-sized park surrounded by upscale shops and department stores. I checked out Macys, I. Magnin, and City of Paris–confronting a blizzard of bathing suits, but nary one by Milady Modest Inc. Finally, I asked a clerk if she knew where I could find one.

"Why on earth would you want one of those?" she asked.

"It's for my aunt. She's rather obese."

"And she sends you out shopping for a bathing suit? Doesn't she want to try it on?"

"Oh, no. She's much too self-conscious for that."

"Well, try Emporium. They go in for that sort of thing."

Emporium was a less snooty department store down on Market Street. They had half a rack devoted to our line. Lots of bold prints in improbable color combinations. Heavy on the frills and flounces that seemed to be missing from the other brands.

"Can I help you find something?" inquired a middle-aged clerk. "These are ladies' bathing suits, you know."

"Yeah, I figured that out. What do you think of these suits?"

"For whom?"

"Just in general. Would you wear one?"

"Why do you ask?"

"Just curious. I'm thinking of buying one as a gift for my girlfriend. I'd like to get a general idea of what appeals to women."

"Is your girlfriend on the heavy side?"

"No, she's slim and beautiful."

"Then if you gave her one of these suits, I don't think she'd be your girlfriend for long."

"That bad, huh?"

"Quite inappropriate. Now, if you'll come with me, we have some lovely styles over here."

* * *

I read the *Chronicle* while munching a burger in Emporium's snack bar. The columnist Herb Caen reported that Alfred Hitchcock will be directing a movie in San Francisco starting in September. His stars are Jimmy Stewart and Kim Novak. Sounds like a great cast. I wonder if he needs any help on the business side? I wouldn't mind helping Kim try on a few bathing suits. She's another sexy blonde that Betty has to compete against. What a tough racket to break into. Like the petroleum biz, it has high barriers to entry. You have to be beautiful, talented, and very lucky. Not to mention willing to be pawed by sleazy producers on the make.

I walked around some more to get a lay of the land. The bankers and business types hang out in the big buildings on Pine and Sutter. Down at the docks I watched ships being unloaded and ferry boats coming and going. Later I rode a cable car over to Fisherman's Wharf and had a shrimp cocktail from an outdoor stand. I walked all the way from there (mostly uphill) to Chinatown, where I had dinner. Lots of places to choose from; I picked one up a flight of stairs–figuring not so many tourists would venture up there. The patrons were mostly local, the food was good, and the tab was under two bucks. I passed a jazz club called the Hungry i, liked what I was hearing, and went in and had a drink. Then it was back to my hotel and a hot shower before bed.

Not a bad day. I like lonely hotel rooms in unfamiliar cities. Places where you know no one. Where you can walk the streets anonymously, not making any waves at all. Where you can board a bus or ship out on a tramp steamer and no one will note your absence.

I was thinking about that–and Juanita's breasts–as I fell asleep.

Chapter 11

My housekeeper stirred her spaghetti sauce and chewed me out for not letting her know I was staying in the city an extra day.

"Sorry," I replied. "I thought you were still off camping. How was that?"

"We had a good time. Did you?"

"It was a business trip. So who was that guy?"

"Peter? He's a very talented ceramicist."

"He makes pots?"

"Yes. And vases and cups and many beautiful objects. He sells them too, which is more than I can say for me."

"And what is he to you?"

"I told you. I met him at school. He's a friend. He lives in Oakland, so I don't see him very often."

"But you share tents with him?"

"We slept outside under the stars."

"That's not answering my question."

"That's because it's none of your business. Your phone was ringing a lot today."

"Did you answer it?"

"Certainly not. I'm your housekeeper, not your secretary."

"If it's not too much trouble, please answer it and take a message. It might have been my father."

"More likely one of your numerous women."

I looked at her and sighed. The lipstick was back and also the perfume. I even liked the apron. She was the dish I really wanted for dinner.

"I missed you, you know," I confessed.

"I opened some red wine for the sauce. I left the bottle on the table if you want some."

"Shall I pour you a glass too?"

"None for me, Mr. Moran. I'm working."

Even Jean admitted that her sauce had benefitted from being left over a day. She served it with a salad made from the tired greens that

I had ignored in my frig. In these small ways am I punished for what–wanting her?

While drying the dishes, I told her about our new designer, then broached a touchy subject.

"Slivmank isn't paying this new girl much."

"That's no surprise."

"She's arriving Friday by bus."

"Too bad. She'll miss the fireworks in the park."

"Norma will be looking for a place to live."

"So?"

"So a hotel is rather beyond her means. Slivmank told her she could stay in my guestroom while she's looking."

"How cozy. What does this Norma person look like?"

"She's, uh, not unattractive in a boyish sort of way. Not my type at all. I wouldn't have agreed, but I wasn't consulted before he made the offer."

"So there'll be an extra guest for dinner?"

"Just for a few days. We can augment your pay if you like."

"And does Juanita know of this arrangement?"

"No. And I'm thinking she may not need to."

"This is a small town, Mr. Moran. She'll find out by Saturday at the latest."

"Oh. That could be awkward."

"Awkward seems to be a theme of your love life, Mr. Moran."

* * *

Betty called later while I was wandering around looking for something to do.

"Hi, Colmy! Did you hear? I did a commercial!"

"I heard, darling. That's great. For Rheingold beer. Are you Miss Rheingold?"

"No, that's some other girl. She's plastered all over the subway. The ad agency wanted a fresh face for the commercial. We shot it at a bowling alley in Brooklyn."

"Were you bowling?"

"No, I was the distraction. I played a waitress in a skimpy barmaid's costume. Every time this cute Italian guy went to bowl, I'd pour a bottle of beer into a glass. He'd look over, I'd flash him a big wink, and he'd roll a gutter ball. Kind of a cute concept."

"I look forward to seeing it."

"God, I must have poured that beer 500 times. I may never wink again. Too bad you live so far away."

"I know. It's killing me to be apart from you."

"They'll only show the commercial in TV markets where they sell their beer. I'm going to be on sports shows: baseball, boxing, and, uh, sports."

"I bet you'll sell a lot of beer."

"I hope so. I just hope all those Broadway producers are baseball fans. So are you seeing someone out there, Colmy?"

Betty was known for her conversational turns on a dime.

"Not me, darling," I lied. "I'm saving myself for you."

"You're a handsome guy, Colmy. I know those California girls are pestering you."

"Oh, not so much."

"Well, keep me posted if you get engaged."

"Yes, and you too, Betty. Though I'm not sure horn players and directors are big on marriage. Are you back on the Cape?"

"Yeah, I'm opening Saturday as Amelia Shotgraven in 'The Solid Gold Cadillac'."

"Is that the lead?"

"No, but it's a nice part. And this play makes sense. So, think of me sometimes, Colmy, when you're kissing her."

"OK, darling. And that goes double for me."

The phone rang almost immediately after I hung up.

"Hi, Colm," said Juanita. "How was your trip?"

"Not bad. I thought about shipping out on a tramp steamer, but decided I'd miss you too much."

"That's good to hear. Are you coming to the parade tomorrow?"

"Do you recommend it?"

"Very much. You're also invited to our potluck picnic. You can meet the rest of my family."

The signs warned of deadly quicksand, but I plunged ahead anyway. "I'd love to, darling. What should I bring?"

"I recommend beer."

"OK, will do."

* * *

Ukiah schedules its July 4th parade first thing in the morning so the majorettes and fez-wearing Shriners on scooters don't pass out from the heat. The last band marched past our corner a little before noon. My first red, white, and blue patriotic parade. By then I had met Ramona and Margarita, their two husbands, their numerous kids, and Mrs. Snyder's husband Earl. Everyone seemed friendly except for Bert, who continues to regard me as a needless intrusion in his life.

Somehow all the children were rounded up and we reconvened in Ramona's back yard. Her husband Dale grilled hotdogs, swilled my beer, and tuned out the kiddie chaos around him. The older tykes were all spinning Hula Hoops, a toy that every kid in America seems to have acquired overnight.

Dale works for his father's company that makes little teardrop travel trailers. He thinks they should switch to larger trailers since modern cars have plenty of power for towing. Both he and Margarita's husband Wayne find it amusing that I'm in the bathing suit business. My standard response now when I'm asked about it: "Hey, it beats working for a living."

Wayne is a lumber grader at a sawmill in Philo. Of course, I asked him if he's a hard grader.

"I'm tough but fair," he replied.

I asked them when I can expect Juanita's dad to warm up to me.

"Probably never," said Dale.

"And maybe not that soon," added Wayne.

"Bert's an old rooster," said Dale. "He likes to be the only cock around the flock. I stay out of his way."

"Me too," said Wayne. "Here's a tip, Colm. Keep it in your pants."

"Yeah, I got warned about that already."

"Go easy on the booze around Juanita," added Dale. "It can impair your judgment."

"And lower your resistance," said Wayne.

"That's what nailed Wayne," said Dale. "I had warned him too."

"Christmas 1951," said Wayne. "Too much rum in the eggnog. It was the season of giving and I got mine. I was married by Easter."

"Well, your wives are knockouts," I pointed out. "And you have lovely families."

"We're lucky guys," agreed Dale. "Notice we both drive station wagons. Hell, in a couple of years I expect I'll be driving a bus."

"That's right," said Wayne. "We'll both be showing up at Greyhound's surplus bus auctions."

"I only hope 40 seats will be enough," said Dale, emptying his beer and tossing the can at a small child. It missed.

Mrs. Snyder came up and told me how pleased she was that her granddaughter and I had "hit it off so well."

"She's a lovely girl," I admitted.

"And so intelligent too," she said. "Anybody in Ukiah who can't take a decent photo, they talk to Juanita and she straightens them right out. Old man Flampert thinks the world of her."

The girl in question came up and kissed me. "Looks like you need another beer, sailor," she said, handing me a cold one. She was dressed for the heat in an outfit that concealed just enough for maximum arousal. I drank my beer and felt my inhibitions crumbling.

* * *

Ramona's oldest kid was an eight-year-old boy named Mark. I cornered him by the air-inflated wading pool to do some market research. Yes, he had seen "Godzilla" at the Saturday matinee. In fact, he had sat through two showings.

"Is that film a topic of conversation among you and your pals?" I asked.

"Yeah, I guess so."

"Did they like it as much as you did?"

"Yeah, I guess so."

"Would you be interested in swim trunks that looked like Godzilla's scaly skin?"

"Yeah, I guess so."

"Would you prefer it to a conventional bathing suit?"

"What's that?"

"You know, like what you're wearing now."

"Oh. Yeah, I guess so."

"Do you think your friends would like it too?"

"Yeah, I guess so."

"Good. You've been a great help."

"Can I have a half-dollar?"

"How about a quarter instead?"

"OK. Thanks."

His mother waddled over to check out the transaction. She was due in August and looked like she had swallowed a small Fiat.

"My son is always asking people for money, Colm. It's very embarrassing."

"He helped me with some marketing questions. We're starting a line of bathing suits for boys."

"That sounds like fun. Juanita says you just graduated from Yale. That's impressive."

"Not really. I was a fairly marginal student."

"I'm sure you had to work hard though."

"That's kind of a myth. It's very, very difficult to flunk out of an Ivy League college."

"Really? Why's that?"

"State colleges are underwritten by taxpayers, so they boot out sluggards. Private colleges are more inclined to keep you around as long as you pay your tuition."

"That doesn't seem quite fair."

"No, I suppose not."

"Well, good student or not you're a nice step up for my sister."

"Thanks, but I have my faults too."

"Oh?" she smiled, "like what?"

What came immediately to mind was lusting after a large pregnant woman after a mere two beers. It's a close contest, but I'd judge Ramona prettiest of the three sisters.

"Oh, I can have trouble making up my mind," I admitted.

"You're just cautious, Colm. Not impulsive. You can delay gratification."

Definitely a plus if you're dating a Howe sister.

Later the kids got dumped on the grandparents while the three couples drove in Dale's Pontiac station wagon to the local speedway, a quarter-mile dirt oval. We sat on wooden bleachers and watched a dozen or so stock-car racers buzz around–stirring up choking clouds of dust and raising a terrific din. A fellow in a '51 Ford won the trophy and got a kiss from a sexy gal, who turned out to be Juanita's friend Alice. By then it was dark and the fireworks show commenced. I'd seen them before, but never up this close. A vivid treat for the eyes, and the lingering gunpowder smells perfectly complemented Juanita's incendiary perfume.

By the end of the evening I was ready to throw caution to the wind and claim what no real man could resist. Fortunately, Juanita had to get up early the next day to go to work. She dismissed me at her door with one smoldering kiss.

Chapter 12

It's frustrating to check the time and find only a bare wrist. As soon as I got paid on Friday I went to the bank, then reclaimed my pawned watch. As I was leaving, the gent behind the counter said, "See you next time, buddy."

He probably will too. When you work for your family-owned business, people assume you're affluent. For example, last night I was buying most of the beer. Juanita and her clan may be a luxury I cannot afford.

At work I drew a non-specific reptile design for our Beachzilla label. Kind of a lizard meets large-fanged snake. Impressed Wendell, who gave it his OK. Speedy Vera drafted the patterns for all three sizes, and Mrs. Snyder sewed up a trio of prototypes. She's taking home the small size this weekend to run past Mark, our youthful marketing consultant. I wanted to have a zigzag edge around the leg openings, but everyone said that would be too complicated (meaning expensive) to sew. I guess parents aren't willing to spend $29.95 to dress junior for the beach.

After lunch I drove to the Greyhound station and picked up Norma Pomeroy, our new designer. She arrived with one suitcase, a small footlocker, and a portable sewing machine. She was impressed with my vintage ride.

"It's a 1938 Packard," I said. "I inherited it from my uncle, who also started the business."

"It's quite extravagant. I'm surprised–considering the hotel where you interviewed me."

"Our Mr. Slivmank is tight with a nickel. For example, he pays me $32 a week."

"Really? How do you manage on that?"

"With difficulty. Have you been to Ukiah before?"

"Never. Are these the outskirts?"

"No. We just passed the center of town."

"Oh."

"Did they name you after Norma Shearer?"

"Sure did. I have a brother named Clark."

"They stuck with M.G.M., huh?"

"Only the best."

"What's does your brother do?"

"Goes to high school back home."

"Where's that?"

"Outside Philly. Can I confess something?"

"Sure."

"I had never heard of your company. Where do you advertise?"

"We don't. My uncle didn't believe in it. He said if your product is good, it will sell itself."

"Could be, but none of my friends have heard of you either."

"Don't worry. We're counting on your designs to put us on the fashion map."

"Good. Bathing suits are an amazing challenge."

"How so?"

"Because they reveal so much. Undergarments do too, but they're mostly hidden from view. Bathing suits are as close as most of us get to being naked in public."

"Our former designer claimed most women hate their bodies."

"I don't know about that. But the challenge is making them feel good about what they see in the mirror. I want women to try on my suits and think, 'Wow, I can't believe I look that great'."

"That's kind of a tall order for some of our customers, Norma."

"Well, that's my job, Mr. Moran. And I intend to do the best I can."

"Good. And please call me Colm."

"OK. So are you my boss?"

"I can't really say. Wendell Slivmank is the manager, but lately he's been agreeing with almost everything I say."

"Sounds like your division of authority is unclear. You could try giving yourself a raise."

"Hmm. That's a thought."

* * *

We dropped off Norma's gear, introduced her to Jean (tense smiles all around), then returned to work for the formal meet and greet. Fortunately, the heat wave had abated somewhat, so the offices were a few degrees below sweat-shop levels. Norma gave no sign of being disappointed by our modest premises, but I noticed she appeared taken aback when introduced to Miss Page, our robust secretary/fitting model.

On the drive back to my place, she brought up this point. "Fitting models usually range from size 7 to 10. Your Miss Page must be at least a 16."

"Could be, Norma. I didn't feel it was polite to ask her. She's quite accommodating should you need to tug and adjust on her. Not at all ticklish either."

"Er, right. She's also rather elderly–requiring rather more support than someone younger."

"I've seen her in the buff, and she's surprisingly . . . uh, nubile for her age."

"You saw her naked? So what is she? Your girlfriend?"

"Of course not. I've only seen her unclothed in her professional capacity. And that was entirely against my will."

"Oh, I see. I don't know if you've noticed, but your housekeeper has a perfect figure. I wonder if she'd be willing to help out in fitting?"

"You could ask her."

A promising prospect, though–knowing Jean–I was sure to be excluded from the fun.

"You didn't show me your office, Colm," she pointed out.

"I'm much too important to have an office, Norma. I generally work at any unoccupied sewing station."

"What happens when things get busy?"

"Oh, I'll find a corner in a hallway or something."

"I don't know, Colm. If you're going to be an executive, you should act like one. They tend not to be modest in their needs."

"You're right, Norma. I'll bring that up with Slivmank."

It felt awkward abandoning Norma on her first evening in town, but I had a date with Juanita. Yes, I'm now seeing her multiple times a week. Good thing I'm too poor to shop for engagement rings.

"Any messages?" I asked my housekeeper.

She flashed me a fake smile. "Just one. From Dial-a-Twit. They have an opening for you on the graveyard shift."

"Very funny. Well, Norma, I'll leave you in Jean's capable hands."

"Where are you going, Colm?" she asked.

"He's got a date," said Jean. "Our Mr. Moran is quite the gay young blade about town."

* * *

When I picked up Juanita, she attempted to hand me a $20 bill.

"What's this for?" I asked.

"It's to help with some of the expenses. I know you don't make much."

"Keep it, dear. I can't take your money."

"Please, honey, I insist. Let me help out."

"No thanks, Juanita. The fellow pays for the dates. That's been the rule since 2000 B.C."

"Come on, Colm. I'm not trying to offend your male ego. Let's be practical."

"Sorry, Juanita. I don't take money from girls."

Rarely can I say no to girls, but on that point I stood firm.

"All right, Colm, if you insist. But I think you should ask for a raise. No one can live on the pittance they pay you."

"That's funny. You're the second person today to suggest that."

"Oh? Who was the first?"

"Norma Pomeroy, our new designer. By the way, she'll be camping in my spare bedroom until she finds a place to live."

"Oh, really? Well I hope your Miss Pomeroy is 45, walks with a limp, and has a bad skin condition."

"Er, no. She's about our age. But she's not my type at all. Anyway she's an employee. You can't make passes at them."

"I understand people have been known to try."

Tonight's movie was "The Incredible Shrinking Man." What a great premise and title (though it barely fit on the theater marquee). Who wouldn't want to see a film with a title like that? Very well executed for a low-budget movie. Good script and well-directed. Nice special effects too. No big-name stars, but the theater was packed. The lead actor (and shrinking man) was a fellow named Grant Williams. Who the hell ever heard of Grant Williams? The guy was probably working for lunch money, yet he did a very credible job. I've noted the name of the producer. When I get to Hollywood, I'm going to look him up. Who knows, maybe we could work on some projects together.

I think Juanita's trying to be a cheap date. She said a burger after the movie was fine with her. Since we couldn't go back to my place, we drove up to the old loggers' parking spot and semi-mingled under the stars. Very intense right up to the point where one encountered the brick wall. Leaves me way more inflamed than I ever was with Betty. I drove Juanita home feeling like all my circuits were scorched and smoking. I think that's true for her too. I'm not sure how much longer this can go on.

* * *

My houseguest got up before I did. She occupied the lone bathroom for a very long time. I finally skipped my morning shower and peed in the back yard. I was eating a bowl of Wheaties when she entered the kitchen. We exchanged "good mornings." She was wearing shorts, a thin sleeveless top, and apparently no bra. The clingy fabric revealed every detail of her small breasts. I kept my eyes elevated politely above the neckline.

She stood for a long time in front of the open refrigerator, letting all the cold air escape. Then she removed the butter dish and walked away leaving the door ajar. I got up and closed it.

"What would you like for breakfast, Norma?"

"Just toast and coffee."

I showed her the bread and toaster, and demonstrated the operation of the electric percolator. Eventually, toast and coffee were produced. She joined me at the yellow metal table.

"A Wheaties eater, huh?" she observed.

"Breakfast of champions."

"You know that's just raisin bran without the raisins."

"I can live without raisins."

Somehow she chewed her toast in a way I found irritating. I hadn't lived with a female since my mother died. I hoped this wasn't a preview of marriage: one small inconvenience and irritation after another.

"How was your date?" she asked.

"Fine. We went to a movie."

"Did you go back to her place?"

"No, she lives with her parents."

"I see. Jean says you're engaged to a girl back east."

"Not officially. We're separated temporarily."

"If I liked a boy, I wouldn't let him get 3,000 miles away from me."

"My working here was my father's idea. There's nothing Betty could do about that."

"You underestimate female tenacity, Colm."

She crunched on, then slurped her coffee. I could never abide slurping.

"Colm, I like the way your kitchen gets the morning light."

"Thanks. I've been wondering why you didn't move to New York after college. Isn't that where all the fashion grads go?"

"There was a designer in California whose work I loved. I wrote her a fan letter. To my surprise she wrote back. We corresponded a bit, and she offered to take me on as her assistant. I thought it was a fantastic opportunity. Except working for her was like being conscripted into the Red Army to face the Germans at Stalingrad. She turned out to be a demanding, egotistical, nitpicking, borderline-psychotic bitch. Partly it was vindictiveness because I proved impossible to seduce. I was considering abandoning ship when I saw your ad."

"I'm glad things worked out." I picked up the classified section of the local paper. "I've been looking at the rental ads. Apartments here go for about $50 and up. Houses start around $65 a month. Do you have anything in mind?"

"I doubt I'll have time to take care of a yard, so an apartment might be better. But I need privacy and quiet, which I'm more likely to get in a house."

"Uh, right."

"Why don't we drive around to give me a feel for the town? I'm very particular about where I live."

"Sounds fine, Norma. But you might want to change your blouse. It's a bit, uh, free-spirited for Ukiah."

"That's a surprise. I wore it all around Berkeley and barely turned a head. Of course, there's not a lot to catch the eye."

"Well, I expect it's a bit much for our local landlords."

"Now I see why your company is called Milady Modest."

"Right. Modesty is what it's all about for us rural types."

* * *

We spent the morning driving up and down the streets of Ukiah. We saw some FOR RENT signs, but Norma found something to fault in every place.

"I'm sorry I'm so picky, Colm," she said over lunch at the Golden Carp.

"Well, I'm sure we'll find you something. Of course, this is a small town and the selection is necessarily limited."

"I could be happy in a cabin in a forest by a burbling brook."

"That might be difficult logistically since you don't have a car. Do you drive?"

"I took lessons, but I made my instructor nervous. I had trouble keeping track of which pedals were for gas and brake."

"That's pretty important to remember."

"I have no trouble with my sewing machine pedal. But there's only one of those. God help me if they throw in a clutch pedal too. Your girlfriend's an actress?"

"Yes, the one back east. She just did a TV commercial for a major beer company."

"We had lots of actors at Emerson. They have a big theater department. I found them to be more than a little self-absorbed."

"Well, you can get that in any profession."

"Do you talk to your girlfriend?"

"Yes, on the phone. But it gets expensive."

"And when you talk, does she ask you about what you're doing?"

"Of course."

"She doesn't just prattle on endlessly about herself?"

"Er, not usually."

"Good. Then she's not like the actors I've met. Hollywood actors as you know have a dismal record at marriage."

"Jimmy Stewart's been married forever."

"And actresses with a similar record of marital longevity?"

I wracked my brain, but drew a zip. Hell, even Shirley Temple was divorced. "Well, I can't think of any offhand, but I'm sure there are some."

"Let me know when you think of one," she replied, slurping her tea. "You say your other girlfriend works around here?"

"Yes, just down the block."

"Good. Let's go meet her after lunch."

I wasn't sure that was such a hot idea, but Norma insisted. Juanita works every other Saturday, so I figured we had a 50-50 chance of missing her. But there she was sorting through incoming photo packets. She greeted me with her brightest 5,000-watt smile. I made the introductions, and the girls sized each other up. I don't think either particularly liked what they saw.

"I hope you don't mind, Juanita," said Norma, clutching my arm, "I'm taking your handsome boyfriend out to dinner tonight!"

That was news to me.

"That's fine, Norma," smiled Juanita. "You two have a wonderful time."

I didn't smile; I suspected I'd have hell to pay later.

Chapter 13

My doorbell rang that afternoon around three. It was Ramona's husband Dale. He had a beer can in one hand and a toolbox in the other.

"Hi, Colm."

"Hi, Dale."

"Your little houseguest here?"

"No, she walked to the grocery store. She didn't care for my selection of eats."

"Good. Mind if I come in?"

"No. Come on in."

Dale entered, took a swig of beer, and gazed about.

"Nice place you got here, Colm. Real, uh, cozy cottage style. Well, here's the thing. What is our job?"

"Uh, I make bathing suits and you make trailers."

"That's what brings in the dough. Our job is to keep the ladies happy. Am I right?"

"You're right, of course."

"So how about I take a quick peek at your bedroom door?"

"Uh, OK. It's this way."

We walked down the hallway to the master bedroom.

"Here's your problem, Colm. You have a doorknob, but no lock. That's to be expected. I'd say this house was built around 1910. It was a simpler time back then. Everyone went to church and generally stuck to the straight and narrow."

"Your point being, Dale?"

"Very simple, Colm. Modern times call for modern locks. Juanita likes you and trusts you, but she's afraid you might fall victim to midnight intruders. I'm the handy guy in the family; I get drafted for tasks like this. Don't worry, this won't take but a few minutes. Best of all, there's no charge for the new hardware."

"I don't know whether to be offended or flattered."

Dale went to work. "If in doubt, Colm, turn the other cheek. It's no reflection on you, pal. You're dating Juanita, and if you're smart you're not getting any. That's a recipe for nervous excitation. Am I right?"

"There's a certain truth to what you say."

"A guy in your state is a natural target for predatory females. Hell, she could be all over you before you even wake up. It's a fact that guys have been known to perform the full smorgasbord in their sleep."

"I don't see how that's possible. You'd need an erection."

"Well, wake yourself up sometime. Chances are you'll have a stiffy. I could pound nails with mine half the night long. OK, that's it. Full security–assuming she's not an expert at picking locks. Now raise your right hand and repeat after me."

I raised my right hand.

"I do solemnly swear . . ."

"I do solemnly swear."

"That I will faithfully lock my bedroom door . . ."

"That I will faithfully lock my bedroom door."

"As long as you know who is staying here. . ."

"As long as Norma Pomeroy is staying here."

Dale handed me his empty beer can.

"Good, Colm. I'll report your oath-taking to my sister-in-law. That should help ease her mind through these difficult times. We like to keep the ladies happy."

"Yes, we do, Dale. And thanks for dropping by."

* * *

Even though she's a girl, I decided to let Norma pay for dinner. I'd paid for lunch, plus it was by no means a date. Not to mention that Norma will be earning about four times more than me. I'm also getting the impression that her family has money. She has that aura about her, and her alma mater is one of New England's pricier colleges.

She occupied the bathroom for over an hour. Hard to figure since she's barely five feet tall and couldn't have that much to wash. I managed a quick shave in the kitchen sink. She finally emerged all dolled up in a slinky silver ensemble. Like something Norma Shearer would wear to a chic Manhattan cocktail party. Rather overdressed for Ukiah, but I said she looked "very nice."

"Thanks, Colm. It's just something I whipped up on my sewing machine."

"Today?"

"Not quite. Have you selected our dining destination?"

"The Peacock Grill has the best food in town. How's your cash situation?"

"Oh, right. You make $32 a week. OK, it will be my treat. I'm going to apply my lipstick now. Would you like to kiss me first?"

Kind of an odd request. I couldn't see any gentlemanly way to decline. So I dive-bombed in for a quick one.

Her lipstick was so red it scorched your eyeballs. She looked quite stunning all made up. She'd gone full Hollywood starlet down to the false eyelashes, diamond earrings, and transparent Lucite shoes that showed off her painted toenails. She'd swooped up her hair and piled it on top of her head. Nose-entrancing perfume too. She couldn't have looked any swankier if we were meeting Mr. and Mrs. Paul Newman for pre-Oscars appetizers at Chasens.

Naturally, all heads swivelled when we entered the restaurant. Norma ordered a martini, but I stuck with a small draft beer. A guy needs his wits about him when he's squiring Norma. She extracted a cigarette from her miniature purse and waited for me to light it.

"Sorry, Norma, I have no matches or lighter."

"Don't you smoke, Colm?" she replied, handing me her lighter.

I did the deed without igniting her dress or precarious hair.

"Gave it up. Bad for your health, you know."

"You're such a boy scout, Colm. Are you sure you went to Yale?"

"I've got the lousy grades to prove it."

I ordered the New York steak and she went with the prime rib.

"I love to dance, Colm. Are there any cabarets with hot dance bands in this town?"

"Out at the fairgrounds they have square dancing one night a week. On Tuesdays I think."

"Oh, please! Spare me that!"

We talked a bit about our families. She said her father was a ditch-digger.

"So you went to Emerson on a scholarship?"

"Not exactly, Colm. You know those subdivisions they're building everywhere? My father started a company that puts in the sewer, water, and gas lines. Endless ditches as far as the eye can see."

"That sounds fairly lucrative."

"It keeps my mother in cigarettes and gin."

"Hi there, Colm," said a familiar sexy voice.

Startled, I looked up.

"Oh, hi, Alice. Hi, Ora."

It was Saturday night, and Juanita's pals were all dressed up and on the prowl.

"We saw your car in the parking lot," said Ora.

"It's kind of hard to miss," added Alice. "So, of course, we had to stop in and say hello." She held out her hand to Norma. "And you must be Miss Ann Blyth."

Norma shook the offered hand. "No, I'm Norma."

"I'm Alice. That's Ora. Gosh, don't you kids look swell. Like you're all dressed up for the senior prom, except Colmy forgot the corsage."

"Where's Juanita?" I asked.

"Out in the car," said Ora. "We should go, Alice, and leave these folks to their dinner."

Alice took a swig of my beer and leaned down to kiss me on the lips. She lingered in the vicinity to whisper in my ear, "Don't mess up a good thing, Colmy."

"I don't plan to," I whispered back.

I liked her perfume and the feel of her smoldering lips.

* * *

When we got back to my place, Jean was mopping the kitchen floor.

"Isn't it rather late for housework?" inquired Norma.

"The thing I like about this job is I can make my own hours," Jean replied. "Sometimes I'm here scrubbing the toilet at midnight."

Not true in my experience, but I let it pass. Nor did I point out that Saturday was her day off.

"Jean," I said, "why don't you make some popcorn and we'll all play cards?"

"I hate cards!" said Norma.

"No problem," I replied. "I inherited a whole closet full of board games."

I cleared the bowl of fake wax fruit off the dining room table and set up a game called Careers. I read out the rules and we commenced play. Each of us had to specify our own "Success Formula," combining the degree of fame, happiness, and money we desired. This we kept secret as we worked our way around the board accumulating points in each category. Manufacturing bathing suits wasn't one of the occupational paths, but "Hollywood" was. I went for maximum money and fame, but lost to Jean who scored big in happiness. Gloomy Norma came in a distant third. She also boycotted the popcorn and Jean's homemade lemonade.

"Well, that was fun," I said as Jean packed away her bucket and mop. "Do you want to stay and clean my toilet?"

"I probably should be going, Mr. Moran. It's getting late."

"It certainly is," agreed my houseguest.

"Shall we go sketching tomorrow, Jean?" I asked.

"That's a thought. Why don't you call me early?"

"Will do. Well, good night, dear."

"Good night, Mr. Moran."

Jean waved a polite farewell to Norma as she left.

"You socialize with your housekeeper?" asked Norma.

"As often as Juanita lets me. Jean's a dynamite girl. Well, good night. Remember to turn out the lights if you're staying up."

Later in bed, I heard what sounded like the doorknob turning. Someone pushed against my door, but the new lock held firm. They uttered what sounded like "Rats!" then slunk away.

I do think it would be interesting sometime to have sex in my sleep. Hell, even sex while awake would make for a welcome change.

* * *

It turned out I didn't have time to go sketching with Jean. Forces were marshaled, calls were made, influential people were consulted, and the ideal rental was located for Norma. Juanita called me with the news bright and early.

"Where are you?" she asked.

"In bed."

"Anybody in there with you?"

"Let me check. . . No, I seem to have passed a celibate night. Your lock did the trick."

"She didn't climb in the window?"

"I expect she was deterred by the thorny rose bushes. I'm not that much of a sex magnet, you know."

"Yes, you are. Well, your worries are over. Meet me at 1217 Sequoia Street at noon. And bring your little friend."

"What's there?"

"The cutest little garden apartment. The rent's only $72 a month. Nicely furnished too. And currently vacant."

"Sounds great. Why don't we rent it and live there in sin?"

"Fine with me. Shall I put my dad on the phone so you can run it past him?"

"Uh, maybe later. See you at noon."

For a gal with no place to live, Norma didn't seem all that excited about this rental opportunity. Considerable hectoring was required to get her bathed, dressed, and out the door in time for our appointment.

1217 Sequoia Street consisted of two pairs of trim stucco cottages facing a garden court. The owner, a Mrs. Rogers, occupied a larger house at the rear of the lot. All four cottages had a small patch of grass surrounded by well-tended flower beds. Small lemon trees lined a sidewalk down the center that led to a bubbling concrete fountain. One of the inner cottages was vacant. Juanita met us on its small front porch. She said hello to Norma and gave me a warm, lengthy, and very public kiss.

The cottage had a roomy living room with fireplace and oak floor, kitchen with dining alcove, bedroom with two big closets, bathroom done in cream and green tiles, and an enclosed porch off the kitchen with a big table that would be ideal for a sewing machine. The furnishings were spare, but tastefully selected. There was even a combo TV-hifi in the living room. Off the back alley was a garage should Norma ever master her pedals.

"Seems very nice, Norma," I said. "What do you think?"

"I'm not crazy about the wallpaper in the bedroom. And the kitchen stove is electric. I really need a gas stove."

Big sigh from Juanita; I took our new designer aside for a private chat.

"Sorry, Norma, but I don't think you'll find anything better. It's a nice street and an easy walk to work. Downtown is just a few blocks farther. Confidentially, Juanita is on the warpath. If you don't take this place, we'll have to check you into a motel this afternoon."

Norma decided she could learn to cook over glowing electric coils. She passed her ten-minute get-acquainted chat with Mrs. Rogers, and wrote out a check for the deposit and first month's rent. She got the key and a gift box of Mrs. Rogers's homemade cinnamon buns.

I invited Juanita to have lunch with us, but she declined. I expect those two girls will never be the closest of pals. We grabbed a burger at a drive-in, then hauled over Norma's gear to her new home. Then I drove her to a supermarket, where she stocked up on necessities. These I helped her arrange in her cupboards. Then she sought my advice on rearranging her living room. We moved her sofa here and there, but it wound up back where it started facing the fireplace. She tried out her new stove: boiling water for tea without electrocuting herself. We sat at her chrome-and-Formica dinette and sampled the cinnamon buns, which were excellent.

"I have a TV now, Colm. You can come over to watch Perry Como."

"I hate Perry Como."

"How about boxing on Friday nights?"

"Brutes punching each other doesn't hold much appeal."

She pensively slurped her tea.

"I don't see Juanita being a long-term thing for you, Colm."

"No? Why not?"

"She's pretty and her figure is noteworthy, but she's much too provincial for a Yale grad. I foresee desperate boredom by Halloween."

"Well, I'll keep that in mind."

Norma got up and surprised me by sitting on my lap.

"Why don't you carry me to the bedroom, darling, and I'll show you what you've been missing?"

I looked at my watch. "Darn, time to go. See you at work tomorrow."

She held on tight and kissed me. I had to admit she was a good kisser. The sugary cinnamon flavors helped. She also moved her cute behind in a fashion that was designed to arouse the unwary.

I unclamped her lips and arms. "That was fun, Norma, but I really have to be on my way."

"I'm not giving up, Colm. We're perfect for each other. I knew that from the first moment I saw you."

"Could be, Norma, but work and romance just don't mix. We have to be professional about this if we are to function well together."

"I think we could function *extremely* well together, and I intend to prove it!"

I hope she puts as much effort into our 1958 swim-wear line as she's putting into marketing her body to me.

* * *

Jean was frying fish in my kitchen when I got back.

"You were gone a long time," she said. "How's her new mattress working out?"

"I wouldn't know."

"Your devastating charm has worked its magic again."

"That was not my intention. Frankly, I'm glad she's out of my hair. Now I can devote my undivided attention to you and your inviting lips."

"I don't recall my lips sending out any invitations. Here's a tip, Colm: Never bother someone working with hot grease."

"Damn, Jean, you're as cold as Norma is hot. Why can't I meet someone in the middle?"

"How about Juanita? She seems pretty middle of the road."

"You should thank Juanita for finding that rental. Otherwise, Norma would have been here helping me decorate my Christmas tree–in 1965!"

Chapter 14

Norma proved to be just as much a take-charge girl at work. She vetoed all of Madame Aranson's new designs and told Wendell to cancel her fabric orders. She also insisted he return all the new stock that had already been received. She set Miss Page to work scheduling appointments with mill reps to review their latest offerings. And powwowed with Vera and Mona, the cutter, over workflow and other issues.

Meanwhile, I buttonholed Wendell about my need for a raise and office. He said he would talk to my father about the former and offered me his old office, which had been converted into a storeroom. I hauled out all the junk, dumped it in the warehouse, and instructed Joe to find a place for it or throw it out. My new office was a windowless space about the size of a rabbit hutch, but I squeezed in a small desk and chair. I hung up a calendar from a zipper supplier that showed monthly hot babes in interestingly zippered apparel. The first call received on my new phone was good news from the San Francisco lawyer: Beachzilla was unclaimed, so he has filed for the trademark.

My second call was to Mrs. Snyder, who reported that young Mark's initial reaction to our prototype bathing suit was just lukewarm.

"He didn't think it was very monster-like," she admitted.

"Right, well that's true I suppose," I said.

"But he liked it much better when he got it wet. He appreciated its lizardly sheen."

"How about we package them in plastic bags filled with water?" I said, thinking out loud.

"Oh, I think that might be a tough sell to Mr. Slivmank," she said. "And I expect all that extra weight would be costly to ship. Plus, there'd be the problem of leakage. And perhaps mold and mildew."

In the end I decided to add this line to the label: "Wow! Looks like real reptile skin when wet!" I hope that does the trick. Wendell OK'd my design, and we sent it off to our label supplier in South San Francisco. Awesome Beachzilla swim trunks soon may be rampaging across the department stores of America.

At noon Norma and I walked to a nearby sandwich shop for lunch. I told her she had Wendell scared half to death.

"Why's that?" she asked, chewing her BLT in an annoying way.

"Your sending back all that fabric."

"I wouldn't dress my dog in those ugly prints. That woman must have been blind or insane."

"Madame Aranson believed bold prints worked as camouflage, serving to distract the eye."

"Hardly, Colm. They just turned our customers into walking billboards for flab. We might as well have dressed them in blinking neon. God, I love your chin."

"My chin has nothing to do with this discussion."

"But everything to do with the tingle I'm feeling right now. Shall I tell you where?"

"Please, Norma. I'm trying to eat."

"If you think Wendell's nervous now, wait until I bring up the B-word."

"What's that?"

"Bikinis."

"Good luck with that, kid. No respectable woman in America will wear one. They've been condemned by all the prim women's magazines–not to mention the Catholic church. The Pope is especially livid on that subject."

"Times are changing, Colm."

"Could be, but they're not changing in Slivmank's withered brain."

"What do guys your age think of bikinis?"

"What else? We think they're great. But we're also inclined to think there goes a slut with her tits hanging out."

"So you wouldn't want your sweetheart such as me to wear one?"

"You're not my sweetheart. And no, I wouldn't want her wearing one."

"Don't you see a contradiction in that attitude?"

"Life is full of contradictions. I wouldn't want my girlfriend showing off her body to the world. Nudity is for the bedroom, Norma."

"I agree. Shall we try it tonight after work?"

"Why don't you practice on your own for a few years, then give me a call."

At least there's one girl on this planet I can say no to. It helps that she's so annoying.

* * *

Today's mail brought a picture postcard of a south Florida beach. Scrawled in blotted ink on the back was this message:

I'm seeing my designs everywhere! You'll be sorry.
Go to hell. –Aranson

It appears our former designer still may be harboring some resentment. Despite the sourness of the sentiment, Wendell tacked the postcard to the employee bulletin board.

That evening I got a call from the old fellow.

"That Slivmank fellow thinks you're underpaid," he said.

"So do I. The dollar doesn't go as far as it did when you were my age."

"Tell me about it. OK, Colm, you are now making $64 a week."

"Gee, thanks, Pop. That should help a lot."

"Anything else?"

"What is your opinion of bikinis?"

"I have no opinions on women's fashions. It is all a fanciful game. Fools dressing sheep, as the saying goes. I was not outraged when Miss Garbo donned pants."

"Then you do not object to them?"

"I object to nuclear war, Communism, and a Democrat in the White House. If there's money to be made in bikinis, I have no objections."

"That's very liberal of you, Father."

"I hardly think that term applies to me, Colm. Keep up the good work. Good-bye."

* * *

On Thursday Mrs. Yeater called in some gals to begin sewing our Beachzilla line. The suits will have elastic waists (as opposed to drawstrings), inner mesh briefs, and no outside pockets (reptiles don't have pockets). Wendell scored a good deal from a wholesaler, so we are buying the inner briefs pre-made. They have an small flap pocket to hold a locker key or coins for the snack bar. (Or a condom for those precociously hopeful older boys.)

Sizes small and medium are to retail for $2.99. The large size will sell for $3.49. The sewing ladies will be paid a flat $.38 per garment, regardless of size. The labels will be sewn in later when we receive them. I'm designing a catalog page to be sent to our sales reps. Wendell says we can't actually mention Godzilla as we'd risk being sued. My ferocious text drops some monster-sized hints, but avoids the G-word.

Norma is producing some outstanding designs. Milady Modest Inc. will have an entirely new look for 1958. She's disguising bulges and fleshy excesses with boldly contrasting patterns of light and dark fabrics. Some of her sketches retain modesty skirts, but they're being simplified and integrated better into the lines of the suit (so she tells me). Meanwhile, reps from textile mills troop in daily lugging thick binders of swatches. Norma asks for my opinion on fabrics, but after a while they all blur together. I did like one sample featuring little fish swimming amid bubbles. Very appropriate for beachwear if you ask me. Norma said she would keep it in mind if she ever designs swim wear for toddlers.

I got a small roll of 16mm movie film in the mail from Betty labeled "Rheingold Beer Commercial #37." Too bad I have no way of viewing it. I phoned Juanita at Flamperts, but they only stock projectors sized for 8mm home movies. She suggested I check the library or high school.

"What is it you're trying to view?" she asked. "Some raunchy stag film?"

"No, Betty's beer commercial."

"Oh, that. How's your engagement to her going?"

"I hardly talk to her now and she never writes. Cross-country romances are extremely difficult to sustain."

"I'm very glad to hear that. Are we having a date tomorrow?"

"Of course."

"And Miss Pomeroy, does she have her claws into you yet?"

"Our relationship is strictly business. It would be helpful if you could find her a fellow. He needs to be relatively sophisticated with a chin like mine."

"That's a tall order, but I'll give it some thought."

"You're the best, Juanita."

"Do keep that in mind, Colm."

* * *

Friday night's movie was "Heaven Knows, Mr. Allison." Normally I avoid films featuring nuns, but this one starred Robert Mitchum, one of my favorite actors. He plays a marine stranded on a Pacific island with Deborah Kerr (the nun). They have to hide out when the Japanese arrive. Quite a bit of flirting, but how far can you go with a nun before you get slapped down by the Hays Code censors? Not very far in this case as chastity triumphed again. After Robert risked his life sabotaging enemy artillery, they were rescued when the Yanks captured the island. It was a big-budget color movie filmed in CinemaScope and stereo sound. Way beyond the financial means of us independents. Perhaps someday I'll produce the first film where the nun actually hops into the sack with the hero. Along the way she can trade her habit for a bikini. That might make a good title: "The Nun in a Bikini."

My flirting with Juanita gets a bit more physical, but some aspects are similar to dating a nun. I was reading in *Vogue* that they have an experimental pill now that's proving effective for birth control. Women take it, not guys. Right now it's only being prescribed for gals with severe menstrual problems. I'd ask Juanita if she had those, but it's a difficult subject to bring up. The pill does have a small failure rate, so you'd still be playing Russian roulette every time anyway. It's too bad our bodies weren't designed with one part for sex and another part for making babies. Having the functions combined puts a real damper on our dates.

Also in the theater was Jean, draped under that clod Elwyn's hairy arm. Plus, I noticed Norma skulking behind us three rows back. I hope she was there to see the movie and not to spy on me. Someday I plan to confess that I probably would have had sex with her had she known how to chew (and drink) like a normal person.

Chapter 15

The name came to me in the middle of the night. I was awakened by some sort of jolt, which I found out later was a minor earthquake. California is prone to those. Naturally, since I was awake I checked to see if I had a stiffy. I did. Too bad Jean didn't choose to enter my bedroom at that moment for some light dusting.

I was trying to get back to sleep, when this name popped unbidden into my mind: Cheeky Swimsuits.

The pure genius of that name astounded even me. Of course, it would be financial suicide to produce a line of bikinis under the name Milady Modest Inc. Bikinis are anything but modest. And "Milady" is as matronly as you can get.

What sort of customer would be interested in a trendy bikini? Cheeky girls with dynamite bodies!

After all General Motors doesn't just make Chevys. They also make Pontiacs, Oldsmobiles, Buicks, and Cadillacs. They make a car for every taste and pocket book. They make Buicks for retired accountants and Corvettes for swinging bachelors. So why should we just make bathing suits for older gals with problem figures?

The concept was so brilliant I had to share it; I immediately dialed Norma.

"Hi, Colm," she said. "You're awake too, huh? What was that bang? Did something blow up?"

"I have no idea. But listen to this great idea I just had."

I laid out Cheeky Swim Wear for her in all of its inspired glory.

"That's not bad, Colm. I kind of like it."

"What it is, Norma, is cheeky. And you have to be plenty cheeky to parade around with 95 percent of your skin on display."

"It also has that nice connotation of ass cheeks, Colm. We could sculpt the bottoms way high in back to expose more of the buttocks."

"Really? You think so?" I asked, shocked.

"Why not? We'd be going for the youth market, and so many of those girls have perfect asses. Just wait until they've hit 30 and had a few kids. Or spend all day in an office pounding a typewriter. Then they'll be grateful for Milady Modest."

"How will we get Slivmank to buy it?"

"We'll have to plan our strategy. Shall I come over now and brainstorm?"

"Norma, it's two in the morning."

"Are you naked?"

"That's none of your business."

"I'm totally and completely nude."

"Congratulations. I hope you don't get a chill."

"I'm yours, darling. Whenever you want me."

"Don't call me darling. And remind me not to call you in the middle of the night. I'll see you at work."

"I'm thinking cheeky, Colm."

"Good. Cheeky it is from now on."

* * *

Saturday morning while getting a haircut it occurred to me that Cheeky Swimsuits needed a logo. Something free-spirited and cheeky. I decided to give it some thought.

The barber did an OK job for a fellow who's probably more accustomed to producing flattops and butch cuts. He said I had a "fine head of hair," which is always welcome news from a professional. It worries me that the old fellow is getting a bit thin on top. I'm happy to inherit his money, but please not his hairline.

While waiting to be served, I read a preview of the new 1958 cars in one of those mechanics magazines. Everyone seems to be going to four headlamps next year. And piling on the chrome with a trowel. The new Packard looks like it was designed by Madame Aranson on a bad day. That company is going downhill fast. Even with my recent 100 percent raise I'm still far from being able to afford a new car. I don't mind my aging Packard, but its ungainly stick shift is one more obstacle between me and Juanita's luscious body.

Too bad Milady Modest Inc. can't produce a new quadruple-bosom swimsuit to keep up with Detroit's latest trends. We're both in the styling biz. Detroit can produce endless variations on automotive grilles. Similarly, even though it's a relatively simple garment, there are an infinite number of ways to style a woman's bathing suit. The key though, is to do it right.

Speaking of which, the magazine offered a sneak peek at Ford's brand new Edsel. Talk about a strange grille design. The barber peered over my shoulder and stated his opinion freely, "It looks like a goddam cunt."

"What does?" I asked, startled.

"The front of that new Edsel."

"You don't think it looks like a horse collar?"

"Yeah, that too. If they sell even one of those damn cars I'll be surprised."

Seeing an opportunity for market research, I asked him what he thought of bikinis.

"Whores and harlots," he replied. "That's who you'll see wearin' 'em."

"Well, they cover everything that's supposed to be covered."

"Just barely. And what happens down there?"

"Er, what do you mean?"

"I'm talkin' cunt hairs, son. Do they shave it or what?"

Considering the source, that was a surprisingly apt question. What do they do?

When I got home, I sketched out the head of a grinning duck. He was winking and had a bit of a leer. Underneath I pencilled in the slogan: "Why be shy? –Mr. Cheeky."

I may be biased, but I think I just created the perfect logo for Cheeky Swimsuits.

* * *

That evening I took Juanita out to dinner at the Peacock Grill to celebrate my rising income. She must have received a description from Alice and Ora of Norma's dinner ensemble last week, because she looked extra ravishing in a new red dress. The rumor is she drove all the way to Santa Rosa to get it. I told her she looked great, but added that as far I as was concerned next time she could skip the false eyelashes.

"I'm glad to hear that, honey, 'cause they're a major pain to glue on."

"Not really worth the trouble, Juanita. Most guys I know rate them down with padded bras."

"Well, you'll never have to worry about that with me, Colm."

"And hallelujah to that," I said.

Juanita liked my Cheeky logo design, but said she doubted she'd ever wear our product.

"Why not, honey?" I asked.

"I've got too much upstairs."

"Do you mean boobs or brains?"

"Both. Plus, I'm too shy, no matter what your duck says."

Juanita had some news. She's thought of a guy for Norma: a Mr. Slade Preston.

"What kind of name is Slade" I commented. "He's the opposite of Harry James. He's a fellow with two *last* names."

"Slade is very nice. And very good looking."

"Oh? If he's so great, how come you didn't go out with him?"

"I did, briefly."

"Let me guess. You gave him the speech and he never called you again."

She laughed. "Yeah, plus he knows my sisters. I can't believe you haven't bailed on me, Colm."

"I like a frustrating challenge, dear. What does your Mr. Preston do?"

"He was a forestry major at Humboldt State, but he can't spend much time in the woods on account of his allergies. His uncle left him some money, so he started a little magazine."

"Devoted to difficult poetry and experimental prose?"

"No, Slade's a practical guy. His magazine's all about plywood."

"Really? How much is there to say on that topic?"

"Apparently quite a bit 'cause it comes out every month. He writes most of it himself too."

"Amazing. How's his chin?"

"As chiseled as Gary Cooper's. He's about the handsomest guy in town–next to you I mean."

"And he doesn't have a girlfriend?"

"Alice gave him a whirl recently, but that didn't work out."

"Why not?"

Juanita blushed. "I'm not at liberty to say."

"How shall we get them together?"

"You run him past Norma, and then we'll pass her phone number on to him. We'll see if he appeals."

"OK. I sure hope he does."

* * *

Sunday morning Jean took pity on me and came over and made eggs for breakfast. We drank our coffee and read the *San Francisco Chronicle*. We get the early edition up here. It has more typos and lacks the final sports scores.

The *Chronicle* had another photo of Eisenhower on the golf course. Someone should remind that guy that he's the President and not just an old retired general. The sports page reported another rumor that the Giants and Dodgers might move to California. That will never happen because there's never been major league baseball west of the Mississippi. The distances are too great for the teams to travel. Besides, the Dodgers have the most loyal fans in baseball. They'd have to be nuts to leave Brooklyn.

I'm beginning to like the *Chronicle's* columnist Herb Caen. He has more to say than just gossip. I noticed he's often quoted in *Reader's Digest*. My uncle passed away, but his magazine subscriptions live on. I read them because I have no TV, and there's too much Elvis on the radio. He has a new song out now about teddy bears that's especially annoying. Improbably, it has risen to the top of the hit parade and is played incessantly.

I switched on the radio briefly to get the news. Our jolt was a 2.7 quake centered up near Willits. Too minor for the locals to get worked up over. Jean slept right through it.

She liked my Cheeky Swimsuits logo, but suggested I add a red fez to my duck. I told her I'd think about it. She thinks there might be a market for our bikinis.

"Would you wear one?" I asked.

"Possibly. I'd have to see how abbreviated you were going."

"I think Norma's planning on being very bold."

"I imagine bikinis will catch on sooner or later. That's how fashion trends work. The new style is widely condemned while appealing to a few risk-takers on the fringe. Then it gradually goes mainstream. You'll recall how scandalous it used to be for men to appear bare-chested at the beach. Both sexes were expected to cover up. I think some men even were arrested."

"That's lunacy. Why would anyone care?"

"I suppose bare nipples were deemed just too objectionable. If you saw a fellow's nipples, you might be tempted to think about the chest of the girl next to him."

"It's a wonder our grandparents ever had children."

"I expect they kept the lights out and got it over as quickly as possible."

"I often think about the chest of the girl next to me," I said with a leer.

"You would in Juanita's case."

"She's not next to me right now."

"How unfortunate for you."

"You have a very nice shape, Jean."

"I'll thank you to keep your eyes to yourself."

"I haven't forgotten that tomorrow's your birthday."

"My youth is over," she sighed. "My decline into old age has begun."

Jean's father is taking her out for a birthday dinner, but I claimed dibs on tomorrow's lunch with her. I'm hoping no birthday time at all will be allotted to that clod Elwyn Saunders.

* * *

Monday at work I ran the concept of "Slade Preston, blind date" past Norma.

"Why would I want to go out with some local rube when I've got you?" she asked.

"Well, for one thing you don't have me. Slade is very nice and as handsome as a movie star. One look at him and you will forget you were ever infatuated with me."

"He's probably as dumb as a stump."

"Hardly. He's a successful magazine publisher."

"Of what? *Popular Tedium for Yokels*?"

I felt I had to fudge on this point. "I forget what his magazine's about, but I'm sure you'll find it fascinating."

"I'll consider going out with him on one condition."

"What's that?"

"It has to be a double date with you and that top-heavy girl you're seeing."

"Why would you want to go out with us?"

"For my own protection. Who knows what sort of creep you're trying to fix me up with. And if he turns out to be a dud, I can devote all of my attention to you. It will count as our second date."

"All right, if you insist. I'll run the idea past Juanita."

"Slade Preston sounds like a made-up name. He probably changed it because he's got a lengthy criminal record under his real name."

"I assure you that's his real name. Juanita's known his family forever."

"If I were you, I'd run a background check on her too. She's probably been arrested for soliciting and God knows what else."

"That's a vicious slander and you know it."

We moved on to business. Shown both options Norma preferred my second drawing of Mr. Cheeky with a fez. She said the idea was inspired, even if it did come from my "floor mopper." We are making a list of all the points in favor of Cheeky Swimsuits for our presentation to Wendell. We are now up to point 14: Gals appreciate bikinis because they can achieve a more all-over tan.

Meanwhile, I stuck my neck out and commissioned our trademark attorney to begin checking for prior claims to the name Cheeky Swimsuits.

* * *

I met Jean at an Italian restaurant around the corner from the courthouse for her birthday lunch. She had dressed sensibly for the heat in an attractive skirt and blouse. More makeup than usual, an extra splash of perfume, and tiny sparkling earrings that may have been rubies. I couldn't have liked her any more if I tried.

"You look great," I said. "As pretty as a birthday card."

"Your simile seems rather forced. The ravioli here is not bad."

We both went for the ravioli, and I ordered a bottle of Chianti.

"Don't you have to go back to work, Colm?"

"Yeah, but I'll just have one glass. So you're 22 today?"

"I wish. I'm 23."

"Wow, you're nine months older than me!"

"Your point being?"

"Uh, just that you're older. We'd have been in different classes in high school. I doubt you would have gone out with me then."

"I'm not going out with you now."

"Right. And why is that?"

"Because you're engaged, you're dating a local girl, and you have another girl waiting in the wings. I'd say your dance card is full."

"Norma is not waiting in the wings. We're fixing her up with Slade Preston. Do you know him?"

"Of course. He's Ukiah's golden gift to the gene pool. I had a severe crush on him when I was 16. It's kind of a miracle that no girl's dragged him to the altar yet."

"Do you think he'll like Norma?"

"I couldn't say. He's tried every other sort of girl. Perhaps he's ready now for a nut like her."

I wound up drinking three glasses of wine to Jean's one. We had a merry lunch, then I handed her a card and gift.

"This is all a bit much, Colm," she said, reading my sappy message in her card. She leaned over and gave me a quick kiss on the lips. "You're sweet."

"I hope you like your gift."

She ripped off the wrapping paper and exclaimed over my gift. It was a lavish tin of English watercolor paints and a sable brush.

"These paints are very expensive," she said. "You shouldn't have. Where did you find them?"

"I got them when I went to San Francisco. Now you can paint as well as J. M. W. Turner."

"How do you figure that?"

"Because now you have the same brand of paints he used."

"Ah, that's the secret is it?"

"It's a well-known fact."

"Too bad I didn't know that earlier. I could have skipped all those years of art college."

* * *

Returning to work, I felt like taking a nap, but called Juanita at Framperts instead.

"Hi, Juanita. I wanted you to know that I took my housekeeper out to lunch for her birthday. When she opened her modest gift, she got a bit carried away and gave me a brief kiss on the lips. It was merely by way of thanking me. It meant nothing."

"Yeah, I heard about that. You went to Luigis and had the ravioli. Much wine was consumed."

"Juanita dear, do you have spies everywhere?"

"My friends see things and report back. I do the same for them. It's not really spying."

"The C.I.A. should be so efficient."

"I appreciate your candor, Colm. And I've got some news for you, honey. Reggie is coming home on leave. He's arriving by bus on Sunday."

"Reggie Dowling the cheeky little upstart who was talking dirty to you in the seventh grade?"

"It was his way of showing he cared. So I guess I'll have to see him some while he's here. I hope you understand."

"I doubt that very much. I'll be seething with jealousy the entire time. Be sure to grill him about those fräuleins."

"I intend to."

I filled in Juanita on Norma's stipulations regarding her proposed blind date.

"I guess we could all go out together, honey, if that's what she wants. It might get a little awkward."

"Awkward is nothing new for me."

"I'll see if Slade is available on Friday, and let you know."

"Too bad Reggie won't be home by then. We could invite him along too."

Chapter 16

When Norma and I went in to face Slivmank on Wednesday, we had marshaled 26 arguments in favor of Cheeky Swimsuits. From the concrete: Bikinis can command high margins while saving on material and labor (#2). To the psychological: Girls desire bikinis to help them get noticed by guys (#17). To the geopolitical: Stylish bikinis will keep us well ahead of the Russians in swim-wear fashions (#23).

Shocked and horrified, Wendell responded with four objections:

1. No decent girl would wear a bikini.

We were ready for that old warhorse. We pointed out that since Victorian times there had been an inexorable trend of bathing suits becoming more revealing. Bikinis were the next logical step in that development. They were now being accepted by fashion trend-setters at all the smart beaches and resorts.

"Besides," said Norma, "whether or not girls in bikinis are indecent, they still have money to spend on flattering swim wear. Why shouldn't we market to them?"

2. Department stores will refuse to stock them.

Even if that were true (and we didn't concede the point), we could still sell to women's dress shops and other outlets.

3. Creating an inventory in all sizes of the new styles would be expensive and add to the chaos in the warehouse.

A tougher objection to overcome. Yes, launching a new line of bikinis would entail a major commitment of time, space, and money. We argued that our warehouse problems needed to be addressed anyway, and perhaps it was time for Joe to go.

4. Failure of Cheeky Swimsuits to catch on could bankrupt the company.

We conceded that moving into bikinis was a risk, but pointed that risk-taking is what separates the most successful businesses from the also-rans.

Of course, the real issue and biggest obstacle is Wendell's cowardice. The guy is old. Not far from retirement, he doesn't want to rock the boat. He wants to slog on making bathing suits for fat gals until it's time for him to get the gold watch and collect his generous pension.

He did say he liked my logo design for Cheeky Swimsuits. He suggested I do one for Milady Modest Inc.

"Like what?" I snapped. "A shy elephant cowering behind a screen?"

"Probably not, Colm," he said, smiling. "Something tasteful and elegant would be nice. Something your late uncle would have approved of. We must always think of him in making any business decision."

In other words, this company is being run from the grave!

So we lost Round One. Norma and I have decided to regroup and give the matter more thought. We are definitely not throwing in the towel.

"Just remember what Einstein said," said Norma, when we returned to her office.

"What was that?" I asked.

"Great flights of genius will always be battled by mediocre minds."

* * *

That evening my long-lost girlfriend Betty called collect.

"Hi, Colmy. Did you get my beer commercial?"

"I did, darling. Thanks for sending it."

"What did you think of it?"

"Uh, I haven't been able to view it yet. A 16mm sound projector is not a common household appliance, you know."

"You can rent them anywhere in Manhattan. I'd have thought you'd make a little effort since I'm starring in it."

"I will, darling, I will. I've been a little busy with business. We're trying to start a line of bikinis."

"I don't know, Colmy. A girl has to be pretty confident of her shape to wear one of those."

"Your shape is perfect, darling."

"I could use some subtractions and additions. Guess what? I'm singing!"

"Singing what?"

"We're doing 'The Pajama Game,' and I got cast as Gladys Hotchkiss."

"Is that the lead?"

"You always ask me that. Jesus, it's not the lead, but it's a nice part. I get some clever lines, and I get to sing and dance. It's a great addition to my résumé."

"I'm sure you'll steal the show, darling."

"Well, I got to go, Colmy. Don't be such a stranger. You could at least send me a postcard so I'll know you haven't forgotten me."

"Will do, darling. I miss you."

"I should hope so. God, Colmy, you've been gone forever!"

She's right. I have been neglecting her. I sat down and typed out a two-page letter. Full of typos, erasures, and misspellings, but I hope she appreciates the effort. They say distance makes the heart grow fonder, but I had to retrieve her framed photo from my grip to recall exactly what she looked like. Oh right, she's that gorgeous blonde who used to electrify my soul.

* * *

There was a Cary Grant movie ("An Affair To Remember") opening at the theater, but Juanita decided our manufactured foursome might have a better chance of getting acquainted by going bowling. I picked up the two girls in my Packard, and we met Slade at the bowling alley. He was easy to spot, being the best-looking fellow in the Western Hemisphere. One of those noble profiles and it all went up from there: movie star hair, manly build, arresting blue eyes, and an infinity of superlatives *ad nauseam*. Dazzled Norma was instantly smitten. Clearly, it was another case of a dream blind date coming true.

Juanita had her own pink ball and matching shoes and bag, but the rest of us had to dredge up a suitable ball from the array of battered alley balls. We rented shoes and were assigned the last alley on the right. Juanita waved to the youth lurking in the shadows behind the pins, who of course she knew and might have gone out with for all I know.

"Some alleys are now installing automated pin-setters that eliminate pin boys," I pointed out.

"That's a shame," said Juanita. "Who are we supposed to flirt with?"

"You could try the fellow who brought you," I pointed out.

Juanita kissed me, then ordered four beers from the waitress.

"Are you extra thirsty?" inquired Slade. "Or are you sharing?"

Norma laughed at his jest like Slade was Bob Hope in bowling shoes. It's kind of painful being subjected to the birth pangs of another couple's nascent romance.

Slade was friendly but rather reserved. I suppose when you have that much physical wattage the addition of a dynamic personality might prove completely overwhelming. He bowled competently and answered Norma's numerous questions. She found it absolutely fascinating that he published a magazine called *Progressive Plywood*.

"Why plywood exactly?" she inquired. "Why were you drawn to that material? Was it because of its inherent pliability?"

"Well, actually most plywoods are fairly rigid. That's one of their advantages. There was no trade magazine devoted exclusively to sheet goods. I studied the market and decided this was an opportunity worth pursuing."

"How very entrepreneurial of you," she replied. "We're making a similar move right now into bikinis."

"Bikinis, uh, right."

"How about a plywood bathing suit?" joked Juanita. "It might be just the thing for shaping and support."

"Yes, I could see where you might need that," said Norma.

"Although support may not be much of an issue for some girls," replied Juanita.

They exchanged insincere smiles.

Juanita was the best bowler, although it helped that she was buddies with the pin boy. At one point she was trying to make a difficult 7-10 split. Her ball knocked the 10 pin sideways, it missed the 7 pin, but a swiftly moving foot picked up the spare for her.

"Did you see that?" yelled Norma. "That's cheating!"

"The pin was wobbling," replied Juanita. "He just helped it along to speed up the game."

Slade and I were fairly evenly matched. We drank our beer and feigned a casual indifference to mask our competitiveness. I rolled more strikes, but he picked up more spares.

Norma had her own unique style. She bowled with both hands, sending the ball moseying down the alley at the speed of a lame turtle. It didn't so much knock down the pins as elbow them politely aside. To her credit she never rolled a gutter ball and scored a respectable 117 her second game.

When Norma excused herself to go to the restroom, I followed behind for a private chat in the hallway.

"You know Slade probably has women swooning over him all the time," I pointed out.

"So?"

"So it might help if you were a bit less, uh, enthusiastic."

"Why do you say that?"

"Because I'm a guy and I know how guys think."

"Oh. When Slade takes me home, should I invite him in?"

"If you want to, but try to keep your clothes on. Guys will take advantage of fast girls, but they won't stick around long."

"I want Slade to stick around forever."

"You don't waste any time falling for guys."

"That's true. God, I can't believe I ever thought you were such a catch."

* * *

Norma called me Saturday morning.

"Damn, Colm, am I that boring?"

"Not at all. You're, uh . . . "

"The word you're looking for is captivating. Or scintillating, that works too."

"Oh, right. So how did it go with Slade?"

"I invited him in for a nightcap, but he said he had to go home and finish an article he was writing on experimental chipboard made from rice straw, whatever that is."

"Well, he's dedicated to his work. That's good."

"Do you think he liked me?"

"Sure. You were having a lively conversation, weren't you?"

"Yes, but you can have that with your grandmother. Did you pick up any vibes?"

"Sorry, my vibe meter is not that sensitive."

"Do you think he'll call me?"

"Time will tell, Norma. You have to be patient."

"Being the girl is always harder. I hope you appreciate that."

"Yes, I know. But we guys get shot down plenty of times by you chicks."

"I'll bet Slade has never been rejected once in his life. He's every girl's dream man–except for his unfortunate plywood fixation. I intend to correct that, of course."

"You'll make him give up his magazine?"

"I'm afraid so. He needs a more suitable and lucrative occupation if we are to have a happy life together."

"Well, don't jump the gun, Norma. You're still pretty far from the altar."

"Yeah, don't remind me."

That evening Juanita and I went to see "An Affair To Remember." This was a remake of the 1939 movie "Love Affair," which I never saw. I was four in 1939 and not much of a film-goer. The modern version has Cary Grant romancing Deborah Kerr; the original version starred Charles Boyer and Irene Dunn. Cary and Charles are quite different, but you'd have trouble finding two actresses who are more alike than Deborah and Irene.

Lots of sniffling in the theater at the end of the movie. On her way to meet Cary at the top of the Empire State Building Miss Kerr gets hit by a car. Cary waits for hours, then assumes she's dropped him. They are coldly formal with each other when they meet months later in her apartment. The clever script has Cary figuring out why she's not budging off the sofa. Loving clinch at the end as the romantic theme music plays.

As the credits rolled Juanita clutched my arm with one hand and her hankie with the other. I sat there envying the producers who were having a big payday from their movie. It helps to have in your cast Cary Grant, who's nearly as good looking as Slade Preston. Casting big stars is not a luxury many independent producers can afford. We have to go out and find our own stars-to-be. I wonder if Slade ever had any inclinations to act? I could team him with Betty in a film set on a beach next to a plywood mill. She could lounge around in a Cheeky Swimsuits bikini while Slade declaims on the wonders of plywood.

Exiting the theater, we came face to face with Jean and her beetle-browed gorilla going in. She felt obliged to make the introductions. Elwyn and I shook hands with the least enthusiasm either of us could muster.

"As your domestic worker Jeanie is entitled to Social Security," he pointed out. "I trust you're paying into it for her."

"I expect so," I replied, icily. Where did that jerk get off calling her Jeanie?

"It's a wonderful movie," said Juanita. "It reaffirms your faith in love, doesn't it, honey?"

"Yes, it certainly does," I said, catching Jean's eye.

After a deluxe dinner for two at the Golden Carp, we went back to my place. Perhaps because this was our last date before the arrival of Corporal Reggie Dowling, Juanita let my probing hand do a bit of exploring below the waist–constrained only by her girdle and garter belt. In a perfect world girls would wear nothing more incommodious than easily removable panties. Juanita was quite wet down there, which embarrassed her for some reason. I don't see why, since I was stiff as a board at the time. Nature prepares us for the act even as society denies us the experience of it.

On the drive home Juanita confessed that Slade had apologized for not calling her again after they went out. He said he had been informed by several friends that she was engaged to Mr. Dowling.

"So are you engaged to Reggie?" I asked.

"I guess I'm as much engaged to Reggie as you are to Betty."

Well, that certainly cleared matters up.

* * *

Sunday morning I walked into town and had breakfast in a café. On the way back I passed the pawn shop and noticed that my lighter and cigarette case were no longer in the window. Perhaps some girl bought the set as a gift for her boyfriend. Good luck to him. Some people have trouble quitting cigarettes, but I had a harder time trying to take them up.

When I got back, Norma called me in a panic.

"Colm! Slade invited me to go swimming, but I don't have a bathing suit! And all the stores are closed!"

"You don't have a bathing suit? How is that possible? You design them for a living."

"Frankly, I have trouble finding one that looks good on me."

"Oh. Well, I have a key to the building. I could meet you there, and you could pick one from the stock."

"Don't be absurd. If I showed up wearing a Milady Modest swimsuit, Slade would never speak to me again. And who could blame him? I need you to call your housekeeper and ask if I can borrow one of hers."

"I don't need to phone her. She's right here cleaning my bathroom."

Jean said she had an old suit that Norma could have if she wanted. It was from when she was a teenager, before she had "fully developed."

"It was back when I was dressing boldly artistic," she added, looking up from scrubbing my toilet.

"How artistic?" I asked.

"Black with purple zebra stripes."

Norma said it would have to do. I asked her where they were going.

"Some place called Johnson's pond. If it's clothing optional, I'll get to see Slade naked. That should be tremendously thrilling. But I'm keeping my suit on."

"It's not a nudist resort, Norma. Coincidentally, Jean and I are headed up there today too."

"You go swimming with your housekeeper?"

"Sure, why not? We're also having a non-picnic lunch. Should we pack extra for you two?"

"OK. But if Slade starts acting amorous, I need you to disappear fast."

"Will do."

Slade and Norma arrived at the pond a few minutes after us. He was driving one of those pointy-nosed Studebakers. Its designer was aiming for modern but achieved ridiculousness instead. Jean surreptitiously slipped Norma the suit, which she donned in the back seat of my Packard. It fit fine, but I'd say the stripes were more a hot pink than purple. They glowed against the black like they were lit from within.

"If you drown, Norma," I said, "the rescuers should have no trouble locating your body at the bottom of the pond."

"Do drop dead, Colm," she replied, tugging at her neckline.

Although it was another warm, sunny day (Ukiah's sole form of summer weather?), we had the entire pond to ourselves. Was Juanita's spy network letting her down?

Slade swam the length of the pond, so I did too. In his reserved way, Slade paid as much attention to Jean as to Norma. I wonder if he suspected that she had once loved him obsessively.

We gathered on our adjoining army blankets and dined on Jean's cold chicken. She is by far the best cook I've ever encountered; Slade and I complimented her effusively.

"Slade, you'll have to try my fried chicken sometime," said Norma.

"I look forward to it," he replied, helping himself to more potato salad. For a guy with the physique of a Greek god, Slade could pack away the calories.

Eventually, the conversation came around to our disaster last week with Slivmank shooting down Cheeky Swimsuits.

"Oh, I've got a solution to that," said Slade. "You don't need bikinis in a lot of different sizes."

"We don't?" asked Norma, surprised. "Have you checked out the female body lately?"

"Yes, quite a few," he replied.

I for one didn't doubt that. Nor, I suspected, did anyone else.

Slade went on. "Now there are four areas you have to cover. Right?"

"Correct, if you're counting the breasts separately," said Norma.

"I always do," he replied. "You could cover all that with four triangles. The triangle is the strongest structure in engineering."

"Four triangles?" said Norma.

"Yes, four triangles of the appropriate size. You connect them with spaghetti straps."

"How do you know about spaghetti straps?" asked Jean.

"I've been to lots of dances," he replied. "One has many opportunities to study the dainty strap holding up the overloaded bodice."

"OK, we have four triangles connected by dainty straps," said Norma. "Now what?"

"Now you pull the straps tight and tie them, thus conforming the triangles to the torso. Having the straps tie achieves adjustability. One structure of four triangles can be made to fit any female, from petite like you to fully stacked like, uh . . ." He glanced at my date's chest.

"Like Juanita Howe," suggested Jean.

"A good example," he acknowledged.

Norma flashed me a tentative look. "I'm not really hating that idea, Colm. What do you think?"

"I'm not hating it either. I'm not hating it at all."

"One size though may be a bit restrictive," said Norma, thinking out loud. "We could do three sizes: with bigger triangles for larger or more modest gals, down to tiny triangles for your extra-small or extra-daring girls."

"Here's another thought," I said. "We could do the larger size in cooler colors and save the warmest colors for the most daring size."

"Damn, I think we've got something here, Colm," said Norma.

"It solves a lot of problems for us, Norma," I replied. "It would be economical with materials, and quick and easy to sew. We could fit the entire inventory on one shelf in the warehouse."

"What about pesky boys?" said Jean, removing a magnificent cream pie from her hamper.

"What about them?" asked Norma, nuzzling Slade to distract him from dessert.

"Might not they be tempted to untie the straps?" she asked.

"Could be," said Norma. "But it could evolve into a new form of flirting. Some girls may like that. Your inhibited girls can just tie double knots."

"Slade, how much do you want for your idea?" I asked.

"Nothing," he replied. "I donate it to the world in the interests of science."

Chapter 17

Norma called me that evening as Jean was applying lotion to my sunburn.

"Are we nuts, Colm?" she asked.

"Very likely, Norma. Can you be more specific?"

"Are we nuts taking fashion advice from a forestry major?"

"He wouldn't be the first guy to have a brilliant idea outside his area of expertise. George Eastman was a bank clerk, but he invented the Kodak Brownie camera. What happened with you and Slade after we left?"

"Not much. He had to go home to work on his damn chipboard article. God, I hate chipboard, and I don't even know what it is. That's the last time I let your housekeeper bring the picnic lunch."

"Didn't you like the eats?"

"I didn't appreciate the competition. Now I have to learn how to make coconut creme pie."

"She could give you the recipe if you like. She's right here rubbing lotion on my back."

"No, thanks. I'll get one from my landlady. Have you two lovebirds had sex yet?"

"It's not on her agenda."

"Good. I need you free in case things don't work out with Slade and me. You're still my backup dream guy."

"Thanks. I've always wanted to be someone's number two."

"You'd have to work at it to be my number two," commented Jean.

After I hung up the phone, I turned around, grabbed Jean, and kissed her full upon the lips. She squirmed to get free, but I held on tight.

* * *

First thing Monday morning Norma and I marched into Slivmank's office with our revised Cheeky Swimsuits proposal. He wasn't thrilled to have us back in his face so soon, but gave us his grudging OK to create prototypes of the "four triangles and straps" bikini. He only agreed to that when I reminded him that my father had given us his conditional approval of bikinis.

"I want to see what they look like," Wendell said. "For example, what's covering the sides?"

"The sides of what?" I asked.

"The sides of the girl," he replied.

"Well, on the sides you've got, uh, straps," explained Norma.

"I thought you said the straps were thin and narrow," said Wendell.

"That's right," said Norma. "They have to be thin so they can be tied."

"So the sides of the girl are naked?" asked Wendell.

"Pretty much," she conceded. "But that's OK, because the triangles cover the controversial areas. There's not much happening on the sides of the body."

"There are the sides of the breasts and the sides of the buttocks," he pointed out.

"It's a sexy look, Wendell," said Norma. "We have to embrace that. We will be offering some teasing peeks at the body. The bikini is not for everyone. Girls with nice bodies to show off are our market. There are millions of them out there."

"I hope you're right, Norma," he said. "Because you're the first girl I want to see in one."

"Uh, I'm the designer, Wendell. Not the fitting model."

"If you expect me to sell them, you have to be willing to wear one. Am I right, Colm?"

"You may have a point there, Wendell."

Dirty look from Norma.

"And I want to see Miss Page in one too," he added.

"Gals with Miss Page's shape are not really our target market," said Norma.

"I want to see it on her," he insisted. "I want to see it on lots of girls!"

Wendell, I was beginning to suspect, was something of a dirty old man.

* * *

After lunch I walked to Flamperts and checked in with Juanita.

"I hear you were up at Johnson's Pond again yesterday with your housekeeper and your former roommate," she said.

"Juanita, how did you know that? There was no one else around."

"I have my ways. Slade was there too. I'm told he looks even better in swim trunks."

"I wouldn't know about that. How's your soldier?"

"I hardly recognized him. Reggie's really filled out. I think the Army's been good for him."

"Any fräuleins to report?"

"He claims not. He wants to get married while on leave."

"What did you say?"

"I said it's hard to support babies on Army pay. He's found out about you."

"Oh?"

"He's not happy. If he comes to see you, don't provoke him."

"Is your Reggie inclined toward violence?"

"His whole family is known for flying off the handle. His older brother Lyle went to jail once for taking a baseball bat to a guy. Just say we went out a few times and then I dropped you."

"Is that what you told him?"

"I had to, honey. I have to keep the peace while he's here."

"How long will that be?"

"Twelve more days. Don't worry, dear. Everything will be OK. I'll see you when he's gone and make it up to you."

"Does he have any guns?"

"Just the usual hunting rifles. Don't worry about that."

"OK, if you say so."

"But do watch out for the blade he straps to his leg."

Just my luck. A sweet grandmother fixes me up on a blind date with an ex-Prune Queen, and the next thing I know I'm in a knife fight with an Army-trained killer.

I got a piece of good news when I returned to work. A store called The Broadway in Los Angeles has ordered nine dozen Beachzilla suits. We're on our way!

* * *

Tonight's dinner was slabs of fried Spam.

I poked at the brownish pods and queried the cook: "Has wartime rationing been reimposed?"

"I found the can in the back of the cupboard," replied Jean. "I thought you should eat it before the date expired."

"I've already apologized for lunging at you yesterday. It was a temporary condition brought on by overexposure to the sun and the silky touch of your hands."

Anyway it seemed like there was a brief moment when she was kissing me back.

"So you say," replied Jean. "You can leave the dishes in the sink. I'll do them tomorrow."

"Where are you off to? You look extra nice this evening, no offense intended."

"I've got a date."

Not good news. And to think I'd assumed she'd dressed like that for me.

"With Elwyn? It must be getting serious with you two."

"Not with Elwyn. A fellow is taking me out to dinner."

"A fellow, huh? Do I know him?"

"You do."

"Is his name a secret?"

"It's Slade Preston."

I lost the rest of my appetite.

"What's that about?"

"He's single. I'm single. Why shouldn't he ask me out?"

"Norma isn't going to like it."

"That is no concern of mine. They hardly know each other. She has no claim on him. I don't mind if Slade wants to see her too."

"Well, have fun."

"I intend to."

She left. I pushed aside my plate. Elwyn Saunders was a nuisance and annoyance, but Slade Preston was trouble an entire order of magnitude greater. Hell, Jean once had a crush on the guy. That meant she was primed to fall for him again. And Slade's already been exposed to her cooking and her scantily clad body. He knows she has much to offer. This could get serious fast. I could see only one small glimmer of hope: feisty Norma was not the type of gal to give up without a fight.

So I called her and gave her the news.

"I should have seen that coming," said Norma, after she calmed down. "Jean deliberately sabotaged me with that horrible bathing suit. I bet she bought it just in hopes that I would borrow it."

"Well, I don't know about that, Norma . . ."

"You underestimate her treachery, Colm. Your housekeeper is a fiend. A calculating and diabolical fiend."

"So what are you going to do?"

"I'm taking off the gloves, Colm. If she wants war, so be it. Slade is mine and I intend to have him. I was sketching some ideas for my wedding dress when you called."

"I think you make a handsome couple," I said by way of encouragement.

"That is so true, isn't it? And to think I was reluctant to take a job this far out in the boondocks."

"It was destiny," I said. "You were destined to meet Slade. That's why you didn't go to New York like all your fellow fashion grads."

"God, Colm, you're right. Fate didn't send me on a 3,000 mile tangent just to lose out to some crummy housekeeper. I want you to be best man at our wedding."

"I'll be there, Norma. I'll be there with spats on."

* * *

Tuesday morning my old Yale buddy Tom Brannan called me again at work.

"Hi, Colm," he said, sounding uncharacteristically low.

"Hi, Tom. It's good to hear from you."

"Is it?"

"Well, it usually is. How are things in New York?"

"Pretty fucking lousy. I popped the question yesterday."

"Good for you. What did Katie say?"

"She said she wasn't over you yet."

"Oh. Sorry to hear that."

"Has she been communicating with you? She claims not."

"No, Tom. I haven't heard from her at all. Not since we broke up. Did she turn you down?"

"She's thinking it over."

"Well, that's good. Just give her time."

"I've been sleeping with her all summer. So why's she thinking about you?"

Flattering to be sure, but I didn't mention that to Tom.

"I have no idea, Tom. I never felt we were that close."

"You're too good looking for your own good, Colm."

"Uh, I have my share of trouble with chicks, Tom. It's not smooth sailing for any of us."

"OK, Colm. Sorry I called. I shouldn't unload all this mess onto you. Just do me a favor and let me know if you hear from Katie."

"Of course, Tom. I'll be glad to do that. I've always wished you two the best."

"Yeah, I hope so. See you around, Colm."

How odd to think Katie is not over me. I hardly ever think about her. We were both virgins when we slept together in that dreary hotel room in Queens. It was an illicit rendezvous by subway. Who knows? I might have married her if my roommate hadn't dragged me to that mixer where I met Betty.

Which reminds me: I never got a reply from that two-page letter I sent Betty. What's up with that? Of course, I haven't viewed her commercial yet either. Damn, I should have asked Tom if he'd seen it.

Love is strange. I traded Katie, an attractive girl who was enthusiastic about sleeping with me, for Betty, a somewhat more attractive girl whose knees were locked tighter than Fort Knox. Now I'm seeing a sexy girl who wants to sleep with me, but doesn't dare, while lusting after another attractive girl who keeps me firmly at arm's length. Meanwhile, I resisted the overtures of another girl, who is now lusting after someone else, a guy who soon may be seducing the very girl I seem to be the most hung up on.

* * *

I was locking up to leave work that evening when I felt a hard object thrust against my spine.

"Don't turn around," grunted a voice. "Unlock the door and go in. Don't make any sudden moves."

I did as directed. He followed me into the lobby.

"OK. Raise your hands and turn around slowly."

I did so. My assailant was a tall guy with a crudely scalped Army hair cut. He wasn't falling down drunk, but I could tell he'd had a few. He smelled of beer, cigarettes, and stale sweat. The gun he was pointing at me didn't look like an Army-issue weapon. It looked like the six-shooter Paladin carried in "Have Gun, Will Travel" on TV. It looked like the toy Colt revolver I once wielded as an eight-year-old pretend cowpoke. Only I didn't think his was a toy.

"You must be Corporal Dowling," I said.

"Don't you worry 'bout who I am. You need to worry 'bout gettin' a load of lead in your stinkin' gut."

"I have no interest in Juanita," I lied. "We're just friends."

"Then why was you takin' her out?"

"It was her grandmother's idea. She thought she looked lonely."

"She wasn't lonely. I was writin' her most every day."

"I'm sure you were. That's why she stopped accepting my invitations. She's been very loyal to you."

"Most guys lie when they's a gun pointin' at 'em. But I got a test for you."

"Oh?"

I hoped it wasn't some variation on medieval trial by torture. Fortunately, Reggie didn't impress me as the type of guy who'd been paying attention in history class.

"You just lead the way to them sewing machines."

"Why?"

I really wasn't in the mood to have my tongue sewn to my lip. Or to my nose.

"You'll find out. Just get movin'."

He followed me into the sewing room.

"Sit down at one of them machines," he commanded, waving his pistol.

I did so.

"Now sew me up one of them bathing suits."

"What?"

"Juanita said you was good at sewin'. I guess I don't need to worry much 'bout a guy what can do that. So you turn on that damn machine and go to work on one of them girly suits."

"Uh, right."

I decided it wasn't wise to confess that I'd never sewn anything more complicated than a potholder. I removed a packet of Beachzilla parts from the box next to the machine. God knew how the parts went together, but I decided to give it my best shot.

"Just let me check my bobbin here. Yes, I've got plenty of thread. Now, I'll set my stitch length and tension. You really should learn to sew, Reggie. It's a very useful skill to have."

"I ain't no chick, dude. And cut the B.S."

Naturally, I started with the straight side seams. I ran the cloth under the needle at my full professional speed. Not as straight as Mrs. Yeater would demand, but I think I was impressing the hombre with the gun. Fifteen minutes later I held up a crude facsimile of a boy's bathing suit."

"Where's the top?" demanded Reggie.

"There is no top," I replied. "This is our new topless model."

"You mean girls are supposed to wear that with their tits hangin' out?"

"It's a training suit for nudist resorts. Girls wear this until they get comfortable with going totally bare."

"Really?"

"Yes, it's quite a popular model. Do I pass your test?"

"I guess so," he said, thrusting the gun into his pants. He held out his hand. "I'm Corporal Reginald G. Dowling, United States Army."

I shook his hand. "Glad to meet you. I'm Colm Moran, draft status 4F."

"I guess I know why the Army didn't want you," he said with a wink.

Chapter 18

Tonight's dinner was Spam hash made with yesterday's leftovers. The cook also was torturing me with a new color lipstick and sultry new perfume. As I was drying the dishes, I suggested to Jean that she should be nicer to me.

"Why's that?" she asked.

"This might have been the last meal you ever cooked for me. Only I wouldn't have been here to eat it."

"Why not?"

I told her about being held at gunpoint by a desperate Reggie Dowling.

"Are you sure the gun was real?"

"It was real all right. I could see the lethal-looking cartridges in the cylinders."

"So why didn't he shoot you? I would have."

"Thanks. Uh, I talked him out of it–eventually. It was a close shave."

"I'm sure your funeral would have been a very somber affair. Plus, I would have had to eat all that hash myself."

Not getting much sympathy for my brush with death, I moved on.

"So, Jean, how was your dinner with Slade?"

"Splendid."

"Where did you go?"

"The Elks Lodge. He's a member you know. They offer a 99 cents all-you-can-eat spaghetti dinner on Monday nights."

"Oh. Last of the big spenders. Did he go back for third helpings?"

"We had a good time. Slade is a very serious young man."

"I hear he's dated every pretty girl in town."

"Then I'm flattered he finally got around to me."

"Are you dumping Elwyn for him?"

"We'll have to see about that."

"Norma intends to fight you tooth and nail for him."

"I'm quaking in my boots."

"Did you hear that Slade came up with a bikini concept that we're developing?"

"He mentioned it. The fellow has hidden talents."

"Well, he's explored every dimension of the female body–in all of its diverse aspects. With many different volunteers. From head to toe. Clothed and unclothed."

"Good for him. I like a guy who knows his way around."

"So you say. We'll need you to model the bikini for us."

"Anything to help realize Slade's vision. Just tell me where and when."

"I'll keep you posted. So did Slade kiss you good night when he dropped you off?"

"I expect he did–not that it's any of your business."

Well, that was a lie. Naturally, I was peering through the drapes after I heard his Studebaker pull up next door. The cad didn't even get out to open the car door for her. He must have been anxious to get back to his wooden prose.

* * *

At work the next day Norma extracted every bit of information I had gleaned about my housekeeper's date with you know who.

"This presents me with a dilemma," she said.

"What's that?" I asked.

"He's coming to my place for dinner Friday night. Do I or do I not make spaghetti?"

"I see your point. Did he take Jean to the Elks Lodge because he's partial to spaghetti or is he just a cheap bastard?"

"I'm sure he's not that, Colm. I think, though, I'll keep to my original plan and grill a steak. All virile men love steak."

"I love steak," I confirmed.

"Therefore, you are a virile man," said Norma. "I believe that is a syllogism."

"Logic is a powerful tool, Norma. He didn't kiss her good night."

"That either indicates Slade is a gentleman or your housekeeper's a cold fish."

"I hardly think the latter is true."

"I do wish Elwyn Saunders, Jean's original creep, would seduce her and subtract her from the dating pool. Better yet, he should marry her fast."

Over my dead body, I thought but didn't say.

Despite her love distractions, Norma has been making progress on our triangular bikinis. She has designed all three sizes, using her own nude body in front of a mirror at home to determine the shape, sizes, and placement of the triangles. This morning Norma selected the fabrics and presented the package to Vera, our pattern drafter, who completed her job in less than an hour. Vera passed the patterns on to Mona, who had everything cut out and ready for the sewers by lunchtime. Mrs. Yeater, however, found the project puzzling. She summoned Norma and me to her lofty command post overlooking the production room.

"There appear to be pieces missing from these garments," she said.

"No, I think everything's there," replied Norma.

"Are we to take the bra cups from stock?" she asked.

"No bra cups, Mrs. Yeater," I pointed out. "We're deleting them."

"But this fabric is so thin," she objected. "Besides the issue of support, it's possible–even likely–that nipples could show."

"Not a problem," said Norma. "Girls have nipples. That's not likely to be news to anyone."

"I see," said Mrs. Yeater. "Then these are lingerie garments, not swimsuits."

"They are very much swimsuits," I said.

"For public beaches and pools?" she asked, shocked.

"We certainly hope so," said Norma. "We hope to sell them by the carload."

"And will not the wearers be subject to arrest for public indecency?" she asked.

"Perhaps in a few backward places," smiled Norma. "I hope so at any rate. The ensuing publicity should be a real boost to sales."

* * *

The scandalized sewing ladies had much to say when Mrs. Snyder was taken off Beachzilla production to sew up our Cheeky Swimsuit prototypes.

"I don't see why girls would even bother putting on these suits," said Mildred. "They might as well go naked."

"Well, that's the goal we're working toward, of course," I replied.

"We're all going to burn in a lake of fire," said Mrs. Cikowich, who may or may not have been joking.

"Not us," said Ida Stipe. "Just young Mr. Moran and Miss Pomeroy."

"No, we're all doing the work of the devil," said Mrs. Cikowich.

"Times are changing, ladies," I said. "In a few years you'll be wearing these suits too. And wishing they weren't so big."

That got a rousing laugh.

"What's that rumbling sound?" asked another woman. "Oh, it's poor Mr. Jonathan Moran spinning in his grave."

Mrs. Snyder held up a completed top. "Well, I could sort of see

Miss Pomeroy in this, but it would never do for any of my granddaughters. Or most girls over the age of 12."

The top was yellow, which meant it was our intermediate size. The modest triangles did look a bit skimpy.

"Mr. Slivmank intends to see it on Miss Page," I announced.

That drew a collective gasp.

"It would fit her like a postage stamp on a balloon!" exclaimed Mildred.

"Like a doily on a couch!" said Ida.

"Like a Bandaid on a blimp!" laughed another woman.

We were having such a merry time, Mrs. Yeater had to come out of her office to shoo me away.

I got back to my office just in time to take a call from our San Francisco lawyer. "Cheeky Swimsuits" was ours to trademark if we wanted. I told him to go ahead and file the papers.

* * *

When I got home that night, Jean was in the kitchen stirring a pan of risotto.

"That smells good," I said.

"Thanks. It's taking longer than the recipe said, so dinner will be delayed slightly. What's in the bag?"

"One of our brand-new, hot-off-the-sewing-machine prototype triangle bikinis. Are you ready to do some modeling?"

"I suppose. Can you wait until dinner's over?"

"Just barely. I'm very interested to see if this thing works."

"I'll bet you are."

She served the risotto with grilled sausage and green salad. A raisin spice cake for dessert. Plus coffee. I scarfed it all down, then had to wait while the dishes were washed and dried. Finally, Jean retreated to the bathroom with my small bag. She was in there for an unconscionably long time.

"I'm not sure this thing is working," she called at last.

"Would you like me to come in and help you?" I asked.

"No thanks. I can manage."

At last the door opened and she emerged. What a letdown. She had donned the tiny bathing suit over her blouse and shorts.

"What do you think?" she asked, twirling about like a professional model.

"Very funny, Jean. Is that your idea of helpful modeling?"

"I just wanted to see the look of disappointment on your face. OK, don't go away."

She returned to the bathroom; I resumed my pacing in the living room. More minutes went by. Then the door opened, and out she came again–this time as the gods of fashion demanded. It may be a cliche, but the sight of her took my breath away. Just enough of her exquisite figure was on display to ring every nerve cell in my body like a gong. What was concealed–which wasn't much–lay just tantalizingly out of sight.

I approached for a closer inspection.

"You can look, buddy," she warned, "but don't even think about touching."

"What if something needs adjusting?"

"Don't worry. Everything's been adjusted just fine. What do you think?"

"You're too beautiful for words."

"I mean about your bathing suit, buster. Is it totally indecent?"

"No, it's fine. Ministers of the cloth and decorous spinsters will find nothing to object to."

"I doubt that. I'm feeling pretty exposed here. I hope this is your smallest size."

"No, it's the middle size. I didn't think you'd feel comfortable in the small size.'

"Your Norma does like to economize on fabric. Have you seen enough?"

"Not hardly. Let's see the back."

Jean did a slow 360-degree turn. Not much was left to the imagination. You could see her nipples, the sides of her breasts, quite a bit of her shapely ass, and her womanly furrow where the front bottom triangle came to a point between her legs. It was by far the most radical bathing suit I'd ever seen. But was America ready for this? I could see Cheeky Swimsuit executives being led away in shackles, and heavy iron bars slamming shut.

"Can I borrow this?" asked Jean.

"I don't know. Why?"

"To show it to Slade, of course."

"In that case you may certainly *not* borrow it."

"Why not? It was his idea."

"Slade is interested in plywood, Jean. That is his profession. It is in no one's interest to distract him from his work."

"Oh, I see. And why am I showing it to you?"

"I'm in the business, Jean. Bathing suits are my occupation."

In truth, I was beginning to see Mrs. Cikowich's point. Clearly this suit was the handiwork of the devil. My senses inflamed as never before, I desired only one thing: to ravish the wearer on the spot. Through a supreme application of will I was able at last to stifle the impulse.

* * *

The next day at work many things happened: First I flipped my wall calendar to a new zippered babe (Miss August). Then I got to see the same yellow suit on Norma in Wendell's office. (Even its creator was too chicken to don the flaming-red small size.) Norma looked only slightly less incendiary than Joan had. It was raw in-your-face sex right there with your morning coffee. Wendell began to perspire and I was getting a bit warm myself. He reached out to feel a triangle, but Norma hopped away like a startled rabbit.

"What do you think, Colm?" he asked.

"Looks fine to me."

"Norma dear, would you mind sitting in my chair and spreading your legs?" said Wendell.

"Why?" she asked, shocked.

"I need to see if everything's covered."

With great reluctance, Norma did as requested. We both bent down to inspect. Yes, everything was covered, but not much anatomical was left to the imagination. It was one small step removed from the bridegroom's view on his wedding night. Clearly, some barbering had been done in anticipation of this event.

"I think we need another layer of fabric here," said Wendell.

I could see his point.

"What do you suggest?" I asked.

"A lining should do it," he replied. "We need one for the top too. That way the nipples will not be quite so obvious."

Exposed as she was, Norma was in no position to object.

Next we viewed the large size on Miss Page. Seldom has such a sight been beheld outside of a burlesque theater. Our serene blue triangles were no match for her extravagant curves. It was like some evil degenerate's parody of a bikini. Thank God Wendell didn't request the between-the-legs view.

"Uh, I don't think this is working," he said, tugging on an upper triangle.

"I never thought it would," said Norma. "Our model here is outside our target parameters."

"What are your thoughts, Miss Page?" asked Wendell.

"It's quite comfortable."

"Would you wear it to the beach?" he asked.

"I'd consider it in a larger size."

"Perhaps, Miss Page, you'd like to view the back," I suggested.

She pivoted to view her rear in Wendell's full-length mirror. "Oh my," she said, "I didn't realize how much of my caboose was showing. I don't think I'd be comfortable with that."

After a heated discussion we agreed to some alterations in the Cheeky Swimsuit line. The yellow version was now the smallest size. The red size was gone, and Norma was to design a new and expanded large size. All were to be equipped with modesty linings.

Next we discussed marketing. Norma thought the suits could command $25 in shops, but Wendell and I held out for a price point of $19.95.

"So we have your OK to go into production?" I asked.

"I suppose," sighed Wendell. "Just remember, Colm, it's your father's company. I don't think he'd appreciate it if we go broke."

"We won't go broke," I said. "Cheeky Swimsuits will put us on the fashion map."

"That's right," said Norma. "From now on the beau monde will look to Paris, New York, and Ukiah. Right, Colm?"

"Uh, that's right. At least for their trendy swim attire."

* * *

A few minutes later Betty called me collect from the east coast. I asked her how their musical was going.

"There seems to be a consensus that I can't sing."

"I'm sure that's not true," I said.

"Well, Colmy, I'm just as blond as Doris Day and Peggy Lee, but there the similarity ends. Did I tell you my mother quit her job with the symphony?"

"I didn't even know she was working. I thought your family was loaded."

"It was a *volunteer* job, Colm. She wasn't paid a dime. Anyway, she's looking around for a project. I thought I'd put her in charge of planning our wedding."

"Oh, are we getting married?"

"Of course. I'm thinking Saturday the 16th of November. How does that work for you?"

"And where are we to live?"

"In New York, naturally. Daddy will pull some strings and get you in the training program at Lehman Brothers."

"I have no interest in becoming a bond trader, Betty."

"It's just temporary, Colm. In a couple of years when you've made your pile, we'll move to Hollywood. I'll have more acting credits then. I'll be ready to make a major splash in the movie you produce. But I'm thinking now it shouldn't be a musical."

"Sounds great, Betty, but we've got some interesting projects going now in bathing suits. I really can't leave here."

"You're joking! Who gives a damn about bathing suits?"

"I do, Betty. I need to prove to my father that I'm not completely useless. And why are you so interested in marriage all of a sudden?"

"I've always wanted to marry you, Colm. You know that. Anyway, of my college friends only three of us are still single. I'm spending all my free time shopping for wedding gifts. You don't want me to wind up an old maid, do you?"

"You're only 22, Betty. A slight delay won't hurt. Your mother can start planning our wedding, but let's aim for the following November."

"November, 1958?"

"That's right."

"Oh, OK. Then we're officially engaged?"

"Oh, I suppose so."

"Shall I pick out a ring at Tiffany's and send you the bill?"

"Why don't you mail me your ring size, and I'll find something appropriate here?"

"All right, darling. But nothing embarrassingly plain and simple, please."

* * *

I saw no reason to tell anyone here about my engagement. Anyway, November of 1958 is so far in the future I can barely conceive of it. It does give me a semi-firm date for one thing. In 16 months at the latest I should be getting laid–assuming Betty can be persuaded to fulfill her wifely duties.

Wendell set me to work designing a hang tag for our new bikinis. One side will have the Cheeky Swimsuits logo with our winking duck in his red fez. The other side will offer care instructions and directions for adjusting it to fit. Norma and I think that's self-evident, but Wendell wants it all fully explained with diagrams. My headline "It Ties To Fit" is so brilliantly succinct I'm amazed I thought of it.

I was interrupted by Miss Page bearing a telegram. I tore it open and read this message: "Ring size seven and one half. Diamond preferred. Loveya Betty."

By combining "Love ya" into one word, she managed to say it all in ten words. Fortunately, it would have cost her extra to specify "big impressive expensive diamond."

"I hope, Mr. Moran, that it's not bad news," said Miss Page.

"Uh, no. It's just a routine message . . . uh, from my broker."

At lunchtime I strolled over to the pawn shop to examine their diamond rings. The gent behind the counter showed me several trays of used rings–most of them far beyond my price range.

"Do people actually walk in off the street and pay you $2,750 for a second-hand ring?" I asked.

"Sure. My customers know a diamond ring is a good investment. It will never lose its value. And it's a good source of ready cash in time of need. You ever have to blow town fast, kid, you'd be thankful to be wearing a diamond on your pinkie."

"I'll keep that in mind," I said. "Do you have anything in the way of a really sparkly fake?"

He put away the big-spender zircons, and brought out another tray.

"These stones aren't glass, buddy. They're the latest thing: genuine strontium titanate. The settings are a nice gold plating over brass. Impressive, huh?"

I nodded. They looked quite sparkly to me.

"How much?" I asked.

"Take your pick: only $39.95. We throw in a nice gift box too."

I selected the ring with the largest and gaudiest stone. As fate would have it, it was Betty's size too. "Can you hold this until I get paid tomorrow?" I asked.

"I can hold it with $5 down."

I paid him the money, and he wrote out a receipt.

For better or worse, it now felt official: I was engaged to be married.

Chapter 19

Friday at work Norma was in a tizzy over her impending dinner with Slade. That's the trouble with falling for a guy so fast: every meet-up becomes fraught with significance. It has to be perfect or your entire future together is imperiled. The sensible alternative is to go out a few times casually and see if anything clicks. Then maybe you can get emotionally involved. That was clearly not Norma's approach.

"I'm worried, Colm, that my place looks too much like a furnished rental," she said, lounging across my tiny desk,

"Well, it is a furnished rental. Slade knows you're new in town. He won't judge you by the state of your apartment."

"I did get some nice new percale sheets."

"Well, try not to rush him into the bedroom. Let him make the first move."

"Can you get me some condoms from the drugstore?"

"I suppose. They always make you feel so guilty though."

"Get some for yourself too. You may get lucky one of these days."

"That's a thought."

"Do you think a girl could be regarded as fast for having her own private condom supply?"

"Better to be fast than knocked up."

"Except if I *were* pregnant, Slade would have to marry me."

"Not the ideal way to begin a marriage, Norma. I recommend using the condom. Or chastity, that works too."

Norma has decided to alter her dinner plans again. She is making the rice dish and vegetable, but has contracted with her landlady Mrs. Rogers for a homemade Gravenstein apple pie. This is an apple grown locally that is said to be the best in the world for pies. Naturally, Norma will be passing it off as her own handiwork. The steaks she has decided to import secretly from the Peacock Grill. She claims home-cooked steaks never taste as good as those from restaurants. She has ordered two Porterhouse steaks, grilled medium-rare, which are to be ready at 6:50 p.m. Since the restaurant doesn't deliver, I've been recruited to transport them to her house. I'm to sneak up the back alley and stealthily enter her unlocked back door at 7:00 while she is entertaining Slade in the living room. I'm to deposit the steaks on a broiler pan in her stove and beat a hasty exit. Kind of a harebrained scheme, but I've agreed to it because I want her evening to succeed as much as she does. I need that guy to fall for her big time.

* * *

At lunchtime I cashed my paycheck at the bank and headed over to the pawnshop. Unfortunately, it was also Juanita's lunch break. As I entered the shop there she was standing by the rings display case with her soldier. Reggie waved a friendly greeting, but Juanita clearly was embarrassed to see me.

"Hey there, Colm" said Reggie, "What ya doin' here?"

"Uh, I saw some cufflinks in the window that looked intriguing."

"Want to help us pick out a nice diamond ring?" he asked.

"Uh, well. . . "

"Oh, hello, Mr. Moran," said the pawnbroker, walking up and wiping his mouth with a paper napkin. "I've got your ring ready. I'll be right with you, folks."

I excused myself and followed the gent to the register. I handed him the cash, he showed me the ring in its plush gift box, placed it in a bag, and said in a loud voice, "I hope she likes it, kid."

"Uh, I expect she will," I muttered.

I got out of there as fast as possible, nodding a perfunctory farewell to the ring shoppers as I exited. I went straight to the post office and mailed a small package to Betty. The cardboard box and rush airmail postage came to less than a buck. Then I went to a drugstore and forthrightly purchased two dozen Trojans without blushing. It helped that the clerk was a young guy around my age.

An hour or so later Juanita called me at work.

"Looks like your plans changed," I said.

"Yeah, I guess they did."

"I think you deserve better, Juanita."

"Reggie told me he ran into you the other day. I hope he was polite."

"He behaved himself. I can't say he left me with a very favorable impression though."

"Was that ring for me?"

I could see no gentlemanly way to tell her it wasn't.

"Uh, who else?" I said.

"So what did you do with it?"

One lie beget another. "I returned it just now and got a refund."

"I'm sorry if I've hurt you, dear."

"I'll live. When are you getting married?"

"Probably around Christmas if he gets another furlough. Or I might go to where he is in Texas."

"He's not going back to West Germany?"

"No, he's done over there. He's been reassigned to Fort Bliss as a tank instructor."

Wow, Reggie as a teacher. The guy must have more on the ball than meets the eye.

"Well, Juanita, I wish you the best."

"My family's not too happy. They all prefer you–even my dad."

"I'm surprised to hear that."

"Oops, I got a customer. I've got to go. You take care, honey."

"Yeah. You too."

* * *

Serving me dinner that evening, Jean wasn't surprised to hear that Juanita had dumped me for Reggie.

"Well, they've been going out since junior high school. That's a lot of noodling behind the gym. I'm not sure what she sees in him–or in you for that matter."

"Thanks, Jean. I can always depend on you for a kind word."

"Keep in mind that she's not just ditching you. She's also withdrawing the 13 children you'd have together."

"Good-bye, little Morans. I'm sorry you won't be fathered by me."

"I wonder how Reggie Dowling intends to support them all. I suppose he can join his brothers in tending their patch up in the woods."

"Their patch of what?" I asked.

"A peculiar plant they grow around here. Robert Mitchum went to jail for smoking it."

"Oh that. Have you tried it?"

"Oh course. Haven't you?"

"Once at a party. It didn't do much."

"You probably had some inferior eastern grade. We grow the real stuff here."

"Do you have any?"

"I thought you took an oath never to smoke."

"I'm not proposing to smoke tobacco."

"I'll see if I can get some."

"Good. I need something to take my mind off my romantic disappointments."

"In that case I'll ask for the extra-potent stuff."

As a gesture of consolation Jean offered to take me out to the movies. I suggested we go to the later showing since I had something to do after dinner. She said that was fine with her.

"I just hope the film is not too inappropriate for you, Colm."

"Why? What is it?"

"A comedy starring Jayne Mansfield. She may remind you too acutely of your lost love."

"That's OK, Jean. At least I'll get to experience magnificent breasts on the silver screen, if not in real life."

At 6:30 I drove to the restaurant. First hitch in the plans: Norma's to-go order had slipped the chef's mind. I had to cool my heels at the bar while he found time on a busy Friday night to grill her steaks. Nor had she pre-paid as I assumed. I had to empty my wallet to pay the $9 tab. It was well after 7:00 when I sneaked in Norma's back door. I was about to deposit the steaks as planned when in waltzed Slade carrying two empty highball glasses.

"What do you think you're doing?" he demanded, eyeing the meat in transit.

I froze.

"Uh . . . good question."

Norma burst in from the living room. She appeared fairly intoxicated and was wearing only a Cheeky Swimsuits bikini. It was the now-banned red model. In my estimation she was at least 97 percent naked.

"Colm!" she slurred. "What are you doing here! Why are you trying to make off with our dinner!"

"Uh, hello, Norma. It was just a little practical joke. Here, I'll put your steaks back."

I scooped the smuggled meat onto her broiler pan.

"There you go," I said. "They smell delicious too. Norma, why are you wearing that bikini?"

"I'm modeling it for its inventor."

"What do you think, Slade?" I asked. "Is it everything you hoped it would be?"

He contemplated his hostess's near-nude body. "I think it's working very well. We've been experimenting with tying and untying the little straps."

Slade also appeared to be well into his cups.

"Good," I said. "That sounds like fun. Well, I'll leave you two to it. Sorry for trying to sneak away with your steaks."

"That was quite outrageous of you," said Norma. "You're lucky darling Slade didn't punch you in the nose."

"Right. Well, have a nice meal. Oh, and doesn't your pie look good too."

A spectacular apple pie graced her kitchen table. Small holes punched by the baker into the top crust formed the outline of a heart. As if on cue Norma's top straps suddenly malfunctioned, and two red triangles fell like autumn leaves to the floor.

"Some boy scout you are, Slade," she giggled, making no effort to retrieve her top. "That was a very feeble knot you tied."

"Hee-hee," tittered her guest. "That was entirely the idea."

I exited at that point, content in the knowledge that her dinner party was going well.

* * *

Tonight's movie was "Will Success Spoil Rock Hunter?" Tony Randall played a nebbish ad man who revitalizes his career by getting glamorous Jayne Mansfield to star in his agency's lipstick commercials. It was another film where she struts about doing a broad lampoon of Marilyn Monroe. I think the joke is wearing thin; Jean wasn't laughing much either. Jayne has quite a pair, but I'd take Juanita's or Jean's in real life. They're both sexy without overdoing it.

According to the credits, the producer Frank Tashlin also wrote and directed it. You don't see that very often. Writing the script yourself would be a good way to save money–assuming you had any talent. I'd give it a try if I had a subject to write about. I can't imagine anyone would want to see a movie about bathing suits for fat gals. As for triple-threat Mr. Tashlin, his movie might have been funnier if he'd hired a real writer.

After the movie, Jean let me buy ice-cream cones, which we licked on the walk back.

"How's your maple nut?" she asked.

"Good. How's your rum raisin?"

"Good. I suppose you're craving ice cream now because of your over-exposure to mammary glands."

"Probably, although I don't think a fellow really can get too much of that."

"Ice cream or mammary glands?"

"Both, I should think. It must be great having breasts."

"I'm sure I wouldn't know."

"You have a terrific body, Jean. It's just about perfect–that is, what I've seen of it."

"You've seen more of it than you were entitled to."

"That's some very bad news. It's been haunting my dreams nightly."

"Now we'll have to find someone else to distract you. I think Norma is your best prospect."

"Norma is seducing your Slade Preston as we speak."

"I doubt that."

"I dropped in at her place earlier tonight, and she was nude from the waist up."

"I don't believe that for a minute."

"It's true, Jean darling. She was modeling our smallest bikini for the guy and her top slipped off."

"Well, there wasn't much holding it up."

"Don't be catty. It doesn't become you."

"I apologize. I'm sure your Norma has a lot to offer."

"She's not my Norma. She's Slade's Norma now."

"Well, I'm seeing him tomorrow."

"Doing what?" I demanded, halting in my tracks.

"We're going to a concert in Santa Rosa."

"Santa Rosa! That's far away. Are you staying overnight?"

"Wouldn't you like to know."

"You're a terrible person, Jean. If you had any compassion at all, you'd be sticking close by me in my time of need."

"Sorry, but I'd rather go hear chamber music."

"How boring! Now I know it's only a ploy by Slade to get you into some cheap motel."

"Slade is a very cultured person. You wouldn't understand that, of course."

"Cultured, my ass. The only thing he's culturing is his obscene sex life."

* * *

Norma called me Saturday morning as I was wallowing in despair.

"I just said good-bye to Slade," she announced. "I sent him on his way with several pieces of my fabulous pie."

"I expect that's not the only form of pie he enjoyed."

"Really, Colm? Do guys refer to ladies' parts as pie?"

"Uh, I believe the exact expression is fur pie."

"Oh, right. I had heard that. It was all quite stimulating. Slade is magnificently equipped for the act."

"I'd rather not hear the sordid details, if you don't mind."

"He has remarkable staying power too. He's especially vigorous in the morning."

"Enough! Enough! God, give me a break. I'm coming over now to collect my $9."

"Why the big rush? I'm good for it."

"Because I have 37 cents to my name."

"What happened to your paycheck? You got paid yesterday."

"Uh, I had some expenses. Do you have your clothes on?"

"Why? Do you care if I don't?"

"I have no desire to see any more of your well-used body. Just have the money ready and I'll be on my way."

"Gee, someone got up on the wrong side of the bed this morning. Are you jealous that I slept with Slade? Is that your problem, bunky?"

"I'm not jealous. Nor am I thrilled that Slade is taking Jean to a chamber music concert in Santa Rosa tonight."

"What!"

"That's right, kiddo. Yours may not be the only pie he's sampling this weekend."

I showed up there about a half-hour later. The dishes from the night before were still stacked in the sink. Norma was looking good in self-designed casual togs. She could be Ukiah's most stylish dresser. She made a pot of coffee and dished me up a piece of her landlady's amazing pie.

"This pie is incredible, Norma. Just keep serving Slade pie like this and you'll win his heart for sure."

"He barely finished one small slice," she replied, slurping her coffee. "I don't think he has much of a sweet tooth."

"Were you distracting him with swimsuit malfunctions?"

"I may have been topless at the time, but that's not much of a distraction."

"You have a tasty little body, Norma."

"You managed to resist it. Do you always lock your bedroom door?"

"Always," I lied. "It's from when I was a kid and was terrified that Nazis were going to invade. How did your condoms work out?"

"Fine. I can't tell the difference, but I understand it affects what you guys feel."

"Yeah. Quite a bit. So you can't feel the difference between skin and rubber?"

"We're not really that sensitive down there, Colm. It's probably a defense mechanism from the old days when rape was the tribal sport. I'm really, really annoyed that Slade is going out with your housekeeper."

"Yeah, it appears your beau is not monogamy-minded."

"Do you think he'll be inclined to stray after we're married?"

"A guy who looks like that? You'll have to watch him like a hawk."

"He's always traveling out of town to investigate new plywoods."

"You'll have to tag along, Norma. You'll see all the lumber centers of North America."

"Shut up! God, Colm, don't make me any more depressed than I already am."

* * *

Jean didn't stay overnight in Santa Rosa. At 11:37 p.m. Slade pulled up next door in his fatuous Studebaker. At some point it had been repainted a dismal lima-bean green. Probably a $19.95 special deal, and they threw in the ugly plaid seat covers as a bonus.

This time Slade escorted Jean to her door. He kissed her without apparent resistance, but no groping was observed. In less than 24 hours the guy kissed two different girls. I've done that a few times myself, but I was in college at the time. No one expects romantic sincerity from college guys. Then they unclinched, and Jean entered her house. Even though I recently became engaged to a beautiful girl back East, I found it all deeply aggravating.

The next morning I stumbled into my living room and unplugged the roaring vacuum cleaner.

"Must you do that so early?" I asked.

"You've neglected your morning ablutions again, Mr. Moran. You look like something the cat dragged in."

"That is my privilege as the head of this household."

"A household of one," she pointed out.

"How was your concert?"

"Quite lovely. Two piano pieces and a string quartet."

"Sounds dreadfully tiresome. Was Slade hopped up on drugs to stay awake?"

"Not to my knowledge. He enjoyed it as much as I did."

"Yeah, I'll bet. Where did you eat?"

"At a restaurant Slade likes in Santa Rosa's Chinatown."

"That burg has a Chinatown?"

"One might conclude that from my previous statement."

"Did he tell you where he slept the night before?"

"That subject did not arise. Nor does it interest me."

"You don't mind that he's doing it with Norma?"

"Most fellows his age do it occasionally with someone."

"Well, I'm not."

"Yes, and I suspect that accounts for the prickliness of your personality."

Chapter 20

Tuesday afternoon was the photo shoot for the Cheeky Swimsuits catalog page and publicity campaign. We all rendezvoused at the modest studio of Hank Herndan, Ukiah's pro photographer. He shoots all of Milady Modest's product stills. Hank's a lanky guy in his mid-thirties, who likes to keep things light with a steady stream of lame jokes. He had hung up a background showing Hawaii's Diamond Head, and raked four bags of playground sand over the floor. Our stunning models were Norma (scorching red), Jean (cautionary yellow), and Juanita (cool blue). The latter two were being paid $25 each, but Norma as an employee was donating her services.

Sparkling on Juanita's left hand was her new (to her) engagement ring. I remembered it as one of the flashier rings on display at the pawnshop. I also recalled its hefty price: $689. The rumor is Reggie paid for it in cash with a fat roll of bills borrowed from his brothers. Naturally, Norma and Jean had to examine it while offering their best wishes to the expectant bride.

"It's a lovely ring," said Jean.

"Yes, uh, lovely," said Norma. "Very dramatic."

"It was Reggie's choice," replied Juanita. "He likes a showy ring."

"OK, girls," said Hank. "I'm sure you'll all have husbands after these photos get out. Wow, Colm, I do like this new look. Milady Modest is letting her hair down at last."

The girls did look spectacular, especially in this semi-authentic beach milieu. But the revised blue style on Juanita seemed if anything a bit too ample in its coverage. (On a real beach I'd prefer her in our yellow model.) And Jean in full makeup looked as striking as any *Vogue* model. How did I ever think she was not as attractive as Betty?

Hank ran four rolls of Kodachrome through his tripod-mounted Rolleiflex–directing the girls in various groupings and poses as a big electric fan ruffled their hair. Occasionally, he'd pause and I'd help him move the heavy photo-lamp stands.

"OK, girls," he announced. "I've got one frame left. How about you untie your tops and wave them at the camera?"

"Not going to happen, Hank," laughed Juanita. "OK, ladies. Let's turn around and give him a new angle on things."

So that was the last photo of the day: Three cute lasses smiling back over three shapely behinds. As Mr. Cheeky reminds us, "This is 1957. Why be shy?"

After the girls got dressed, we rode in my Packard back to Norma's place for coffee and dessert.

"Excellent pie," commented Jean.

"Thanks," said Norma. "It was better a few days ago. I made it for my boyfriend Slade Preston, and he loved it."

"What's your trick for getting such a flaky crust?" asked Jean.

"Gee, that's kind of a family secret. My granny would never forgive me if I told anyone."

"I was talking to Slade's sister at the store the other day," said Juanita. "Now that his magazine is well established, he wants to get married and start a family."

"There's a lot of that going around," said Jean. "Colm wants to get married in the worst way."

I choked on my pie.

"Is that true, honey?" asked Norma.

"Marriage has crossed my mind," I confessed. "As has suicide, becoming a monk, and playing center field for the Brooklyn Dodgers."

* * *

So many Beachzilla orders have come in that by Thursday Wendell was trying to scrounge up more lizard cloth. What a shame that all those surplus rolls had been cut up into potholders (which, alas, were not rocketing out of the warehouse). At my suggestion we are now offering stores two free potholders with every dozen Beachzilla suits ordered. Slivmank is also looking into the possibility of hustling them to toy stores as dollhouse rugs.

Right before lunch I got another collect call from Betty.

"Hi, Betty. They really don't like me to accept collect calls here."

"Why not? You own the company don't you?"

"Well, my father does. What's up?"

"That's what I'd like to know. What's up with that ring you sent me?"

"Oh, you got it, huh? You never know how long the Post Office's going to take."

"I had it checked out by a local jeweler. Did you find it in a box of Cracker Jacks?"

"I'll have you know I paid for that ring with money I earned myself."

"How much do you make? Five cents an hour?"

"OK, I admit it's not the fanciest ring on the block."

"It's a total fake, Colm! Either you're a patsy who got taken or you care nothing for my feelings. Which is it?"

"Neither, darling. That ring is kind of a placeholder."

"A what?"

"It's serving as a symbol of a ring until I can afford to replace it with the genuine article."

"Hmm. Well, that's a new one on me. Why didn't you borrow money from your father?"

"I'm trying to make it on my own, Betty."

"And I'm supposed to walk around wearing a ring that looks like it dropped out of a gumball machine at Coney Island?"

"It's not that bad, Betty. That stone is the latest technology in simulated diamonds. Its refractive index is virtually identical to the real thing."

"Right, Colm. I'll be sure to mention that when I'm showing your fake to my friends."

"I guarantee I'll replace it with a beautiful ring by our wedding day. From Tiffany, Cartier, Van Cleef & Arpels–you name it."

"Is that a promise?"

"Of course. We're doing well now. Our new bathing suits are starting to catch on. Shall I send you one?"

"What are they imitating? Chinchilla? Gorilla hair? The dusky hide of a seal?"

"Don't worry, darling. I guarantee you'll love it."

"OK, send me one. So what did you think of my beer commercial? You *must* have seen it my now."

"I loved it, honey," I lied. "It was so cute the way you were distracting that bowler."

"Did you like my wink?"

"I loved it. Do one for me right now."

"Colmy, we're talking over the phone."

"I know, but flash me a wink."

So she sent me a wink long-distance, and I told her I loved her. That's a difficult admission to make in the workplace.

* * *

When I got home that evening Jean was chopping mushrooms and frying strips of beef in a large iron skillet.

"That smells good," I said.

"You've got a guest."

"A guest? Where?"

"In the living room."

I poked my head around the door. Seated on my Morris chair was Juanita clutching a large straw bag. She didn't look pissed, so I felt it was safe to enter the room.

"Hello, Juanita. What a nice surprise."

"Hi, Colm. I suppose you've heard the news by now."

"Uh, what news?"

She held out her hand. Being a gentleman of the old school, I kissed it.

"Notice anything missing, honey?" she asked.

"Damn, Juanita. Did you lose your expensive second-hand ring?"

"How can you not have heard, Colm? It's all over town!"

"What is?"

"A gal got off the Greyhound yesterday. A Miss Birgit Vogel. She wasn't speaking English so hot, but she made it understood that she was looking for an Army corporal named Dowling."

I swallowed hard and sat down. "Uh-oh. Was she a fräulein from Germany?"

"You guessed it, darling. A fräulein with a little gift from N.A.T.O. in her oven."

Jean entered with a small bowl of mixed nuts.

"Anyone care for something to drink?" she asked.

"Not right now, Jean," I replied.

She put down the bowl, smiled, and returned to the kitchen.

"And Reggie's the father?" I asked.

"He will be in about three months."

"And he was planning on deserting her?"

"I guess 'out of sight, out of mind' was his strategy."

"Where is she now?"

"Staying with me, if you can believe that. Reggie's mom refuses to have her in her house."

"And where's Reggie?"

"He went to Santa Rosa today to consult an immigration lawyer. I guess he's going to do the honorable thing now and try to marry her."

"Doesn't the Army frown on that?"

"Not as much as they did right after the war. Plus, a baby changes the situation."

"So are you upset?" I asked.

"Well, I'm angry, of course. I feel very betrayed. But I've decided to look on the bright side."

"Which is?"

"You, you silly boy. I'm accepting your proposal of marriage!"

Jean entered with a small bowl of mints.

"Will there be a guest for dinner, Mr. Moran? I'm making beef stroganoff."

"Are you staying for dinner?" I asked my possibly future wife.

"No, sorry. I have get back and tend to Birgit."

"Only one for dinner, Jean. Could you delay it for a bit?"

"Certainly, sir."

She deposited the candy, smiled, and returned to the kitchen.

Juanita removed a bulky publication from her bag.

"Good God, what's that?" I asked.

"Don't be so jumpy, Colm dear. It's only the Sears catalog. I've got the page marked. To tell you the truth, honey, I didn't care much for any of those pawnshop rings. Now Sears has a nice one-quarter carat diamond solitaire in a 14k gold setting for only $145."

"$145?" I asked, feeling dazed.

"And the diamond is flawless. They have some cheaper ones, but I think this is a better investment."

"It may take me some time to save up $145," I pointed out.

"Not a problem, dear. It's only $8 down and $10 a month."

"Well, that's certainly reasonable."

"So I'll phone in the order and pay the $8 C.O.D. charge. You can reimburse me for that, and I'll give you the bill to pay every month."

"Right. That sounds eminently doable."

Jean entered carrying an ashtray.

"I don't smoke, Jean, and neither does Juanita."

"I'll leave this here in case anyone wants to start. Should I put the noodles on?"

"Please, no noodles, Jean. I'll alert you when I want noodles."

"Anything you say, sir."

She smiled and returned to the kitchen.

Juanita put away her catalog and stood up. I stood up as well.

"Then it's all settled about the ring, Colm darling. That's a start. Of course, you'll still have to ask my father for my hand, but that's only a formality."

"Your father despises me, Juanita."

"No, you'll find his attitude has changed after my near-miss with Reggie. Of course, he's not in a very good mood now as he regards all Germans as possible Nazi war criminals. I don't think we should schedule your visit until after Birgit leaves."

"Yes, that's probably wise."

"I'm thinking September for our wedding."

"September, 1958?"

"No, silly, next month. I see no reason to wait. It has to be after Ramona delivers because she doesn't want to look enormous in the wedding photos. And before Margie gets too big for the same reason."

"Who the hell is Margie?"

"My sister Margarita. You've met her."

"Oh, right."

"The good news is we don't have to wait any more."

"Wait for what?"

"You know. I mean since we're going to be married soon anyway."

"But what about–you know?"

"Not a problem. I'll probably get you know right away. But I won't be showing at our wedding. And I won't be the first girl in Ukiah to have one a bit prematurely."

"Uh, I'm not sure I can do that, Juanita."

"Well, aren't you the old-fashioned gentleman. I can wait if you want to, dear. You just seem a bit frustrated at times."

"Right. That's true."

"Well, give me a kiss and I'll be on my way."

So I kissed her. In five minutes I went from being distantly engaged to imminently married with a kid practically on the way.

I used to think asking someone to marry you was a fairly daunting undertaking. But all I had to do was answer the phone or tell one small lie.

* * *

Eventually Jean got tired of waiting and put the noodles on to boil. She dished up my dinner, but I found I wasn't very hungry.

"Is there something amiss with my stroganoff?" she asked.

"Uh, no, Jean. It's excellent as usual. I'm a bit disturbed at the moment."

"May I offer you my heartiest congratulations, sir."

"Don't be an ass, Jean. Sit down and help me figure out what to do."

She pulled out a chair and joined me at the dining table. "You don't want to marry Juanita?"

"Not really."

"Then why did you just become engaged to her?"

"That's what I'm trying to figure out. I've discovered that I have difficulty saying no to girls."

"You said no to Norma."

"True, but it helped that she was vastly irritating."

"You'll have to tell Juanita that you changed your mind."

"How can I do that? I'd sound like a total cad–especially after she just got betrayed by Reggie."

"How do you get in these fixes, Colm?"

"I really don't know. One thing leads to another and there I am in the soup. Are girls still suing men for breach of promise?"

"Only if his family has money."

I got up to answer the ringing telephone.

"Colm, honey, I forgot to ask. Do you prefer white gold or yellow gold?"

"What?"

"For the ring. I have the choice of white or yellow gold. Which do you prefer?"

"Do I have to decide that right now?"

"Well, I want to order the ring. And since I hope to wear it for 60 or 70 years I want to make sure you like it."

"I think gold should look like gold, Juanita."

"Good. I prefer the yellow gold too. That's what I'll order. My family is thrilled, darling."

"Great. I'm thrilled too."

I hung up and returned sheepishly to the dining room. Jean gave me a severe look.

"Didn't you just miss an opportunity to correct your misunderstanding?"

"I couldn't do it, Jean. Only a cad breaks off his engagement over the telephone."

"You're too nice for you own good, Colm."

"I've always dreamed of shipping out on a tramp steamer. This may be the time to begin my maritime career."

"Don't be a coward, Colm You just have to face the music and do the right thing."

I'm not sure Jean was helping. Of course, I didn't dare tell her that I was also scheduled to marry Betty in 1958.

* * *

I spent a restless night mulling over my options. I had no doubt that given a choice between me and Slade, Jean would opt for the cultured and handsome plywood publisher. I stood a better chance against Elwyn Saunders, but he had been supplanted by a much more formidable rival. That left Juanita and Betty.

Did I wish to marry a possibly self-centered actress or the possible mother of my 14 children? That was my dilemma.

Whopping big families: could they in some ways be rewarding? Most Catholics I knew did not seem oppressed by their numerous relatives. For example, there was that extensive Kennedy clan that was always getting written up in *Life* magazine. One son had become a U.S. senator and was being talked about as a possible Presidential candidate. They all looked happy enough in their photos. I imagine it helped that their pater had made a fortune in the liquor business.

Humans are animals after all, and every animal is driven genetically toward reproductive success. Perhaps that's why I sometimes feel an overwhelming desire to plant my seed in Juanita. Few females in the history of the human species ever have offered as much promise of reproductive success as the Howe sisters. Note, however, that I felt just as turned on during that all-too-brief clinch with Jean. And planting my seed in Katie had proved quite stimulating–even though my seed never traveled farther than the end of the condom.

I also thought about that pill the drug companies were working on. Perhaps it would get perfected in time so that Juanita and I could stop at only six or seven kids. That seemed like a more manageable number. You might not need a commercial-size kitchen, and you'd have a better chance of remembering all their names. I might not need to learn how to drive a bus.

I certainly cared for Juanita. I wouldn't like her to move to Utah and marry someone who was only interested in her breeding capabilities. She had a good sense of humor and was easy to get along with. She was pretty and had a body the likes of which men have fought and died over for eons. She appeared to be fond of me too. She was sensible and had proven her worth in her job. She would make a good hostess for the parties I'd be giving for my Hollywood friends. She was not likely to desert me the first time Errol Flynn made a pass at her. Plus, she had offered to sleep with me *as soon as I wished*.

Since Betty was so far away, I could let matters hang fire with her while seeing how things worked out with Juanita. Why rock the boat now and get everyone and everything in an uproar? Keeping my mouth shut and going along with the program seemed like my best option at this time. With that decided, I rolled over and went to sleep.

* * *

Juanita called me as I was looking over the slides from our recent photo shoot. Hank had given us dozens of terrific shots to choose from.

"Colm darling, do you read the local paper?"

"I do, dear. I read it to stay informed and to keep up with the Brooklyn Dodgers. Duke Snider's hitting pretty well."

"You might want to skip it today."

"Why?"

"In all the uproar no one thought to cancel my engagement announcement. I never expected them to print my photo so big."

"It's announcing your engagement to Reggie?"

"Are you totally angry, humiliated, and embarrassed?"

"Probably not."

"I phoned the editor, Colm. They're running a correction tomorrow."

"Stating that you're not engaged to Reggie?"

"That and correcting the name of my intended fellow. What's your middle name?"

"I don't have one. We Morans believe that middle names are a needless appendage."

"OK, if you say so. I need you to phone the editor right away with your parents' names and home city. Can you do that?"

"Uh, OK."

"You'll be happy to know that Reggie and Birgit just left by bus for Texas."

"They're gone?"

"Out of my hair and life, I hope. It looks like the Army is going to let them get married. But she'll have to go back to Germany and apply for a different visa. She's here on a tourist visa now. Where should we go for our honeymoon?"

"I don't know . . . Fresno?"

"God, what a romantic I'm marrying. We'll see you at my house tonight at 7:45."

"What for?"

"To ask for my hand in marriage. Don't be late. My dad always watches 'The Life of Riley' at 8:30. He's a big William Bendix fan. That gives you less than an hour to talk him into it."

Of course, I immediately went out and bought a newspaper. A very flattering photo of Juanita ran across two columns on Page 5. As I was reading the notice my phone rang. It was the newspaper's society editor requesting Facts for her story. I answered all of her questions, digging myself in deeper with each reply.

Norma flounced into my office a few minutes later.

"That Justeen Snyder woman is spreading a vicious rumor that you got engaged to Juanita Howe."

"There is some truth to that," I admitted.

"Why, pray tell? It's obvious you're stuck on your housekeeper."

"No, I'm not," I lied.

"God! Have you knocked her up?"

"I've never even slept with Juanita. Honest Injun."

"Then what was the point of going out with her?"

"Lay off Juanita. She's a very fine person."

"You can't marry her, Colm! I need you to keep distracting Jean so she doesn't tighten her grip on Slade."

"Well I'm sorry I can't live my life to suit your needs. Have you heard from Slade?"

"My telephone is as silent as a tomb. I even called the phone company to make sure it was working. Is he going to drop me because I put out?"

"It's been known to happen. You'll recall I warned you about that."

"God, I hate men! Girls have sex with guys to give *them* pleasure you know."

"I imagine it's quite an imposition, if you think about it."

"That's why you can all drop dead as far as I'm concerned."

* * *

It occurred to me as I was driving to Juanita's house that if ol' Bert turned me down, it would solve some of my immediate problems. After all, what's the point of asking for his daughter's hand, if the father doesn't have the right of refusal?

Both Juanita and her mother kissed me when I arrived, then excused themselves to "take a little walk." Bert glanced over contemptuously from the recliner where he was watching TV. I walked over and switched off the set.

"Hey, buddy! I was watching that!"

"My name's Colm, not buddy."

"I know that," he sneered. "What kind of a puny ass name is Colm?"

"It beats the hell out of Albert. I'd like to marry your damn daughter."

"You just met her a few weeks ago. All you want to do is get in her pants."

"If that's all I wanted, I wouldn't be here facing an old fart like you."

"How would you like to get decked right here in my living room?"

"You start something, Pop, and I'll finish it. But take off your glasses first. I don't want to blind you with the broken glass."

"Oh, so you're a tough guy, huh?"

"I've been in my share of bar brawls. I'll hit you hard if I have to. Stand up now if you want to fight."

"Jesus, I'm trying to watch my program, and some hothead walks in and tries to pick a fight. You got an attitude problem, kid."

"No, you've got the attitude problem, Bert. You treat Dale and Wayne like dogs. Well, I've got some news for you. If I marry Juanita, you're going to treat me with respect. So the choice is yours: You can stop acting like a jerk, or I walk out of that door for good. What's it to be?"

Long hard stare from Bert. I glared back at him. I figured a mild pop to his nose might get me banished from Juanita for life. But could I hit an old guy?

"You like William Bendix, Colm?" he asked.

"Yeah, I like William Bendix. What's it to you?"

"How about I get you a nice cold beer, and you can stick around and watch 'The Life of Riley'?"

Damn. No way I could hit him after that gracious offer.

"OK, Bert. I could go for a beer."

"You got to treat Juanita good though. She's a peach."

"Uh, right. If you say so."

"I think you got more on the ball than that Reggie kid did. Can you imagine knocking up some Kraut?"

"Well, love is a mysterious thing."

"I doubt much love was involved in that tangle," he chuckled.

"Where's that damn beer, Bert?"

"Coming right up. Make yourself at home, Colm."

The gals returned and we all watched Bert's favorite TV show. William Bendix plays an aircraft factory worker married to a gal who I had seen somewhere before. About midway through the show I placed her: she was the actress who played the love interest in that Bing Crosby movie "Holiday Inn." Bendix and his neighbor pal spend their workdays staring straight up and power-riveting aircraft wings. Kind of a subtle joke because if you tried doing that for longer than five minutes, your arms would get too tired to hold up the tool. After that we watched "M Squad," "The Thin Man," "Colt .45," and "Person to Person." It was the most TV I'd seen in months. I suppose it was a good preview of married life.

* * *

Saturday morning I was washing the Packard when my housekeeper strolled over from next door.

"Did you see the paper?" she asked.

"Yeah, I did."

"I confess I find this mystifying, Colm. Why are you announcing your engagement in the newspaper if you don't intend to marry her?"

"I've decided to make the best of the situation I'm in."

"What does that mean?"

"It appears I'm getting married next month."

"Oh, really? You're going to marry a girl you don't love?"

"I'm fond of Juanita."

"What about your fiancee back east?"

"Her I sort of loved, but I'm having second thoughts. She didn't think much of the ring I gave her. I expect she's tossed it into Cape Cod Bay by now."

"I didn't know you'd advanced to the ring stage."

"It was a recent development."

"So you're engaged to not one but two girls–neither of whom you love."

"Uh, more or less."

"You don't think love is a necessity for marriage, Colm?"

"The girl I care for isn't having much to do with me."

"Perhaps that's because you weren't free. And are even more ensnared now."

"She should have put up more of a fight."

"Perhaps that's not in her nature."

"Then she shouldn't be surprised if the train leaves the station without her."

"You're something of an idiot, Colm."

"Right. You've mentioned that before."

A car horn beeped down the driveway. It was a slime-green Studebaker.

"So where are you off to, Jean?"

"We're going to an art show at the fairgrounds."

"You should remind him to call Norma. She's wondering why he hasn't phoned."

Chapter 21

I walked into town and had the budget lunch for one at the Golden Carp. I sipped my tea and thought about what Jean had said. It seemed to me she was sort of implying I might have had a chance with her. Or was she?

I wish I'd thought to point out that Slade's heavy involvement with Norma hadn't prevented someone from kissing him on their front porch last weekend. Except if I mentioned it I'd probably have been raked over the coals for spying. It's hard to win with chicks.

That kid named Steve brought his bowl of garlic over and sat at my table.

"Do you like peeling garlic, Steve?" I asked.

"It's boring and it makes my hands stink."

"Then why do you do it?"

He shrugged. "It's my job."

"You're kind of young for restaurant work."

"I help out. Everybody in my family does. I mop the floor too–that's the worst. What's your job?"

"I make ladies' bathing suits."

Steve laughed. "That's pretty funny. Do you really?"

"Well, I help sell them. Someone else sews them."

"That's the stupidest job I ever heard of!"

"You may be right. I'm in the same boat as you. I do it to help my father."

"You're lucky."

"Why's that?"

"Any job is better than working in a dumb restaurant."

* * *

In line at the theater that evening, we spotted Norma waiting with Slade. Looks like the cad finally called her.

This week's movie was "Fire Down Below," a suggestive title if ever there was one. It's also something you can get from dining in the wrong restaurant.

Robert Mitchum and Jack Lemmon were partners in a South Seas smuggling operation when they get hired to sail shady-lady Rita Hayworth over to another island. They both go for her and have a predictable falling out. Not the most engrossing plot, but Rita looked good in her swimsuit. I'm thinking she's about a decade too late now for a Cheeky Swimsuits bikini. I doubt though she'll ever be wearing anything from our Milady Modest line. She had a big dance number in the movie, but 40 is kind of pushing it for sultry hip-swinging. The kids in the balcony weren't too impressed either. Independent producers can sometimes afford big stars on their way down, but I think you should put them in parts that fit their age.

I offered to take Juanita out to eat after the movie, but she suggested we go back to my place and raid the refrigerator. She made a bacon and cheese omelet, which we ate at the kitchen table.

"I guess you didn't care for the movie, huh?" I said.

"Why do you say that?"

"Every time I looked at you, you were watching Slade and Norma."

"I'm curious to see how they're getting on. That girl had him in a vice-like grip. He could barely eat his popcorn."

"So how many times did you go out with Slade?"

She blushed. "Not that many, honey. Nothing happened, so don't you worry."

"I'm not worried. Did you like him?"

"What's not to like? I told you he disappeared after my little speech."

"Which upset you?"

"Does anyone enjoy rejection? So don't you try it. Remember, my ring is coming in the mail."

"I know. Yellow gold with a flawless diamond."

"Well, flawless when examined up to a power of ten. That's what the catalog says. I won't be sticking it under a microscope. Are you still committed to marrying a virgin?"

"My resolve is weakening by the minute."

"Now that you've got my dad tamed I don't think he'd blow a gasket if I came home a little late tonight. I understand you were buying condoms the other day."

"Your spies are everywhere. I was buying them for Norma, but I kept a stash in reserve."

"I suppose you've had other girls and know how it's done?"

"A few times. It's a relatively simple procedure. Would you like to check out my bedroom?"

"Let me hit the bathroom first. I'll join you there."

My bedroom decor was strictly 1910, but when Juanita dropped her towel, we rocketed into the Atomic Age. Her body was as modern as tomorrow and primed for contemporary passions. (I may use that line on the posters for my first movie.) We took it slow and didn't have much trouble. We fit together nicely, and she seemed to be having a good time. We took a brief timeout, then went at it again.

"That was pretty neat," she said, when we finished. "It slides right up there, which is kind of amazing considering how big it is."

"You never experimented with carrots or cucumbers?"

"Not even tempted. I wonder if it feels different without the rubber?"

"It seems like it would, but maybe not. We could try it sometime when we want to make a baby."

"Don't kid yourself, honey. We're probably making a baby right now."

"But all my baby fluids went into the condoms. Every last drop."

"There's probably a stray one on the sheets from your last wet dream."

"I don't think they live that long."

"I like it when you kiss me when you're inside me. It's like a two for one special."

"You must work in retail."

"Some people do this and then go to sleep. Can you imagine that?"

I tried, but I was already dozing off.

"Don't pass out on me, honey. I need you to get me home pronto."

* * *

My housekeeper was bustling about with her dust rag when I emerged from the bathroom Sunday morning. I gripped my towel tighter.

"Shall I hang the bloody sheet out the window, Mr. Moran?"

"I have no idea what you're talking about."

"Wasn't that Juanita I saw leaving here with you late last night?"

"Uh, possibly. How was the art show?"

"Not bad. I sold a painting."

"You should have told me you were exhibiting there. I would have gone to see the show."

"I figured you were busy, what with your bachelor life coming to a screeching halt."

"Who bought your painting? Do you know?"

"Let's just say it will soon be hanging in the offices of a popular trade magazine."

"Oh, I see. Another way for Slade to weasel his way into your . . . uh, heart."

"My father got a big kick out of your betrothal announcement in the paper yesterday."

"He would."

"I'm thinking of giving you a painting as a wedding gift."

"Why don't you keep the painting and give me yourself instead?"

"Why, Mr. Moran, what do you mean?"

"You know what I mean. I love you and I want to marry you."

"Three marriage proposals in one month. I wonder if that's a record for a Yale grad?"

"You may have been third on the list, Jean, but you're number one in my heart."

"Now there's a line to cause a girl to swoon."

I adjusted my towel, which was beginning to slip.

"I mean it, Jean. We could pack our bags and run away together today."

"Don't even think of dropping that towel, buddy. Sorry, I'm busy cleaning your kitchen. Someone left a mess of dishes in the sink. And I really think I should change your sheets. I'll let you empty the waste-basket."

"Oh, sorry."

It's a bit sticky sharing the details of one's intimate life with a housekeeper whom you happen to adore.

* * *

Monday at work was show time for Norma's latest Milady Modest creations. That girl is doing amazing work. Miss Page never looked better as she modeled one flattering suit after another in Norma's office.

"I really like the satiny sheen of this Lastex fabric," commented Norma, fingering a duo-tone floral print suit that was subtly disguising Miss Page's bulk.

"What's Lastex?" I asked.

"A cotton/acetate blend with some rubber for stretch," she replied. "It can stretch up to six inches to adjust to different torsos."

I can do the same, I thought but didn't say.

"Very good," said Wendell, fondling Miss Page's right breast.

At Norma's insistence Miss Page retreated to the ladies' restroom to change into the next suit. This was a cream and red windowpane check with matching red trim around the mock pockets and neckline. No straps, but Miss Page was being safely contained within. Norma tugged and pulled, so Wendell did the same. I kept my hands to myself.

"Notice here I went with loose leg shorts to trim the hips and slim the thighs," said Norma.

"Looks great," I said. "What's holding up the second floor?"

"A strapless inner bra that adjusts to B, C, or D cups. Miss Page, of course, is at the maximum for this size."

"Any risk of slippage during a high dive?" asked Wendell.

"I doubt it," said Norma. "But do our ladies do much diving?"

"I never do," commented Miss Page. "I leave that to Esther Williams."

The next suit had tapered halter straps and a top that flowed smoothly down to a short skirt.

"Here we've totally integrated the six-gore skirt into the lines of the suit," said Norma. "It's covering a separate self-fabric panty that shapes like a girdle."

"I love this one," said Miss Page. "And it's comfortable too."

"The contrasting trim is another step for production," Wendell pointed out.

"True," said Norma, "But look how it's tying everything together and flattering the waist."

We were reviewing suit number eight when I got called away to answer the phone.

"Hi, darling," said Juanita. "Are you free on Friday?"

"Sure."

"You're not taking your housekeeper to the movies that night?"

"No, I'm devoting myself to you."

"That's nice to hear. Ramona wants to throw an engagement party for us."

"Fine. I'll be there. I hope you can make it too."

"Of course I'll be there, silly boy. I had a very good time Saturday night."

"Really? I thought the movie was only so-so."

"I was referring to the activities that came later."

"Oh, that. Adding the crispy bacon to the omelet was a great idea."

"No, even later. Those activities."

"Oh, right. We should try that again sometime."

"I agree. Sometime soon, I hope."

* * *

That afternoon Norma and I went out to lunch to get caught up on each other's love lives.

"Did Slade spend the night?" I asked.

"He did. I hinted that he was welcome to go down on me, but he looked quite shocked. So much for California guys being wild and uninhibited."

"This is the sticks, Norma. You're lucky he's willing to sleep with you before marriage. Did he say why he didn't call?"

"Press of business. Same excuse my father's been laying on my mother for a quarter century for his unexplained absences."

"You think your dad's fooling around?"

"My father lays pipe as his business and he lays pipe as his hobby. 'Nough said?"

"I get it."

"Now that you're foolishly engaged, Colm, did you get any honeymoon previews?"

"If I answer that, you'll blab it to everyone."

"Oh, so you did. How was it?"

"Pretty darn fabulous."

"She wasn't a virgin?"

"No, she definitely was."

"Another notch in your gun, eh?"

"I'm not that kind of guy, Norma."

"All guys are that kind of guy. Was it a difficult passage?"

"Quite the opposite."

"You're kinda small, huh?"

"I'm told I'm above average."

"So how can you be sure you were first across plate?"

"Because I trust her."

"You used a condom?"

"I did, but she expects to get pregnant anyway."

"You were sloppy?"

"Hardly, but she comes from a very fertile family. It'll be a miracle if she gets her period."

"That's frightening."

"It's total Russian Roulette every time you take Juanita to bed."

"Her backsliding last week to Mr. Primitive. Did she explain that?"

"She blamed it on temporary nostalgia for their teen romance. And to keep Reggie from calling me out for a gunfight in the center of town."

"So tell me, Colm. Do you go down on your girls?"

"Jesus, Norma. You need to work on your boundaries."

"Had you not locked your bedroom door, I'd have gone down on you. And swallowed."

All in all I'm glad I missed out on that fun. She probably would have slurped that too.

* * *

By Friday I was feeling pretty discouraged. Our sales reps were loving the new Milady Modest and Beachzilla lines, but had nothing positive to say about Cheeky Swimsuits. It was all the same old objections we'd heard from Wendell. One guy even complained about the red fez on my duck. Trying to do something new in this business is like sticking your head in a red-hot guillotine.

Plus, Betty had called to say the bikini I sent her was "only appropriate for lounge wear in a house of ill repute." I debated that point with her but got nowhere. Some Vassar girls are modern in their outlooks, but I got stuck with one as rigid as your grandma. She mentioned that the *New York Times* would be printing an announcement of our engagement "any day now." It's a good thing that paper doesn't circulate much on the west coast.

As requested, I went to Ramona's house directly from work. Parked in their driveway was a shiny new aluminum travel trailer hitched to a pale yellow Mercury convertible. It would have made a grand wedding present, but no such luck. It was a prototype trailer Dale's factory had just built for demonstration purposes. The spiffy tow vehicle belonged to his dad. Dale took a break from the barbecue grill to give us a tour.

"Have you met my baby brudder Ryan?" he asked, tossing me a can of beer.

"I don't think so," I said, shaking Ryan's hand. He was a friendly kid a few inches shorter than me with a deep tan and an Elvis pompadour. He looked a bit like that actor who died in a car wreck, James Dean.

"Ryan just graduated from Chico State with a major in female anatomy," added Dale.

"Actually business administration," said Ryan.

"They teach them how to make change and put a new ribbon in the cash register," said Dale.

"Can we go inside the trailer?" asked Juanita.

"Let me do my spiel first," said Dale. "What you're looking at is a compact 16-foot trailer that sleeps five. You know how we accomplished that?"

"You only sell them to midgets?" I replied.

"Not in the least, Colm. Our innovation is moving the entry door from in front of the axle to behind it. This gives you a much more efficient interior."

"And whose idea was that, Dale?" asked Ryan.

"It was little baby Ryan's," he replied. "When he's not fixating on girls, he's thinking about trailer interiors."

Ryan pulled out a metal step and opened the trailer door. "This is the first one we've built," he said. "So we welcome your comments and suggestions."

I followed Juanita into the trailer, paneled in a varnished blond wood. On the left as you enter was a double-door closet with drawers below. Beyond that was a small corner bath complete with toilet, tiny sink, and stall shower. Then you turned right to go down a center aisle. To the left was a sink and gas stove, with a small propane-powered refrigerator mounted below. All done in a matching pink enamel. Opposite this kitchen area was a dinette that seated four. Yellow starbursts swirled across its pink Formica tabletop. A built-in sofa extended across the front of the trailer.

"The dinette converts into a bed that sleeps two," said Ryan. "And the front gaucho pulls out to sleep two more."

"Where's the fifth guy sleep?" asked Juanita. "Standing up in the shower?"

"Not hardly," said Ryan, flipping a latch above the sofa and releasing a hinged Pullman-style bunk.

"I can stick at least two of my kids up there," said Dale. "Maybe three if I pack 'em in sardine-style. And four if I grease 'em up first."

"I like it," said Juanita. "It feels roomy, and I love all the storage cabinets. Not much counter space around the sink though."

"That's all we could squeeze in," said Ryan, "unless we went to a smaller sink or a two-burner stove."

"No, I'd want the four burners," said Juanita. "What do you think, honey?"

"Very nice," I said. "Do the occupants take a vow of chastity?"

"There's a guy with his priorities straight," said Dale.

Ryan unlatched a folding accordion door and demonstrated how it could close off the front sleeping area.

"As you see, we do provide a measure of privacy," he said.

"Don't worry, Colm," said Dale, "with a houseful of kids you'll soon master the art of doing it quickly and silently. Hell, half the time I'm done before Ramona even notices I've begun."

* * *

The house and yard soon were jammed with family, friends, and the usual mob of manic kids. I shook dozens of hands and promptly forgot all the names. I sipped my beer, smiled, and listened as person after person assured me I was a big step up from Reggie Dowling. I only hope it's true. Reggie may not be admired for his urbane sophistication, but I had no doubt he loved Juanita.

I got introduced to Juanita's white-haired boss, who walked with a cane and looked to be at least 90. He said he opened his first store in 1911 and successfully held his own against Woolworth, Kresge, and W.T. Grant.

"You know what the secret of success is, young man?" he asked.

"No, what?"

"Never let your guard down. Always be alert for shoplifters. People will steal you blind, if you let them."

"Oh, that's a good tip."

"I hired Juanita when she was still in high school. A real cutie pie. In my younger days I'd have been chasing her all over the store."

"Uh, right. Well, she certainly admires you."

"Yes, sir. I'd have got her in the storeroom and showed her what's what. And I'm not just talking about a hand up her skirt."

I edged away. "Uh, I think Margarita wants me to help her move some chairs."

I wandered into the back yard and found Norma and Slade by the beer cooler.

"Nice party," said Norma. She was dressed in some sort of exotic caftan with matching turban. Her beaded shoes looked like something out of the Arabian Nights.

I nodded at Slade, who was so handsome no one ever noticed what he wore.

"Dale just put some steaks on the grill," he pointed out. "You could go swipe a few."

"I can never get enough meat," I said. "It's a legacy of wartime rationing."

"Your future sisters-in-law are both expecting," said Norma. "I feel like I've ventured into some extreme fertility zone."

"It's the 1950s, Norma," I said. "Having babies is what it's all about. How many children do you want, Slade?"

"I think two should be sufficient."

"An heir and a spare," said Norma. "That's customarily the minimum for royalty. I expect Colm will be going for an even dozen."

"At the very least," I smiled. "All the males destined for Yale, of course."

"You'll have to sell a trainload of bathing suits to pay those tuition bills," said Norma.

Since they had not yet toured the trailer, we walked over and I introduced them to Ryan. He gave them the spiel while I checked out the nifty convertible. It had a red and white interior and red top. The odometer registered just over 27,000 miles. Then Ryan strolled over and opened the hood so I could inspect the big 256 cubic inch V-8.

"Is this a '55?" I asked.

"No, it's the '54. They didn't change much. It was the first year for this engine."

"What's the rated horsepower?"

"Stock is 161, but we made some modifications: dual carbs, upgraded exhaust, heavy-duty shocks, tranny cooler, etcetera. It has no trouble pulling the trailer."

"It's a beautiful car."

"You know what car my dad really likes? The 1938 Packard Super 8. Ever think of selling?"

"I'm not sure it's mine to sell. I'm just borrowing it from my uncle."

"I thought he died."

"Yeah, he did."

"Nice trailer," called Slade, exiting.

"I like it," said Norma, following him out. "But I'd need a bathtub and four times more closet space. And those pink appliances and curtains have got to go!"

* * *

When I pulled into my driveway after the party, I noticed Jean sitting on her front porch. So I walked over to say hello.

"How come you weren't at the party, Jean? You were invited."

"I'll try to make it to your next engagement party."

"That was the only one scheduled."

"I mean for your next fiancee. I expect there will be others."

"I wish."

"I broke the law for you tonight."

"How so?"

"By purchasing an illegal substance."

"Great. Shall we try it?"

"We better go to your place. I don't want to get my father arrested."

Jean had already rolled the fragrant weed into fat cigarettes. We sat in my dark living room with the blinds drawn and lit one. I puffed away, then handed it to her. Soon it felt like someone had taken a can-opener to my skull.

"Wow, this stuff really works," I said.

"Just another way California is superior," she said.

"They grow this locally?"

"Up in the woods. Don't go looking for it or you risk getting shot."

"Weird things are happening inside my head."

"That's nothing new."

"God, I want to kiss you."

"You tried that before and got a very poor reception."

"How can you smoke this and not want to make love?"

"You must have been drinking at your party. I fear I've unleashed a monster."

"I love everything about you, Jean, from your feet to your ears."

"What's wrong with the top of my head?"

"Absolutely nothing. I loved that time we kissed. I think about it all the time."

"Like last weekend when you were entertaining Juanita in your bedroom?"

"I kept wishing it was you instead."

"I wish I could believe that."

"It's true. I've never even told Juanita I love her."

"Why not?"

"I have trouble with insincerity."

"And does she say she loves you?"

"Not so far. The subject really hasn't come up."

"You continue to amaze me, Colm."

"Don't you like me just a bit, darling?"

"You're better than a terminal disease."

I chuckled and puffed the butt down as far as I could, then snuffed it out. "Shall we light another, Jean?"

"OK. One more and then I'm leaving."

"Tell me a secret, Jean. Tell me all your secrets."

"I have no secrets. I'm an open book."

"Well, that's a big fat lie. You're the most unrevealing person I've ever met. I never have a clue what's going on inside your head. Not since the day I met you."

"Then why do you like me–if indeed you do?"

"How can you doubt it? I like you because I love you."

"Thanks for clearing that up."

"I love you because you do something crazy to my soul. It's so powerful, it hurts."

"Like sticking your finger in a lamp socket?"

"Yeah! Very similar to that!"

* * *

I woke up sometime before dawn. I had a stiffy and I was feeling very hungry. I lay there scratching my privates and thinking my life had jumped the rails. I used to be so care-free. Now my life was one big mind-gnawing worry after another. Now I understood why people took vacations. They got out of town to keep from going insane.

Then I had another one of those flashes of genius.

What I really, really needed to do right now was go on a Cheeky Swimsuits publicity tour.

Chapter 22

My housekeeper showed up and with some pleading made me a big breakfast. I ran my idea past her; she said she would think about what I proposed.

After breakfast I called Dale and laid out my plan. He said it sounded intriguing to him, but he would have to consult his dad. Meanwhile, I worked out a tentative budget. I calculated that we could do a two-week trip for $680. Dale called back and said his dad liked the idea, but had one condition: Ryan would have to come along to do the driving. I said that was fine by me. Adding Ryan raised my budget by $70 ($5 per diem for meals times 14 days). Could I chisel $750 out of Wendell? The prospect seemed dim, so I decided to bypass him and phone the old fellow. Fortunately, it was raining back east so he wasn't on the golf course.

"I've been reading about you in the *New York Times*," he said.

"Don't worry about that, Pop. It was all a big misunderstanding."

"They spelled your mother's name wrong. Nor did they mention that she's deceased."

"It won't happen again. I'm not marrying that girl."

"I'm sure her parents are just as pleased by that news as I am."

I told him I needed his OK for a $750 bikini publicity tour.

"Does your budget include legal fees should you be arrested?" he asked.

"Don't you worry about that, Pop. We're not doing anything indecent."

"I'll need a receipt for every expenditure."

"Will do, Pop. We have a bookkeeper here who watches me like a hawk."

"I'm glad someone is. That girl's mother left a message with my secretary. Shall I ignore it?"

"Right. You don't have to talk to her. The marriage is off. Shall I send you a photo of our new bikini line?"

"Please don't, son. Ignorance is bliss is my motto where ladies' garments are concerned. Not to mention your activities."

"We're putting your little company on the fashion map, Pop."

"How fascinating that will be for all concerned. Good-bye."

One thing about the old fellow: he never talks your ear off. Next I phoned Norma and Juanita; Norma agreed enthusiastically, but Juanita said she would have to check with work to see if she could take time off.

"Don't you have some vacation time coming?" I asked.

"Yes, but I was saving that for our honeymoon in Fresno."

"I was kidding about that, dear. We'll go someplace nicer. Maybe Modesto. I really need you on this publicity tour."

"OK, but I'll have to come back early if Ramona has her baby."

"Why? She has babies all the time."

"I still want to be here for her. And you don't have to worry."

"About what?"

"I got my period today."

"Really? That's amazing."

"I know. It's pretty unprecedented for my family."

* * *

I finally convinced Jean to come along on our trip. I'm paying her $50 a week (same as Juanita) in addition to her housekeeping wage. She's also helping with the banners. I'm painting the ducks and she's doing the lettering. The cloth we got at a fabric store downtown after a search of the warehouse turned up nothing suitable. Dale and his brother are doing their own signs.

Wendell is skeptical, but he's hoping for the best. Being a cautious fellow, he's given me half the funds in cash and half in travelers checks. He also supplied me with rolls of dimes and quarters to use in payphones in case of disasters.

"Two single men will be traveling with three single girls," he pointed out. "The girls will at times be scantily clad."

"True, but Juanita and I are engaged," I replied.

"Signifying what?"

"Uh, signifying that nothing immoral will transpire."

"I hope so. Remember, you all will be representing Milady Modest Incorporated."

"I prefer to think we're serving as goodwill ambassadors for Cheeky Swimsuits."

"Are you sure you don't want me to come along as chaperone?"

"We'll be fine, Wendell. Remember, we're aiming for the youth market. Besides we need you here to coordinate publicity for our 1958 line."

"Madame Aranson sent me another irate postcard. I'm thankful now I never got overly familiar with her."

"Don't worry. She's far away in Florida."

"I wish. She's back in Ukiah. I saw her lurking across the street from my house yesterday. I was quite unnerved."

"Are you sure it was her?"

"It was her all right. I recognized the bust line."

* * *

I hoped to leave on Wednesday, but last-minute details delayed our departure until Thursday morning. Ryan and Dale pulled up in front of my house as specified at 9:30. Large professionally painted signs had been mounted to both sides of the trailer. They read: "**Introducing the New Ukstream Trailer. Sleeps 5 comfortably! Full kitchen and bath! Affordable travel for the entire family! Taking orders now!**"

"What do you think? asked Dale.

"Looks great," I said.

"Thanks. Ryan waxed the Merc. I had him take a toothbrush to every crevice."

"Good job, Ryan," I said. "The shine is dazzling."

"It should turn a few heads," he admitted.

I hung my clothes in the closet next to Ryan's and placed my socks and underwear in a drawer. Fortunately, there were five drawers–one for each of us. Then Juanita arrived with Norma, and Jean brought out her stuff. My gear and Ryan's was moved to the trunk of the car so that the girls could jam their lavish wardrobes and other necessities into every cranny of the trailer. What was left over filled the rest of the trunk. God help us if we ever need to get to the spare tire and jack. Sadly, there was no room anywhere for the beer cooler.

I noticed Juanita had something new on her finger. Not the biggest diamond in the world, but it sparkled and was not embarrassingly puny. I gave her a kiss and slipped her eight bucks. Only 15 more payments to go. Both Jean and Norma said they liked it better than her previous ring.

Eventually, we were ready to depart. I handed the Packard keys to Dale.

"Tell your dad it's a little balky going into second," I said.

"Don't worry, Colm. We'll bring it back in just as nice condition. I wish to hell I was going with you."

"You have your new baby to look forward to," said Juanita, taking my arm.

"Another reason to blow town," said Dale. "Remember, Ryan, if you take any orders, we need $500 down. And try to sell them the standard package. Custom changes are a pain."

"I know, Dale," he replied. "I heard all that from Dad."

"And keep it in your pants, pal," he added.

"I'll try," said Ryan without much conviction.

A slime-green Studebaker sped around the corner and screeched to a stop behind the trailer. Both Norma and Jean assumed Slade had arrived to say good-bye to her. I saw no reason why he had to butt in, but at least he donated a bottle of wine to the cause. Later I discovered that the label was marked "Courtesy of the American Plywood Association."

So as not to play favorites the cad kissed all three girls, including my fiancee and the girl I love. Next time I hope he restricts his farewells to Norma.

We climbed into the car: guys in front, girls in the back. Ryan started the big V-8, shifted into gear, and stepped on the gas.

"She feels a lot heavier now," he commented. "I hope we haven't overloaded the trailer axle."

"It's only a few clothes," said Norma. "They can't weigh much."

Some of us waved to Slade, looking forlorn and abandoned at the curb; I waved to Dale.

A mile down the road we pulled over to put up the convertible top. The girls were complaining that the wind was mussing their hair. To minimize ill will they have agreed to a rotational system for occupancy of the middle seat (with its impinging drive-shaft hump).

* * *

Our first stop was Santa Rosa, home of boring chamber music. It used to be a small cow town, but according to Jean has been booming since the war years. The Hitchcock film "Shadow of a Doubt" was filmed there. That's the movie where Uncle Charlie (Joseph Cotton) starts creeping out Teresa Wright. I saw it when I was eight and fell hard for Miss Wright. If I squint my eyes, Jean sort of reminds me of her.

They were having a gas war at an outlying intersection, so we pulled in and topped off the tank for 19 cents a gallon (for premium). The gas jockey tried to give us a free cut-glass tumbler, but Ryan declined on account of its weight.

We parked near downtown, and the girls retreated to the trailer to change, while Ryan put down the top and I hung our banners on the sides of the car. They read: "**Exciting New Beachwear! Cheeky Swimsuits. Ask for them by Name!**" Beside that message was a winking Mr. Cheeky with his slogans "***Why Be Shy?***" below and "***It Ties To Fit***" above. The girls emerged from the trailer in their respective red, yellow, and blue bikinis.

"So what's the plan, Colm?" asked Norma. "God, I wish I was more of an exhibitionist."

"You're the biggest exhibitionist I know," I replied. "Now you girls get in the car and sit on the boot above the folded top. Ryan's going to cruise slowly down the main drag while you wave to the enchanted throngs."

"I did that when I was Prune Queen," said Juanita. "Only I wasn't half-naked at the time."

"Don't complain," said Jean. "At least you're wearing the biggest suit."

"You girls look terrific," said Ryan, getting an eyeful. "I've never seen bikinis that small. Are they legal?"

"We're about to find out," said Norma.

"And what will you be doing, Colm?" asked Jean.

"I have a very important job," I replied. "I'll be sitting in the car and handing out flyers to interested parties."

Ryan pulled into traffic, and we cruised slowly down the main drag. Startled pedestrians stared in amazement. A few returned our waves. Small children gaped and pointed.

"Drive slower," I said to Ryan. "We need people to be able to read all our signs."

We were proceeding at a sedate pace, when a siren sounded behind us. A city cop on a motorcycle pulled us over. He parked his bike and sauntered back to the car.

"Hello, officer," smiled Norma, pulling up a strap.

"What is this" he asked, eyeing the girls. "A parade?"

"We're doing a promotional tour for our new swim wear and trailer," I said.

"Well, you were impeding traffic flow. I could cite you for that."

"It didn't seem like anyone minded," said Juanita, flashing him a radiant smile.

"Say, Miss," he said. "Weren't you queen of the Prune Festival?"

"Why, yes, I was."

"I thought so. Is that a bikini?"

"Yes, it's our new triangular model," I said. "Would you like an informational flyer?"

"Got any literature on that trailer?" he asked. "The missus and I were talking about getting one."

"Right here," said Ryan, handing him a fact sheet. "Sleeps five. Comes fully equipped for only $1,399. Built right up the road in Ukiah."

"Thanks," said the cop. "I'll look it over. Well, keep up with the traffic next time, and good luck on your tour." He tipped his cap and returned to his bike.

"Let that be a lesson to you, Ryan," I said.

"What's that?" he asked.

"Always have three girls in bikinis in your car, and you'll never get a ticket."

"Can we get dressed now?" asked Jean.

"Not now," I replied. "The day has just begun."

* * *

After a quick lunch at a drive-in, we drove to the local newspaper office. I told the girls to go in and ask for the city editor.

"Why?" asked Norma.

"So they can do a story on us," I said. "We're making news here."

Jean and Juanita looked skeptical.

"I can't walk in there," said Juanita. "I'm only half dressed."

"You just rode through the center of town like that," I pointed out.

"That's different," she said. "Theoretically, we could have been headed to the beach."

"I know people who read that paper," said Jean. "I don't want to be in it like this."

"Me neither," said Juanita. "Mr. Flampert reads it and so does my dad."

"We're trying to get publicity here, girls," I said. "That is the point of this trip."

"Fine," said Jean. "But let's get publicity in newspapers my friends don't read. I'll be sitting this one out in the trailer."

"Me too," added Juanita.

Only Norma was brave enough to go in. We didn't get a reporter, but a photographer came out and snapped some photos. He took down our names and accepted our informational flyers. He seemed disappointed that two-thirds of our bikini-modeling team was hiding in the trailer.

"Are they shy or what?" he asked.

"It's the first day of our tour," I explained. "We're still working out some kinks."

After that near debacle we drove south over the hill to Petaluma, a town that's big in chickens and eggs. Hatcheries there ship out thousands of live chicks to farms around the country. Giant henhouses produce eggs by the millions. We did our parade through the center of their Victorian downtown, this time at a speed that didn't impede traffic. We parked at a prime intersection and handed out flyers to curious passers-by. Then the local high school let out, and we had to depart quickly to escape a pack of rowdy teenagers.

"Those kids were sure obnoxious," said Juanita.

"This is making me very self-conscious," said Norma. "Receiving catcalls in a bikini is not something Coco Chanel ever had to endure."

"You're doing great, girls," I said. "Those kids were just jealous of how much fun we're having."

"And when does that start?" asked Jean.

"Right now," I replied. "Ryan, find us a campground."

We checked into a trailer park located in rolling hills north of town. Our assigned space required a tricky dodge around a big tree, but Ryan backed up the trailer in one go.

"Good job," I said.

"Thanks," he replied. "I've been moving trailers since I was 12."

"And what else have you been doing since you were 12?" inquired Norma.

"Hoping to meet someone cute like you," he said with a wink.

Even though it was a warm day and the park had a swimming pool, the girls immediately changed into blouses and shorts. This may not augur well for the broad acceptance of Cheeky Swimsuits. They set out to explore the park while Ryan finished leveling the trailer and connecting various hoses and cords. After that he unhitched and drove back to town for beer and groceries. I hope we can squeeze everything into that midget refrigerator. I don't mind dressing out of a car trunk, but I'm not prepared to guzzle warm beer.

* * *

Since it wasn't the weekend yet, the campground was pleasantly uncrowded. Quite a few of our neighbors dropped by for trailer tours. Ryan demonstrated all the features and gave his best sales pitch. He had to counsel the girls about keeping their stuff put away to make a good impression. Since his dad hopes to sell the trailer as new, we are also under orders not to scratch or spill anything. I left a stack of bikini flyers on the table, but these older mid-week campers were more in the Milady Modest category.

Dinner was barbecued chicken cooked by Jean over a grill that Ryan retrieved from the trailer's exterior storage compartment. We sat around the provided picnic table, and Jean proved again that everything tastes better eaten outdoors. We talked about our previous camping experiences. I had none to report since I had been expelled from the Boy Scouts without ever earning a badge.

"What on earth did you do, honey?" asked Juanita.

"We went on a hike at Coney Island, and I ditched the troop to sneak into a freak show. The Scoutmaster had to call the cops when my absence was discovered. Asked to explain, I told him I'd rather watch a guy pound nails up his nose than learn the names of trees. He told me not to come back."

"I did better," said Ryan. "I made it all the way to Eagle Scout."

"How are you in the woods?" asked Norma.

"Prepared for most anything," he replied. "Even you."

I bought a bundle of wood at the campground store, and Ryan made a fire after the sun went down. We sat around the campfire and roasted marshmallows on twigs. No mosquitos to swat since California summers are so dry. We opened Slade's wine, which was just passable paired with blackened blobs of sugar. Jean had the poor taste to propose a toast to its provider.

Eventually, it was bedtime. I had assumed that Juanita and I would be sharing a bed, but that was not to be. The ladies decided that it would be girls up front and guys on the dinette bed. The trailer may sleep five, but we discovered that no more than two can move about at any one time. Four of us waited outside while Ryan made up the beds (all the bedding had been stowed under the front sofa). Then we sat on the beds while everyone took turns making their solo trips to the dinky bathroom. Teeth were brushed, pajamas donned, and it was time to settle in.

"How wide is this bed?" I asked my bunkmate.

"Forty-two inches. Cozy, huh?"

"Was that as wide as you could make it?" I asked.

"Dad likes roomy aisles since a lot of our customers are on the heavy side."

"Do you snore?" I asked.

"Not much, Colm, but girls tell me I like to snuggle in my sleep."

"There will be no snuggling tonight!"

"I sincerely hope not. Just poke me in the ribs if I try anything."

Norma as the most petite got elected to sleep up in the bunk. She enlisted Ryan to give her a boost up to her perch.

"Goodnight, girls," said Ryan, closing the accordion door. "Pleasant dreams."

"We'll all be dreaming of you," said Jean.

I didn't care for that remark. I asked Ryan which of us was going to sleep landlocked against the wall.

"How many beers did you have?" he asked.

"Three cans plus some wine."

"Well, I had more than that, so I get the aisle," he said, switching off the light.

We settled into our bed like sardines in a can. This was my first experience sharing a bed since those few nights with Katie. I suppose people do it, but I found relaxation difficult. I could hear Ryan's every breath and feel his every movement. I lay there wondering how Jean and Juanita were getting on in their cramped sofa bed.

I woke up sometime later because I was hot. A steamy body was plastered against me and a hand was cupping my right breast. I lashed out with an elbow.

"Omph," muttered my bed-mate.

I climbed out over him, grabbed my robe, and spent the rest of the night in the back seat of the car. The Mercury is a fine automobile, but it wasn't designed to provide a comfortable night's sleep for a six-foot, two-inch guy. Seats in some Nash models fold flat to make a generous bed for two, but that feature hadn't crossed over into Ford products. My robe was warm enough, but my feet got cold, I got a crick in my neck, and generally had a miserable time.

Ryan apologized as we showered in the park's restroom. I apologized back for giving him a bruise on his chest. When we returned to the trailer, we found the door was locked. Ryan knocked on the door.

"What's happening in there?" he asked.

"Juanita's taking a shower and Norma's getting dressed," said Jean from inside. "How much hot water do we have?"

"Six gallons," he replied.

"Oh dear," she said.

At breakfast we discussed the sleeping accommodations.

"We're all living in a small box," said Norma. "We're like shipmates on a submarine. Under the circumstances I think we should dispense with conventional privacy concerns. Juanita can sleep with Colm. I'll sleep with Ryan. And Jean can take the bunk."

"Sounds fine to me," I said.

"OK by me," said Ryan.

"Why can't I sleep with Ryan?" asked Jean.

"That's easy," I replied. "Norma is smaller. She won't crowd Ryan as much."

"Well, I may crowd him a bit," she leered.

"I'd prefer not to listen to people having sex," said Jean.

"Right," I said. "Sex is off the menu. Agreed?"

The vote by show of hands was 3 to 2, so the measure carried.

Chapter 23

Getting five people ready to go took forever. It just goes to show what a feat the D-Day invasion was. We did a quick cruise down the main street of San Rafael in Marin, then crossed the new bridge to Richmond. At over five miles, it's one of the longest in the world. Nice view of San Francisco Bay and the distant city from the top. Our destination was the hillside campus of U.C. Berkeley, teeming with coeds eager for the latest in trendy swim wear. We parked on Telegraph Avenue, a busy street just south of campus. Not only can Ryan back up with aplomb, he effortlessly parallel-parked our combo into an impossibly tight space.

"That was amazing," said Norma. "You're a genius at parking."

"So the girls tell me," he replied.

The girls lounged on the boot and answered questions as Ryan kept the frat boys back and I passed out flyers.

"How far are you going?" asked a coed.

"To the tip of South America," Norma lied. "We started in January in Alaska. My first winter in a bikini."

"Do you all sleep in that trailer?" asked her friend.

"We do," said Juanita. "It's very comfortable."

"Who sleeps with whom? asked a fellow in sunglasses.

"We rotate partners," said Norma. "That way no one gets jealous."

"Do you really?" asked a fat girl.

"She's kidding," said Jean. "It's strictly business. We're all just friends."

"Have you had any trouble with cops?" asked a frat boy.

"Not at all," said Norma. "Our bikinis are accepted everywhere. I even wore one to church last Sunday, and the preacher complimented me from the pulpit."

That got a laugh from the crowd.

"Who designed them?" asked a girl. "They're kind of radical."

"I did," replied Norma. "They come in the three color-coded sizes you see here and adust to fit anyone."

"I like them," commented a pretty girl, "but I'd have to hide it from my mother."

"I wouldn't be caught dead in a bathing suit that I didn't have to hide from my mother," said Norma.

"What do you do for fun?" asked an older gent.

"Fun," said Norma, "Uh, let's see . . . We *must* have done something fun . . ."

"We had a cookout last night," said Juanita.

"And I brought along some books to read," added Jean.

"Have you read *The Catcher in the Rye*?" someone asked.

"I not only read it," replied Norma, "I dated Holden Caulfield all through college."

"How was he?" asked a girl.

"Kind of depressed when I met him," said Norma. "But I soon set him on a sunnier path."

"Is the girl in blue available for lunch?" asked a husky guy in a varsity jacket.

Juanita held out her hand to show off my ring. "Not any more. Sorry."

"Who's the lucky guy?" he asked.

"He is," said Norma, pointing to Ryan. "But I'm trying to break them up."

"Are you getting paid to do this?" asked a fellow who looked like an accounting major.

"We're getting paid $500 a week," lied Norma. "And next year we'll be hiring lots more girls–but only if they send us a photo of them wearing a Cheeky Swimsuits bikini."

* * *

At noon we drove straight down Telegraph Avenue to Oakland. You don't hear much about that burg, but they have a real big-city downtown. We did our parade, then ate lunch in Oakland's Chinatown. The Santa Clara and Central valleys send vast truckloads of fruits and vegetables to Oakland for processing in their canneries. I'm told the East Bay also makes cars and bulldozers, and has a busy port and big Navy base. After lunch we crossed the Bay Bridge and did our parade around San Francisco. We were hoping to park near Union Square, but on a busy Friday afternoon not even Ryan could find a spot big enough for a car and trailer. So we found our way to Highway 101 and headed down the peninsula to Palo Alto. We parked outside the gates of Stanford University and chatted up the passing students. Those kids must have more money than Cal students. Several girls wanted to buy suits on the spot. Too bad we hadn't had the space to bring along some inventory.

We parked for the night in a trailer park off 101 in a little town called Sunnyvale. Mostly orchards and small farms around there. According to our road map, we were at the southernmost tip of San Francisco Bay. A path led down to some mud flats along the water's edge. Ryan got out his fishing pole and went to try his luck. Jean and Juanita hiked along the shoreline, while Norma and I relaxed on the patio with beers.

"So, what do you think of our driver?" I asked.

"He's P.D.S."

"What's that?"

"Pretty damn sexy."

"Enough to make you forget Slade?"

"Slade is the kind of man you marry. Ryan is the kind of guy you have fun with."

"Will you be able to keep your hands off him in bed tonight?"

"My hands maybe. I'm not sure about the rest of me."

"Don't forget Jean will be right above you."

"We'll wait 'til she's asleep. She's kind of a prude, Colm."

"I don't think so, Norma."

"She looks good with her clothes off, I'll concede that. Too bad you'll never get to sleep with her."

"I haven't entirely given up hope."

"She's too upright to let you cheat on Juanita with her."

"God, you're depressing me, Norma. Let's change the subject."

"I've got some new ideas for Milady Modest designs."

"Good."

"I'm really getting into swimsuits for problem figures."

"Why do you suppose that is?"

"Anybody can design a suit for somebody like Jean or Juanita. But getting our Miss Page dressed for the beach and looking good, now that's a challenge."

* * *

We played poker for matchsticks until bedtime. Ryan was the big winner, and is now fully equipped to start fires or take up smoking. Then the beds were made up and pajamas donned. I assisted Jean in her assent to the bunk; I didn't want Ryan feeling up the girl I love. I closed the accordion door and climbed into bed with Juanita. Clearly a vast step up from Ryan as a bed-mate. Except quite a few days had passed since our interlude in my bedroom. Juices had accumulated and tensions built up. Being confined horizontally with Juanita in a mere 42" of space was not conducive to sleep–or continued abstinence. She kissed me goodnight and rolled over to face the wall. I nuzzled the back of her neck, and slipped an arm over and grasped a breast.

"What are you doing?" she whispered.

"Getting comfortable," I said, pressing my erection against her.

I pulled up her nightgown, and my wandering hand found the mound between her legs. I slipped a finger into her wetness and began gentle stroking.

"You shouldn't do that," she whispered.

"Shhh," I replied, not stopping.

She came without making a sound, then rolled over and returned the favor with a warm hand inside my pajamas. I gushed out extravagant quantities.

"Uh-oh," she whispered. "Now what am I supposed to do?

"I don't know," I whispered. "Wipe it on my pajamas, I guess."

"There's too much."

"What's going on back there?" inquired Jean, her voice resounding from up on high like some celestial divinity's.

I faked a sneeze. "Nothing," I said. "I'm just getting up to get a tissue."

I hopped out of bed and retrieved one from the bathroom for Juanita.

"If this were a movie, you'd be dying in the next reel," observed Norma.

"Not for a sneeze," I replied. "The movie convention is a cough signals the person has a fatal malady. Is everyone comfortable?"

"I am," said Ryan.

"Me too," said Norma.

"The mattress up here is awfully thin," said Jean. "I suggest you sleep in the bunk tomorrow, Colm."

"I'll think about it," I lied.

I fell asleep soon after and slept soundly until morning. Whether anyone else was fooling around in the dark I couldn't say.

* * *

We were no faster getting on the road the next day. After the usual scramble for the midget shower, Jean made a big breakfast. Then came lingering over coffee, idle chatter, and clean-up. Then the stowing away of stuff and hitching up the trailer.

Our first stop was in nearby San Jose. We paraded through its compact downtown, then found the newspaper office. This time we got both a reporter and a photographer. Since none of us knew anyone who read the San Jose paper, all the girls participated in the interview. The reporter was a state-college journalism major hired for the summer. She seemed more taken with the trailer than Cheeky Swimsuits, but she said she'd try to get our story on the front page of the local news section.

Should I ever decide to live in the Bay Area, I might pick San Jose. It's a small city of pleasant neighborhoods surrounded by serene, unspoiled country. Everywhere you go are lovely views of hills to the east and west. San Francisco is an easy drive up uncongested Highway 101. Not much industry except for a few small electronics companies doing something with transistors. I don't expect that will amount to much.

Leaving the Bay Area, we headed west over a narrow, winding mountain road to the seaside town of Santa Cruz. Some fellows in this town have adopted a curious Hawaiian water sport called "surfing." They haul long boards into the surf and attempt to stand on them while riding the crests of waves. Ryan and I agreed that might be fun to try sometime.

We rolled through downtown, waved to the few pedestrians (Jean said everyone was at the beach), then drove up into forested hills and checked into a state park. Festooned with mighty redwood trees, the campground was more scenic than typical trailer parks, but provided no electric outlet for the trailer's power cord. We would have to make do with the trailer's built-in propane lantern for light.

We decided to try something new in this town: showcase Cheeky Swimsuits on an actual beach. We unhitched and drove back to town. Since it was a busy summer weekend, the streets leading to the beach were clogged with cars. We parked blocks away and hoofed it. The beach was like a mini Coney Island: a broad swath of sand with a fishing wharf and small amusement park. We had lunch in a seafood restaurant at the end of the pier, then headed back to the beach. Hordes of people lounged on the sand, but only a few little kids were splashing in the water. We found a spot and spread out our blankets and towels. Mechanical organ music wafted over from the distant merry-go-round, and we could hear screams from the plunging roller-coaster cars.

"How big do you think this crowd is?" I asked.

"I'd say two or three thousand at least," said Ryan.

"OK, girls," I said. "You can remove your blouses and shorts now."

"Do we have to?" asked Jean.

"That is the whole point of this expedition, Jean. It's why we're paying you the big bucks."

"What big bucks?" asked Norma.

"You're getting a free vacation," I pointed out. "Plus, valuable insights into what girls at the beach are wearing these days."

"They're all wearing more than us," said Juanita. "A lot more."

"Strip, girls," I commanded.

They did so reluctantly. Necks swivelled as nearby beach-goers turned to stare.

"You're getting a nice tan, Jean," said Norma. "I look like someone dating a mummy in his crypt."

"Can't you tan?" asked Ryan, sporting one of the supreme tans on the beach.

"Nobody in my family can. We just burn and blister, then perish from sunstroke."

"Well, try not to do that today," I said. "A corpse makes a very poor model for a bikini."

"Are we going in the water, honey?" asked Juanita. "I'm getting hot."

"Maybe later," I said. "Right now we're going to walk casually around the beach. I'll pass out flyers to anyone who inquires. Ryan, you stay here and guard our stuff."

"How about I stay here and guard Ryan?" said Norma.

"This way, girls," I said. "On the double."

My plan might have worked had we come on a weekday. I had neglected to consider the perverse psychology of crowds. As we walked along we began to be followed by several young rowdies, calling out taunts. This grew into a pack of ruffians who got bolder in their comments. Hoping to escape them, we ducked into the park's arcade, but were quickly ejected by a security guard. As the mob swarmed toward us, I threatened to slug several drunken oafs who were daring each other to grab and pull bikini ties.

We kept backing away, then the girls escaped into a ladies restroom.

"OK, guys, the show's over," I said. You can go back to the beach now."

"They ain't gonna be in there forever," said one smiling tough.

"I got no place to go," said another. "I can wait. I think that girl in blue likes me."

"I got dibs on the doll in yellow!" someone shouted.

A guy peered around the restroom entrance. "Hey, girlies," he called. "Come on out! Everybody went away!"

"Yeah," yelled another lout. "We have dispersed!"

Right then Ryan arrived with our gear. Now I felt slightly less outnumbered.

"Take a powder, guys," he said. "The cops are on their way."

"We ain't doin' nothing," someone muttered.

"Yeah," said a kid who looked to be about 14. "This here is a public beach."

A middle-aged lady in what could have been a Milady Modest suit emerged warily from the restroom and was greeted by several ironic wolf whistles. At Ryan's request she took the bags inside to the girls. After several minutes they came out dressed again in street clothes as a pair of city cops showed up. As if on cue, the crowd melted away.

"What's the story here?" asked the taller of the cops.

"I don't know," I said, indignantly. "We were walking to the refreshment stand, when we were accosted by a pack of hoodlums. I thought this was a family park."

"You didn't say anything or do anything?" asked the other cop.

"Not at all, officers," said Ryan. "We were minding our own business."

"Were you dressed like that, Miss?" the first cop asked Juanita.

"Yes, I was," she lied.

"We're here with a Christian youth group," added Norma. "We always dress modestly. Bathing suits are the work of the devil!"

The cop shrugged. "Well, I apologize for the trouble. It should be OK now. Let us know if anyone bothers you again."

"We shall!" said Norma. "And my pastor will be writing a letter to the authorities!"

Chapter 24

Juanita sighed, "Well, that was discouraging." Back at the trailer we were drinking beers. Jean had made an avocado snack called guacamole that we were scooping up with corn chips. It was a food unknown on the east coast, but I rather liked it.

"I fear you may be ahead of your time with this mini bikini idea," said Jean.

"I'm not so sure about that," I replied.

"You aren't discouraged by the riot we almost started?" asked Juanita.

"I don't think the circumstances were typical of most beaches," I said. "For one thing they sold beer there. Plus, jerks are always bolder in big crowds. Plus, we had three of you in bikinis. That's a lot of skin on display."

"Colm's right," said Norma. "If we'd stayed put on the beach, we probably would have been OK. Things are always more provocative in motion. But we're doing something new here, so you have to allow for a few problems."

"Like almost getting attacked?" asked Jean.

"We were there to protect you," I said. "Right Ryan?"

"We would have fought to the last man," he affirmed.

"I feel very safe with Ryan nearby," said Norma, taking his hand.

"How about making the triangles bigger?" suggested Juanita.

"The triangles are fine," I replied. "It just takes time for people to get used to seeing them. Remember, we're showing our bikinis on three very attractive models. On your average-looking girls the reaction won't be so extreme."

"He's right," said Norma. "We're too beautiful and sexy for our own good."

"You're all gorgeous," conceded Ryan. "So far I haven't sold a single trailer, but I hardly give a damn."

"You're so sweet, Ryan," said Norma. "I can't think of anyone I'd rather share a trailer bed with."

"I'm sleeping with him tonight," said Jean.

"Over my dead body," replied Norma.

"That's enough, girls," I said. "I'm captain of this ship. I'll determine who sleeps with whom."

Someone knocked on the open trailer door.

"Can we look at your trailer?" asked a fellow camper.

"Sure," said Ryan. "Come on in!"

* * *

We decided to stay put the next day, which was Sunday. I made that executive decision after a miserable night tossing about on the thin mattress in the bunk. I slept up there to free Jean to bunk with Juanita instead of Ryan. I like Ryan, he's a great guy, but the prospect of his snuggling all night with Jean was too painful to contemplate. As it was I had to listen to some suspicious sounds from directly below. Perhaps not actual intercourse, but clearly he and Norma were up to something.

After breakfast we aired out the bedding, swept the trailer, and Ryan and girls hauled the laundry down to a coin-op place in a town called Felton. I snoozed on the sofa in between giving trailer tours. An elderly couple in a teardrop decided they'd had it with vacationing in a small tin can, and agreed to move up to a roomy new Ukstream. They couldn't wait for Ryan to return, so I had them fill out a contract and took their check for the $500 deposit. I told them a closet could *not* be substituted for the shower, but said we might be able to do yellow appliances instead of pink. They were thrilled, and I was relieved to return to my nap.

Ryan was impressed with my salesmanship. He said he would check with his dad about the appliance change.

Norma had scrounged up a San Jose paper in Felton. We found this small story on an inside page of the second section:

> **Bikini Innovators**
> **Visit Here on**
> **State-wide Tour**
>
> SAN JOSE – How small can a swimsuit go? Apparently, much smaller than current styles. That is the hope of Colm and Norma Moran, a young married couple who are touring the state in a trailer to introduce their new Cheeky Swimsuits.
>
> Their innovation is a tiny bikini formed of triangles held together by thin straps. "It can adjust to any body shape and size," said Mrs. Moran, 22, a petite gradu-

> ate of Boston's elite Emerson College. She was modeling their red suit, featuring the barest minimum of fabric. Two larger sizes were demonstrated by professional models Jean Valland and Juanita Howe. All are from Ukiah, Mendocino County, where their new firm is located.
>
> Also touring with them is Ryan Deming, 24, whose family builds the trailer. A recent graduate of Chico State College, he said that travel trailers represent "the wave of the future" for family vacations.
>
> The enterprising young business people expect to reach San Diego by next week.

Accompanying the article was a blurry photo also squeezed down to one column. The only things clearly discernable were Juanita's scantily clad breasts.

"Why do you suppose she thought we were married?" asked Norma.

"Colm looks like the marrying kind," said Jean. "That's why he's forever getting engaged."

"Well, he's engaged to me now," said Juanita. "I'm flattered that she thought I was a professional model."

"You're all pretty enough to be models," I said. "Too bad they ran the photo so small."

"You can't see the trailer at all," complained Ryan. "My last name has two 'M's and I'm 22 not 24."

"Give her a break, guys," said Norma. "She's only a student. This is really fantastic."

"Why exactly?" asked Jean.

"It proves we're making news," said Norma. "Los Angeles here we come! Fame and glory await us!"

* * *

Our accommodation problems seem to have become intractable. It was Ryan's turn to take the bunk, but Jean and Norma refused to sleep together. Juanita didn't want me to sleep with either of the other girls. I, of course, objected to Jean sleeping with Ryan. All of which left me with three choices: the bunk, the car, or back to cuddling with Ryan. So at bedtime I found myself once again with my nose a foot from the ceiling on the thinly padded bunk.

"This mattress is a joke," I complained.

"It's intended for kids," said Ryan, snuggling below me with you know who.

"I'm going to sue your father for sleep deprivation," I said.

"We can stop in the next town and get you an air mattress," said Ryan. "That should make it more comfortable."

"Right. And put me even closer to the ceiling. I don't see why I can't take the front bed with Norma."

"I'm more than willing," she replied.

"We've already discussed this," said Juanita. "I'll take the bunk if you'll sleep with Ryan."

"Ryan can't keep his hands to himself," I pointed out.

"I'm not minding that at all," said Norma.

"Enough!" hissed Jean. "Don't be a baby, Colm. Go to sleep."

"I wish I were a baby," I said. "A baby would fit up here better."

After a long night, morning finally arrived. I drank four cups of coffee and eventually became semi-awake. We hit the road, and did our wave tours through Monterey, Salinas, Paso Robles, Atascadero, and San Luis Obispo. After that last town Highway 101 veers back to the coast. We stopped for the night at a trailer park right on the ocean in Pismo Beach. The waves rolled in just a few dozen feet from our campsite. A couple of seagulls strolled over to watch Ryan back in the trailer and level it.

"This is very pleasant," said Norma. "It's like the California you see in postcards."

"Why don't you girls go swimming?" I suggested.

"Do you see anyone in the water?" asked Jean.

"You mean the water's cold all the way down here?" I asked.

"It might be a degree or two warmer," she replied. "But inviting it's not."

We had beers on the patio, then walked into town for dinner. We ate in a Mexican restaurant a block up from the beach. They may have Mexican restaurants back east, but I never encountered any. The food is quite a bit different. Interesting spices, but my dish was spoiled by a nasty green herb called cilantro that tasted like soap. I picked it out as best I could. I did like the Mexican beer though and a custard-like dessert called flan.

After dinner we strolled along the beach. The setting sun lent a golden glow to the palm trees waving in the breeze above our trailer. It all seemed exotically tropical to me.

Bedtime was not as rancorous tonight as Jean was willing to try out the Army-surplus air mattress we'd bought in Salinas. She went back up to the bunk, and I went back to Juanita's welcome embrace on the dinette bed. We got reacquainted as silently as we could, then fell asleep in each other's arms.

* * *

Sometime after midnight we were awakened by a knock on the door.

I leaned over Juanita and looked out the window. Parked outside was an unpleasantly familiar car. I got up and opened the door.

"Hello, Slade," I said. "What brings you here in the middle of the night?"

"Can I come in?" he asked.

"Sure. Why not? All we were doing was sleeping."

Slade entered, and I switched on a light. Norma slid open the accordion door and attempted to give her man a kiss. He pulled back and held her at arm's length.

"Hello, Norma," he said. "I, uh, need to talk to Juanita."

"What about, honey?" Norma asked.

"Uh, it's kind of personal. Juanita, could you see me outside?"

Juanita looked stricken. "Has something happened to Ramona?" she asked.

"Not at all," he replied. "Everything's fine. I just need to discuss something with you."

"All right, Slade," she said, reaching for her robe.

"What's this all about?" I asked.

"It's, uh, a personal matter," said Slade. "I'm sorry to disturb you all. You can go back to sleep."

"As if," said Norma. "Slade, honey, you're acting kind of strange."

"I know," he said. "This isn't really like me. But it's important I talk to Juanita."

Exiting the trailer, the two of them went and sat in Slade's Studebaker.

"Shall I make some coffee?" asked Jean.

"Might as well," I said. "We're all awake now."

"I was having a great dream too," said Ryan, yawning.

"What was it, honey?" asked Norma.

"I was designing this terrific trailer. It was 50 feet long and two stories high."

"I hope it had real beds for everyone," I said.

"It did," he replied. "It had a rooftop swimming pool too, but I was still working out how to support the weight."

"Sounds tremendously boring," said Norma. "I hope Slade didn't mind that I was sleeping with you, Ryan dear."

"If you wish, Norma," said Jean. "I can say I was."

We were sitting on the beds sipping our coffee when they returned.

"Well, what was that all about?" I asked.

"I'm sorry, Colm," said Juanita. "We have an announcement to make that's going to upset some people. We don't wish to hurt anyone."

"Juanita and I are in love," said Slade. "We intend to get married."

"What!" exclaimed Norma.

I was stunned. "Uh, isn't this rather sudden?" I gasped.

"I'm sorry, Colm," said Juanita. "We discovered that the feelings we had for each other were mutual. I have to break off our engagement. I'm sorry to hurt you like this."

"I smell a rat," said Norma. "Jean, is this your handiwork?"

Jean sipped her coffee. "I discovered quite unintentionally how each of them felt about the other. I thought it was my duty to help bring them together."

"It was a series of misunderstandings between us," said Slade. "Somehow our communication was totally off. We've corrected that now."

"And where do I fit in?" demanded Norma.

"Face it, Norma," I said. "You don't. And neither do I. Well, I wish you both the best. You've got a great girl there, Slade."

Norma clutched Ryan's arm. "Hey, Slade! Here's a bulletin: I like Ryan better anyway. I've been sleeping with him all this trip!"

"That's fine," said Slade. "I'm glad you found someone."

"And here's another tidbit for you," continued Norma. "Colm here has been screwing your new bride to be."

"I know that," said Slade, coldly. "She already told me."

"It was only the one time," noted Juanita. "And we were engaged at the time."

"So, what are your plans?" asked Jean.

"Slade's tired," said Juanita. "He's been driving all day. He's going to a motel. I guess I'm going with him. We'll be back in the morning to collect my stuff."

Juanita handed me some folded bills.

"What's this?" I asked.

"It's your eight dollars, Colm. I have 30 days to return the ring, so I'm sending it back to Sears."

"I'm giving her my grandmother's ring," said Slade.

"I'm glad you're marrying someone else," said Norma. "I wouldn't want to be stuck with a guy who mugs his own granny for a ring."

"My grandmother's dead," he retorted.

"What did you do, strangle her?" she asked. "And chop off her ring finger with an ax?"

"Let's go, Juanita," said Slade. "Some people are not very understanding."

* * *

Between the coffee and the wrenching alteration to my life, I didn't get much sleep that night. Jean went back up in the bunk, so I did have 42 inches of expansive bed all to myself. I kind of missed Juanita though.

She returned as we were finishing breakfast. So as not to spark further discord, Slade remained in his car while she packed

Norma had a question for her. "If you were so stuck on Slade, how come you fixed him up with me?"

"You specified someone with a great chin, Norma, and he was all I could think of."

"Right, except it would also give you a chance to see him again," she pointed out.

"Actually, I didn't want to see him again. I agreed to the double date, but only reluctantly."

"That's right," I confirmed.

"I wasn't trying to be devious, Norma," said Juanita. "Although I would have been surprised if it had lasted with you two."

"Hah!" she replied.

"I'm sorry to leave you short of a swimsuit model, Colm."

"That's OK, Juanita. Ryan knows a girl from college who lives in L.A. She might work out for us."

So we said good-bye to Juanita. I gave her a farewell kiss and carried her bag out to the car. Despite this setback, I would always regard her as my best-ever blind date. Some of us waved as they drove off. I turned and looked at Jean.

"I hope this means we're now engaged," I said.

"Hardly. Last I heard you're still set to marry Girl Number Two back east."

"I'm planning on terminating that."

"Well, there's a payphone by the office. Do you need some change?"

"I've got rolls of quarters and dimes for emergencies."

"Good. I'll go with you."

"You intend to listen in on my call?"

"I do, Colm. Otherwise, God knows what she'll get you to agree to."

Betty was there when I called. I told her the news in no uncertain terms. She did not get me to reschedule our wedding to next week, join a bank training program, or adopt any children. Our relationship is now over, even though her mother already had put down a hefty deposit on the Waldorf Astoria ballroom. Betty was understandably upset, but I didn't hear any tears. She did say I was a "lightweight" who "would never amount to much." I told her I would still keep her in mind when I was casting my future films. On that note, the conversation ended.

"There's only one girl in my life now," I announced as I hung up the phone.

"Oh?" said Jean. "Anyone I know?"

I grabbed her and kissed her. This time she kissed me back.

Chapter 25

Since it was so pleasant by the ocean, and we were sort of on vacation, and some of us were getting over love disappointments, we decided to stay another day in Pismo Beach. It was fortunate we did because Ryan sold another trailer. So far the trailer business is looking a lot more lucrative than abbreviated bikinis.

After lunch Norma suggested that Jean and I take in a matinee at the movie theater in town.

"Oh, what's playing?" I asked.

"I have no idea," said Norma. "But I'm sure you'll enjoy it."

"I think we may be in the way here, Jean," I said.

"Yes, I'm getting that feeling too."

I took Jean's hand as we walked toward Pismo's compact downtown. This felt like the right time to bring up a touchy subject.

"Considering that I was engaged to Juanita, I think I'm owed an explanation for what happened."

"I can tell you what I know."

"Please do."

"OK, Slade inherits this old Leica camera from his uncle. He starts taking photographs for his magazine. He buys his film at Flamperts."

"So being a handsome flirt, he chats up Juanita. Had she known him before?"

"*All* girls in Ukiah know Slade. Or at least know of him. She's thrilled when he asks her out."

"Right, like you were."

"Exactly. So they go out for a while, and they like each other. Everything's going swimmingly for both of them. One thing leads to another, and she tells him she can't sleep with him because birth control doesn't work for her and her sisters."

"Right. I got the same speech. So Slade acts like a cad and ditches her."

"Wrong. He decides she's telling him that because she's saving herself for Reggie. He figures he's serious, but she's not. And I suspect his male ego was offended."

"OK, touchy Slade stops phoning. Then what happens?"

"Slade is having trouble getting over Juanita. He asks out her friend Alice Thorton to try and find out what's up with her. Juanita hears about that and concludes Slade is a frivolous guy only interested in sex. And then you show up and start taking her out."

"I hope that pissed him off."

"Strangely it did. Even stranger, he decides he can't compete with you because you're a handsome Yale graduate with family money."

"Quite a sensible reaction. So why did he decide to butt in now?"

"I don't know if you've noticed, but I'd been going on walks with Juanita. With a bit of coaxing, she confided that she was marrying you to make the best of her situation."

"Hey, that was my reason for marrying her!"

"Yeah, tell me about it. I got her to confess that the guy she really loves is Slade Preston. Naturally, I called him with that news."

"But didn't you want Slade for yourself?"

"To put it bluntly, I did not."

"Then why were you going out with him?"

"Because he asked me to."

More confirmation that women are unfathomably mysterious.

"So why did he sleep with Norma if he loved Juanita?"

"She got him drunk and then took off her clothes. He did what most guys would do in that situation. Wouldn't you?"

"I don't think so–not with Norma. Not unless I were really drunk. It would take a lot of booze to neutralize her high annoyance factors. So does Slade mind that I slept with Juanita?"

"He's not thrilled about it, of course. Nor is she too happy that Norma got her claws into him."

"Do you mind that I slept with Juanita?"

"Of course, I mind. Nor did I appreciate all that fooling around in the trailer. You were supposed to be sleeping."

"Well, we were sleeping most of the time. And I'm accepting that you slept with Peter the horny potter."

"Who says I slept with him?"

"Didn't you? You went camping overnight with him."

"I told you, Peter's just a friend. I don't think he's particularly interested in girls."

"Oh. Why didn't you tell me that at the time?"

"Why do you think?"

"To make me jealous?"

"Hmm. You're smarter than you look."

* * *

The movie playing in Pismo was "Loving You," a Technicolor musical starring that pelvis-gyrating rock and roll singer. Jean was more than willing to see it, but I refused. I was not going to spend 90 cents (for two tickets) to underwrite that smirking redneck's movie career.

"What should we do instead?" asked Jean.

"I don't know if you noticed, but we just walked down a street lined with budget motels."

"We have no luggage and I'm not exhibiting a wedding ring."

"This is a resort town, darling. They may not care."

We stopped at a drug store first. Jean waited outside while I secured the goods. This time the clerk was a grandmotherly type who seemed personally offended that I was proposing to wallow in sin. She rang up the sale grimly and dropped the change into my palm without touching my hand.

We got a $5.50 room overlooking a parking lot. It was clean though and the double bed looked inviting.

"It's come to this has it?" said Jean. "An illicit afternoon rendezvous in some nameless motel."

"It's not nameless, darling," I said, embracing her. "It's called the Capri Lodge, named after the pants."

"I'll be sure to note that in my diary. And to think I owe all of this to Elvis Presley."

"With some help from Slade Preston," I pointed out, kissing her.

The activities commenced. I don't think anyone was disappointed. As for me it was the greatest afternoon of my life. Every time I thought of getting up and putting on my clothes, I decided that more nuzzling, fondling, etc. was required.

"Is this a casual fling or do we have a future?" Jean inquired as I nibbled on an earlobe.

"I thought we were engaged."

"Well, no one's asked me about that."

"Will you marry me, darling?"

"I suppose I should. Otherwise, you'll probably become engaged to someone else."

"There's always that risk," I admitted. "We could get married here tomorrow. Norma and Ryan could be our witnesses."

"I don't think so. You'll need to discuss this matter with my father."

"Damn. What a gruesome ordeal that's going to be."

"Very likely. It's a shame your uncle reported all your youthful escapades to my father."

"I'm the victim of vicious gossip."

“You’ll just have to convince him that you’ve matured.”

“Fat chance of that. Why are girls’ fathers such ogres?”

“My dad has only my welfare at heart. He may warm up to you in time.”

“If you ask me, he seems entirely too possessive.”

“He’s just being protective. He doesn’t want me to marry some idiot.”

“Well, I’m not an idiot.”

“No, dear, most of the time you’re not.”

When we got back, Norma and Ryan looked as satiated as I felt.

“How was the movie?” asked Norma.

“Not bad if you like that Presley kid,” I replied. “Did you hear the news?”

“What news?” asked Ryan.

“Jean and I are engaged,” I replied.

“Damn, Colm!” exclaimed Norma. “You must have a morbid fear of being single. How many hours were you unattached?”

“Too many,” I said.

“Congratulations,” said Ryan. “This calls for a celebration. How about you take us all out for steaks?”

“OK,” I said, “but it’s going to put a dent in our travel budget.”

“Don’t forget we’re saving Juanita’s salary and per diem,” said Norma.

“That’s true,” I said. “And how often does a guy get engaged?”

“Only once so far to me,” said Jean.

* * *

We got back very late. The restaurant featured a quartet that played jazzy standards, so we danced. I may be a useless parasite on society, but at least I dance well. Ryan did OK too. I danced mostly with Jean, but sometimes we switched partners. Norma tried to kiss me during a rhumba, but I told her to behave. Nothing like becoming engaged to enhance one’s attractiveness to other females.

Tonight I shared my 42" bed with Jean. She’s a more restless sleeper than Juanita. At one point I got a sharp elbow to the nose; it didn’t bleed that much. After we’re married, we may have to have twin beds like those chaste couples on TV. Or I could learn to sleep in a catcher’s mask.

We hitched up and resumed out trek south. For our waving tour through the sleepy town of Santa Maria, the girls moved up a notch in modesty: Norma wore yellow and Jean blue. I think we still woke up a few folks. An hour or two south of there we passed through a tunnel and came out by the ocean again. On this stretch of coast the highway parallels railroad tracks. Must be a scenic ride for train passengers.

We had a picnic lunch by the side of the road on the outskirts of Santa Barbara. We were less than a hundred miles from Los Angeles, but this area looked so inviting we decided to spend the night. We got a space in a little trailer park right on the beach. The old guy in the shack of an office charged us four bucks, which is double what we had been paying.

After getting parked and leveled we walked up to town. With its red-tile roofs Santa Barbara resembles a hillside town in Spain. I'm told movie stars have weekend homes in the area. We encountered none on our stroll up the downtown's classy main street. We went into a women's dress shop, and Norma took off her clothes. With some prompting so did Jean. The owner of the store was so taken with the Cheeky Swimsuits they were modeling, she ordered a dozen of each size.

"These are unlike anything I've ever seen before," she said. "They're daring but practical too."

"We're getting a tremendous response to them," said Norma. "We've also completely revamped our Milady Modest line. Shall I have our rep call with samples when they're ready?"

"Why not," she replied. "I might be interested if they're as innovative as these."

"Norma's doing miracles now with problem figures," I said.

"Most of our clientele work hard to maintain their trim figures, but we do get our share of difficult cases."

"We can fit anyone up to 400 pounds," I said.

"Thankfully our ladies are seldom that extreme," she laughed.

To make up for blowing the budget, Jean made a thrifty dinner tonight in the trailer. We opened a bottle of wine to celebrate Cheeky Swimsuits' first sale.

"This has been a fun trip," said Ryan, refilling everyone's glasses. "It'll be tough going home and getting back to work."

"We should just stay on the road forever, honey," said Norma. "You can take orders for trailers, and I'll mail my new designs back to Ukiah. How does that sound?"

"Sounds fine to me, but my parents may have a different opinion. What about Colm and Jean? Are they coming with us?"

"Nah, we're dumping them. We need our privacy, baby."

"I'd miss Jean's cooking though," he replied.

"Hey, I can cook too," she said. "You should have seen the pie I baked for Slade."

"That's curious," said Jean. "Your landlady is famous for her pies. She always takes the blue ribbon at the county fair. She decorates her top crust with a heart like you do."

"Just one of those coincidences, I guess," said Norma. "So, Colm, should we stop in Sears tomorrow and pick out a ring for your latest fiancee?"

"No need to," I replied. "Jean's going to wear her mother's ring."

"Letting him off easy, huh Jean?" said Norma.

"Never," she replied.

* * *

Figuring we'd have a busy day in L.A., we got an early start the next morning. Along the way we stopped for breakfast in a town called Ventura. Going into the restaurant, I paused to buy a *Los Angeles Times* from a rack. I divvied up the sections, which we read over our eggs. Scanning an inside page, I spotted a small item near the bottom. The headline read:

Fire Destroys
Clothing Firm

Even though there are probably hundreds of clothing firms in the state, I sensed immediately it was Milady Modest. Too bad my intuition proved correct. Only two small paragraphs of information, all of it bad. The fire had started at night and swept the premises. The loss was believed total. No one was injured. Authorities were investigating. Arson was suspected.

I got my rolls of coins and used the restaurant payphone. The Ukiah operator connected me to Wendell's home number. He answered on the second ring and gave me one new piece of news. A neighbor had spotted someone loitering near the building right before the fire. The description matched Madame Aranson.

"Have they arrested her?" I asked.

"Not yet, but the police are looking for her," he said.

"Did anything get salvaged?"

"Nothing, Colm. The fire was too intense. All the inventory and stock are gone. All the patterns, all the equipment, and all the business records. A couple of walls are still standing, but that's it."

"Did you call my father?"

"I did. The next morning."

"How did he take it?"

"Surprisingly well, Colm. Your father is remarkably unflappable. Of course, I assured him that our insurance was up to date. I'm meeting with the claims adjuster today."

"Good. We'll turn around now and head back. We should get there tonight sometime."

"I'm sorry this happened, Colm. I never imagined that woman could be so vindictive."

"Yeah, I guess she didn't appreciate being replaced. She must be a little crazy."

"More than a little, I should think."

Ryan was shocked, Jean was sympathetic, and Norma was pissed.

"I never met the bitch," said Norma as we sped back up Highway 101. "But you could tell she was nuts. All you had to do was look at her psychotic bathing suits."

"Some of them weren't that bad," I said, feeling guilty for instigating her dismissal.

"Colm, the woman was an arsonist before she lit the first match," she replied. "Her designs were like setting your eyeballs on fire."

"I hope, Norma, you made copies of your designs," I said.

"All my copies are in my head, Colm. I never forget a design. The problem is in recreating the patterns. That's a huge task. Am I out of a job, Colm?"

"Of course not. We're going to work hard and be back in production before you know it."

"I hope so. Otherwise, I may be picking out fabrics for trailer interiors. No offense, Ryan baby, but those trailer curtains make me want to vomit."

"Don't tell that to my mom, Norma. She does all our interior designs."

"Oh, am I meeting your mother sometime?" she asked.

"Uh, if you want to."

"I'll think about it."

Chapter 26

It was nearly dark when we rolled into Ukiah. We dropped off Norma first.

"Will I be getting a paycheck tomorrow, Colm?" she asked.

"I hope so. I'll talk to Wendell and see what's up."

"Will I ever see you again, Ryan?" she asked.

"Sure thing, kiddo. I'll call you tomorrow."

"I hope so, baby. In the meantime, you can carry my bag to my door."

"Oh sure."

He was gone a long five minutes. I asked Jean if she thought it would work out for those two.

"Hard to say, dear. There's someone out there for all of us. Norma could be Ryan's fated mate."

"They seem fairly compatible. And they're both designers."

"That's true enough. She could be hard to take on a daily basis, but then I'm not Ryan."

"How do you think we'll do on a daily basis?"

"We'll have to see, won't we? I'm sure some adjustments will be required–mostly on your part, of course."

Ryan returned and drove on to our street. He helped us out with our bags.

"Thanks for the fun trip, old buddy," he said, shaking my hand. "We'll come back tomorrow with your Packard."

"Good. Just leave it in the driveway if I'm not here."

"Will do. It was nice seeing you again, Jean. You've filled out some since high school."

"Well, you're in a good position to know. Thanks for doing all that driving."

"My pleasure. Well, good night."

We waved as he drove away.

"Are you sleeping in my house tonight, darling?" I asked.

"Certainly not. I'll see you tomorrow. I'll try to prepare my father for the disastrous news."

"Good. I love you far more than I can say."

"Unaccountably, I find myself returning the sentiment."

She said she didn't need any help carrying her bag. I kissed her good night on the sidewalk and walked into my dark house. We had been gone a week, but it seemed far longer than that.

* * *

Jean returned the next morning in her housekeeper role. She offered to make me breakfast, but I said I was hungrier for her. She's boycotting my bedroom (scene of alleged "debaucheries" with Juanita), so we retired to the guest bedroom to burn through more rubber goods. All in all a very satisfying way to start your day. Afterwards, we held each other and were in no hurry to get up.

"Did you tell your father about us?" I asked.

"I decided I should break it to him gradually. I only told him you broke off your engagement to Juanita."

"How did he react?"

"He wasn't surprised. He thinks you're too much of a scamp for marriage."

"A scamp, huh? Well, I'll show him."

We were startled by the sound of footsteps in the hallway.

"Jean?" called a voice that sounded like Dr. Valland's.

"Oh, shit!" gasped Jean, diving under the covers.

Her father, looking shocked, peered in from the doorway. "Jean! What on earth are you thinking!"

Jean reemerged from under the spread. "Hello, Father. You should have knocked."

"I did," he replied. "No one answered. So I let myself in."

"It's not what you think," I said. "I love your daughter, Dr. Valland. We plan to get married."

"Really? And didn't you love someone else last week? And what about your blond actress?"

"Could you wait in the living room, Father?"

"I don't have much time, Jean. I have a full schedule of appointments this morning."

"We'll be right there, Father. Please wait."

We threw on our clothes and joined him in the living room. I immediately stated my case.

"I'm not as flighty as you assume, Dr. Valland. I loved your daughter right from the beginning. My engagement to Juanita Howe was a mistake that I've corrected. I also broke off with Betty, my actress friend. Jean and I both care for each other very much. We'd like to get married soon. Next month if possible."

"Why so fast?" he demanded. "Jean, are you pregnant?"

"Not at all, Father. We're being careful."

"And you love this character?"

"I do, Father. Very much."

"You don't care about his sorry record of . . . immaturity?"

"I believe he's sincere about changing."

"We would like your blessing, Dr. Valland."

"And how will you support a wife, young man? Didn't your business just burn to the ground?"

"We're going to rebuild. We were fully insured. We hope to be back in business by next week."

"I think you should wait, Jean. I think you should wait at least a year. If Colm is financially stable and you're still committed to each other at that time, then I'll not oppose your marriage."

"I'm sorry, sir, but that is not acceptable to me. Jean and I are both adults. We're free to make our own decisions."

"He's probably right, Colm. We could wait a bit. But I agree a year is too long. Would six months be acceptable to you, Father?"

He sighed. "Six months. Yes, well, I suppose. That will give you time at least to think about what you're doing. And maybe learn something about each other."

"I could live with six months," I said. "Thank you for your understanding, sir."

Dr. Valland looked at his watch. "I've got to go. This is a big disappointment to me, Jean."

"It's all going to work out, Father. I promise you that."

"I hope so. I apologize for disturbing you. I suggest next time you lock your door."

"Yes, sir."

I collapsed on the settee after he left. Jean sat down next to me, and put her arms around me.

"God, what a nightmare!" I sighed.

"That was awfully embarrassing. I'm sorry, dear."

"Well, at least it's over. He knows about us now."

"That he does."

"My father is 3,000 miles away, Jean. That's where parents should be kept: at least a continent away. If we live here after we're married, he's going to be right next door."

"We could sell and move elsewhere."

"You know I wasn't kidding that night when he heard me call you darling. I meant it. I called you darling because I loved you."

"I know. I thought it was very sweet of you."

"Six months, huh? It looks like we're going to have a winter wedding. What's Ukiah like in February?"

"Cold and rainy."

"We should go someplace warm on our honeymoon."

"We could go to Hawaii. And invite my father along too."

For that remark I had to wrestle her down for a kiss.

* * *

At 10 a.m. I met up with Wendell at the lunch counter in Flampert's. He's using it as his temporary office. On the way in I stopped by the photo counter to say hello to Juanita. She seemed pleased to see me.

"How's Ramona?" I asked.

"Doing well, Colm. She delivered a healthy baby girl Wednesday night. Seven pounds, three ounces. They named it Daisy."

"Daisy Demming, huh? That's kind of a fun name."

"Colm, I need to talk to you. Can we meet soon? Say for lunch today?"

"Uh, sure, OK. Should I be here at noon?"

"Make it 12:30. I'll see you then. And I'm sorry about the fire."

"Yeah, it was quite a shock."

We all sat at the counter: Wendell, me, Norma, Mrs. Yeater, Vera the pattern drafter, and Hazel the bookkeeper (who began by passing out paychecks). Taking that as a positive sign, I splurged on a donut with my coffee. Wendell brought us up to date: the insurance adjuster mentioned a tentative settlement figure of $72,000. But because the fire was clearly arson, they are bringing in their own investigator. The settlement has to wait for his report. In the meantime, they are offering to pay toward renting temporary premises and some limited expenses.

"Why the wait?" asked Norma. "Do they think we torched it intentionally?"

"That's been known to happen," he replied. "Companies get in a financial bind so they try to collect on their fire insurance. Our case will be helped when the police arrest Aranson."

"How seriously are they looking for her?" I asked.

"They're serious," said Wendell. "But they think she may have fled the area. They've put out a bulletin for her arrest."

"What about those nasty postcards she sent?" said Norma. "Isn't that proof for the insurance company?"

"Burned up in the fire," said Wendell.

We discussed getting back into production. It was agreed that Norma and Vera are to work on new designs at Norma's place. New fitting-mannequins are to be ordered for delivery as soon as possible. Orders for replacement fabric and machines will be placed pending our conference this morning with Mr. Morgan at the bank.

"What about our Beachzilla line?" I said. "We have a backlog of orders and the patterns are simple. We could start making that first."

"Many of my ladies have their own sewing machines," added Mrs. Yeater. "They could do piecework at home for the time being."

"Unfortunately, the lizard fabric is out of production," said Wendell. "The mill is willing to make more, but their minimum order is a thousand yards."

"That's a lot of bathing suits," said Vera.

"I think we've got the demand," I said. "We should do it."

"And where would we take delivery?" asked Wendell.

"Hell, you can stack it in my living room for the time being," I said.

After that meeting, Wendell and I walked over to the bank. Mr. Morgan was not encouraging. He was reluctant to extend more credit. Wendell pointed out that our accounts receivables more than covered our current debt to the bank. Morgan was unmoved. He judged that a significant portion may be uncollectible. Our only other collateral was a city lot now encumbered by the remains of a burned-down building.

"What we'd like to see, gentlemen," he said. "Is a capital infusion by the owner."

"You want my father to chip in more money?" I asked, shocked. "How much?"

"We'd like to see $25,000 deposited to your account," he replied. "Then we'd be reassured that you're serious about continuing in business."

"OK," I said. "I guess we'll make the call."

Wendell was all for phoning right away, but I said we should wait until the market closed. For a call like that, you don't want to start off on the wrong foot. He went back to his house, and I walked the few blocks to Milady Modest's former premises. I squeezed past the temporary wire fence the insurance company had strung across the front. The many synthetic fabrics stored in the warehouse must have burned at super-high temperatures. The building interior had been almost entirely reduced to a fine white ash. The sewing machines in the production room were now hard puddles of twisted metal. Of the front offices the only one not obliterated was mine. My desk was gone, but a smiling (though somewhat charred) Miss August was still unzipping her sweater on the wall. I took down the calendar to save as a souvenir.

* * *

Juanita and I went to the sandwich shop for lunch. We chatted about Ramona's new baby, then Juanita changed the subject.

"Colm, honey, I'm thinking now I made a mistake."

"About what?"

"About us. I was kind of in a daze that night. It was flattering that Slade drove all that way to say he loved me. And I was excited to see him. But I wasn't thinking all that straight."

"Jesus, Juanita, are you changing your mind about Slade?"

"I don't know, honey. I'm totally confused. He's so serious. I don't know if he's cracked a smile since we've been back. You always made me laugh. Have I made a big mistake?"

"Juanita, there's something you should know. Jean and I are engaged."

"Oh, my. Well, I was afraid of that. You always liked her more than me, didn't you?"

"I don't know. I liked you both. But I love her and I'm not going to change my mind about that."

"I appreciate your telling me this, Colm. That simplifies matters, doesn't it? I'll marry Slade and do my best to make him happy."

"You don't have to marry him, Juanita, if you don't love him."

"Oh, I think I will. He certainly loves me. I think, though, we could have been happy together."

"I think so too. I was looking forward to marrying you."

"Were you really? You weren't just settling for me because you couldn't have Jean?"

"Not at all," I said, fibbing a bit. "I think Slade will lighten up. Give him time. He has a sense of humor. It's good that he's serious about accepting the responsibilities of marriage."

"I'm still annoyed that he slept with Alice and Norma. And all those other girls too."

"I'm sure he won't be straying after you're married. He's not the type. He'll be a good father. You'll have beautiful babies."

"Can you keep all this confidential, Colm? I wouldn't want Slade to hear that I was having doubts."

"Of course, dear. My lips are sealed."

"I'm glad we had this talk. I was feeling things weren't settled between us."

"Me too. Have you set a date for your wedding?"

"We're thinking October at the latest. Margie is starting to show, so we can't wait too long. How about you?"

"We promised Jean's father we'd wait until February."

"Why so long?"

"He's hoping she'll get over me. He thinks I'm a major flake."

"You're a lovely guy, Colm. Jean is very lucky to have you."

"And Slade is lucky to have you. I'll tell him that the next time I see him."

* * *

When I got back home the Packard was in the drive. It had been washed and waxed. You have to like people who return your car in better condition than they received it. The gas tank was full too.

Jean was putting away groceries. I kissed her and gave her the latest updates. I also mentioned that I'd seen Juanita at Flamperts. I told her the news about Ramona's new baby, but didn't divulge that we'd had lunch together. I'm hoping Jean's spy network isn't as efficient as Juanita's.

"I talked to my father," she said. "He would like you to do something."

"What? Move to Tibet? Commit ritual harakiri?"

"He wants you to get a blood test. He's already set it up at the hospital lab. You can go there anytime."

"He thinks I'm going to contaminate you with some vile disease?"

"He's just being cautious. I'm his only child."

"Fine. I'll go. I'll open my veins and bleed for your father."

"They don't take that much, darling. Just a small vial."

"He must think I've seduced hundreds of women. And visit prostitutes daily."

"I'm telling him nothing but good things about you."

"Glad to hear it. He may even warm up to me in about 200 years."

At precisely 3:30 I phoned the old fellow. I figured he was home by then and had downed his first cocktail.

"Have they caught your arsonist yet?" he asked.

"Not yet, Pop. They think she blew town."

"It would be just like my brother to employ an insane person. I believe life in California can do that to you."

"Pop, we're having trouble with our banker."

"Oh?"

"He would like to see a good-faith cash infusion into our account."

"Wouldn't we all?"

"The figure he mentioned was $25,000."

"How droll."

"Can you do that, Pop?"

"The question, son, is not can I, but will I? You know it has never been my ambition to own a bathing suit company."

"We were doing really well before the fire, Pop."

"Accepting the payoff from the insurance company would be a convenient way of liquidating the company. No mess, no fuss."

"But we want to stay in business, Pop. People depend on us for their jobs."

"I'm impressed with your dedication, Colm. My proposal is to split the payoff with you, fifty-fifty. You can go make your little movies, and I'll never have to hear from that Slivmank fellow again."

"Wow, Pop. That's a generous offer."

"Or, I can put $25,000 into bathing suits. But that will be the limit of my investment in your enterprises. The choice is yours: bathing suits or movies."

"Gee, Pop, I don't know what to say."

"You can think about it over the weekend. Call me back this time on Monday. Anything else?"

"I got engaged."

"To whom this time?"

"A girl named Jean Valland."

"Good. Well, good-bye."

As William Bendix would put it, what a revolting development this was. To get the cash we need for Milady Modest, I'd have to forget my dream of producing movies. Damn!

* * *

I did get one piece of good news today. Elwyn Saunders called Jean to invite her to the movies, and she told him she was out of circulation–for good. That creep will have to find someone else to drape his gorilla arms around.

Jean wasn't much help with my $25,000 question. She said it was a decision I'll have to make myself. She's willing to move to Los Angeles with me, but I think she'd miss her dad and friends. I suspect she's staying neutral because she doesn't want to start off married life with me blaming her for the choice I made. It could be she regards my getting into movies as a wild pipedream, but is too tactful to point that out. As usual she's playing her cards close to her vest. Juanita, I know, would have had us stay in Ukiah so all the cousins could grow up together.

To distract myself we went to the movies. Tonight's feature was "The Pride and the Passion." It had Cary Grant, Frank Sinatra, and Sophia Loren fighting Napoleon by lugging a giant cannon around

Spain. I could sort of see Grant as a Royal Navy captain. But you wonder who got the bright idea of casting Sinatra as a Spanish guerilla leader. Over two hours long and as plodding as the peons dragging the gun. Sophia Loren was worth the price of admission, but they killed her off at the end. Which also killed off the romance angle of the story. The big-name producer, Stanley Kramer, also directed, so he gets a double dose of blame.

"You give me that cast and that budget, and I could make a better movie than that," I said to Jean as we headed toward the Golden Carp.

"I bet you could," said Jean. "I can't say much for the plot, but the scenery was pretty."

"I won't be able to afford scenery, darling. Technicolor more than doubles the cost of your movie. I'd be starting out in black and white with unknown actors. Want to star in a movie?"

"What's your plot?"

"Which would you prefer: a horror film where you get menaced by a monster? Or a spy movie where you infiltrate a cell of Communist subversives?"

"Is your monster a guy in a rubber suit?"

"Probably."

"In that case I vote for the spy movie. It sounds more appealing–as long as I don't have to wear a bikini."

"You in a bikini is what I'm counting on to sell tickets."

"I'm no Sophia Loren."

"You're better."

"Liar."

More disappointments later: Jean promised her dad she wouldn't sleep with me again until he had the results of my blood test. So she kissed me good night on my porch and crossed the yard to sleep in her house.

The perfect ending to a rotten day.

I went to sleep thinking that running a bathing suit company was not unlike hauling a giant cannon across Spain. Only this one is being dragged by picky older gals with problem figures.

Chapter 27

Six months later

I met the train at the depot. My father is of the generation that thinks only daredevils like Lindbergh fly. The old fellow greeted me with the usual Moran handshake.

"How was your journey, Pop?" I asked, hoisting his bag.

"A pleasant respite from the ringing telephone."

"I have about 30 messages from your secretary."

"We'll just ignore those for the time being. I find the absence of snow here heartening."

"December and January were colder than I expected, but it's been fairly springlike lately. Did you remember today's Valentine's Day?"

"I mailed a card or two before I left."

"Oh? To anyone I know?"

"Very likely not."

"Just a card or did you include a bauble or two?"

"Nothing very extravagant. You know me. Is this my brother's Packard?"

"That it is, Pop. Still running fine."

"Which is more than we can say for Jonathan."

"No dents either. I've been careful."

"So you have. That's reassuring."

On the drive to my place I told him I was looking forward to his meeting Jean.

"Oh, I've met her," he said. "When I was here before. She very competently managed my brother's funeral. Pretty as a picture too. I said there's the daughter-in-law for me. That's why I suggested you work for my brother's company. And why I kept her on to be your housekeeper."

I nearly ran into a telephone pole.

"You're kidding, Pop."

"No, Colm. I don't kid. My only fear was that she'd have too much sense to fall for you. But the Moran charm is not to be underestimated."

"I can't believe what you're telling me. Was Jean in on this deal?"

"Certainly not. I'm sure she wouldn't have worked for you had she been aware of my intentions. I admit I was disquieted when I read the announcement of your engagement to that other girl in the *Times*."

"Have you seen a beer commercial set in a bowling alley?"

"For Rheingold beer?"

"That's the one. Betty is the girl in that commercial. The one doing the sexy wink."

"Well, she's pretty enough. One may dally with actresses, but one doesn't marry them. You should thank me for all the alimony I'm saving you."

"You're pretty smart, Pop."

"I'm hoping it runs in the family."

* * *

We had a dinner for the family tonight at the Peacock Grill. These can sometimes be big affairs, but in our case it was just the four of us. Dr. Valland has been friendlier toward me these days. It helped that my blood wasn't crawling with spirochetes, and I didn't sell out the company and drag his daughter down to L.A.

It was Jean who suggested the solution to my dilemma. She said if I accepted the $25,000 it should be with the understanding that I now owned half the company. I didn't think the old fellow would pay *me* money to take half of *his* company, but to my surprise he agreed. So now I'm pretty much running the show. We're turning a profit, and Slivmank no longer bugs my father with unwelcome phone calls. It helped that the insurance company finally forked over our money even though Madame Aranson is still on the lam. We have some pension checks for her if she ever drops by.

We were digging into our steaks when Juanita's friends Alice and Ora dropped by our table.

"Hi, Colm," said Ora. "Getting nervous yet?"

"Not so far."

I made the introductions.

"You can still change your mind, Colm," said Alice. "I have gas in my car. If we leave now, we can be in Mexico tomorrow."

"Uh, I think I'll stick with the program here. But thanks for the offer. How's Juanita?"

"Not pregnant yet," said Ora. "And she's been married four whole months."

"She may be calling on you for some assistance," added Alice.

"I'm not planning on renting him out," said Jean.

"We were both expecting Valentine cards," said Ora. "You've disappointed us."

"I'm sorry," I said. "It won't happen again."

"Well, enjoy your last night as a bachelor," said Alice. "And have fun on your honeymoon without me."

"We intend to," said Jean.

"Charming girls," said the old fellow when they'd left. "Who's Juanita?"

"One of Colm's many ex-fiancees," said Jean. "He came very close to marrying her."

"She was Miss Runner-up," I explained. "Close but no cigar."

"Well, she did sample the cigar," said Jean. "But I'm overlooking that."

* * *

The next morning I made breakfast for the old fellow. We sat at the yellow table in the kitchen and sipped our coffee.

"You could fix up this place you know," he said. "You could toss my brother's outmoded furniture and get something modern."

"Sounds fine to me, Pop. I suggested it to Jean, but she goes for this vintage stuff. I said why look like we're living in 1910? Let's replace those drafty wooden windows and upgrade to low-maintenance aluminum siding. Let's install a big picture window up front. At the very least let's brighten up the joint. Let's paint all this dark oak woodwork and ditch these Persian carpets."

"What did she say?"

"The usual. She said I was an idiot."

"She's a girl with strong opinions."

"She knows her mind. I should resent your arranging my marriage, you know."

"I didn't arrange it. I merely facilitated it."

"How did you know I'd take the bait?"

"You'd have been a fool not to. If I were a decade or two younger I'd have gone after her myself."

"How come you never remarried, Pop?"

"Your mother set a high standard. I'm not one for compromising."

"That's what I figured."

"Dr. Valland tells me we're in for an unusual wedding."

"We were planning a small one, but the guest list kept expanding. That's why we're having it at the Legion Hall. Any more and we'd have had to rent the cow barn at the fairgrounds. Want to go see our new offices?"

"If I must. Is Jean coming over?"

"Nah, I'm not supposed to see her. Bad luck and all that. Her friends will be there soon to help her get ready."

We headed off in the Packard. We drove by the vacant lot where all the fire debris had been cleared away.

"That building had an interesting history," I said. "First it was a place where they repaired wagon wheels. Then it was a chair factory. Then it was a wholesale grocery warehouse. And then Uncle Jonathan bought it."

"Any nibbles on the sale?"

"Not so far. The neighbors would prefer a house or two, but the lot is zoned commercial."

I drove three blocks south to our new location. Milady Modest Inc. had moved into a former convalescent hospital that had sat vacant for years. Fearing he had a white elephant on his hands, the grateful owner had given us a good deal on rent.

Although it was the weekend, Mrs. Yeater was there with a busy crew of sewing ladies. I introduced the old fellow to them, then continued with our tour.

"This was the hospital's activity room," I said. "It makes a good production space. The entire building is air-conditioned, which is helpful for maintaining productivity. Ukiah gets really hot in the summer. We're using the former patient rooms as offices. There's a fully equipped kitchen we turned into a lunchroom. In the back is an attached four-car garage we've made into our warehouse. I hired a Negro classmate of Jean's to run that department. He's very efficient and organized."

"Most impressive, Colm. Why are these gals working on Saturday?"

"Trying to fill orders, Pop. Our 1958 lines are doing great."

"Even those bikinis of yours?"

"We haven't been pushing them much, but they're in a few stores. Norma's still enthusiastic, but I'm beginning to think we're too far ahead of the crowd with those. Right now they've been eclipsed by our expanding line of novelty bathing suits for boys. They're selling phenomenally well. And boys are so much easier to fit than gals."

"It appears you are on a sound financial footing at last."

"I believe we are. You can discuss it with Wendell Slivmank if you like. He'll be coming in soon."

"Then by all means let us exit hastily now."

* * *

The white-haired minister was in the act of marrying Jean and Ryan, when two bikers swinging motorcycle chains burst in through the door. Wedding guests screamed and retreated to the other side of the hall.

"What's the meaning of this?" demanded the minister, standing his ground.

All eyes turned as Norma, dressed in black leather, swaggered into the room and pushed the two thugs aside.

"Unhand that bride, Cody!" she shouted.

"I'm marrying her," replied Ryan, icily. "And you can't stop me, Babs!"

"Wise up, Cody," Norma replied. "Your bride Lois was racing your brother that night. *She* was the driver of that mystery deuce coupe! It was Lois who crippled your twin brother!"

Ryan staggered back from shock. "Is that true, Lois?"

Jean wept into her bouquet. "It was an accident, Cody. I dropped in a hot new cam, and that fool Jody tried to pass me on dead man's curve."

"We're done here, Lois," said Ryan. "Blood is thicker than motor oil."

"Well, that's not technically true," noted the minister.

"Butt out, Bible-man," said Ryan. "So long, Lois. I'll be riding with Babs from now on."

"No, Cody! No!" exclaimed Jean.

"It's over, Lois," he said. "And never try to pass me again. Because I'll always be the king of the highways."

He walked over, kissed Norma passionately, lifted her into his arms, and carried her from the room. Swinging their chains menacingly, the two bikers followed them out.

"Cut!" I yelled. "Very good. How was the sound, Dale?"

"Good," replied Dale Demming, removing his headphones. "I could hear everyone that time."

"That was the fourth take, dear," said Jean. "Can we get married now? My bouquet's starting to wilt."

"Fine," I said. "I think we've got all the coverage we need."

We'd been shooting "King of the Highways" on weekends for several months. My script called for a scene at a wedding, so I decided to shoot it today. The minister looked authentic (because he was), and our guests seemed happy to participate. Dr. Valland, giving away the bride, looked convincingly outraged, and the old fellow muttered curses right on cue.

"OK," I shouted. "Everyone return to their seats. We're not filming this next part. It's for real."

And so we got married. I was all over in about 15 minutes. No one burst in swinging chains this time. I didn't fumble the ring; Jean didn't chicken out. Then the party started.

The inspiration for my movie was a film we'd seen at a drive-in theater. "The Delinquents" was written and directed in Kansas City by a fellow there named Robert Altman. It was done totally on the cheap with unknown actors, mostly locals. I figured if they could do it and get their movie seen, so could we. So I bought a used 16mm camera and some sound-recording gear. With the assistance of friends and the local hotrod club, Cheeky Films was in business. Ryan starred as two brothers (Cody and Jody) with a need for speed. His acting was surprisingly competent, and his stunt driving was impressively professional. His love scenes with Jean were a trial, but I kept those takes to a minimum.

* * *

The party went on into the night. Things became somewhat muddled after a while. I remember the old fellow gave us a big fat check. He also said he was turning over the rest of Milady Modest Inc. to me. And signing over my uncle's house to Jean. It appears I'm to be a tenant of hers. Norma slurped a lot of champagne and proposed to Ryan. He said he'd have to think about it. Slade kissed the bride, so I kissed Juanita. She said they were happy and trying for a baby. For inspiration she brought along a photo of Reggie's chubby little N.A.T.O. baby named Gottfried Meinhard Dowling.

The band played many lively tunes. I danced with numerous partners, including quite a few of the sewing gals. Ramona and Margarita both took me aside to say they liked Slade, but wished Juanita had stuck with me. Madame Aranson did not show up with a gun and shoot anyone. Then it was well past midnight, and I was back home with my new bride. The old fellow was camping next door with my father-in-law.

"We should go to sleep," said Jean. "We're supposed to be driving to L.A. in the morning."

"A honeymoon on the beach in Santa Monica," I said. "Are you sure you're OK with that?"

"I'd prefer one in a hotel."

"We'll be in a hotel, darling. I've reserved the honeymoon suite. How does that sound?"

"It would sound better with William Holden, but you'll do."

"I'm hoping to sober up enough to consummate this marriage."

"It's OK if you can't, dear. We'll spill ketchup on the sheet and hang it out the window tomorrow."

"My father wanted me to marry you, right from the start. Did you know that?"

"And my father wanted me to marry anyone but you."

"That means my side won," I said, competitively.

"Perhaps. But my side gets to exact revenge for the next 50 years."

I kissed her, and then one thing led to another. We'd done it before, of course, but this time it was legal. We didn't bother with a condom. Like everyone else these days we're trying to get launched in the diaper derby.

Author's note:

To everyone's surprise Juanita Preston did not become pregnant until 18 years later. The fertility specialist they consulted discovered that Slade's sperm, although conveying glorious DNA, lacked motility. They named their son Trent after Trent Dzieduszycki, an early experimenter with plywood resins. Elwyn Saunders went to law school and years later married a woman he met at a revival meeting. They had two children whose histories are related elsewhere.

38108797R00137

Made in the USA
Lexington, KY
22 December 2014